HER BRAVE WARRIOR

OMEGA SKY
BOOK 6

CAITLYN O'LEARY

To Titan, the Greatest Black Russian Terrier I Ever Knew

SYNOPSIS

What Happens When You Might Be Sleeping with The Enemy?

Navy SEAL, Mateo Aranda, was used to fighting the good fight. He had successfully carried out missions in dozens of countries, and he never once wavered.

The thought of terrorists following his team home and targeting their families was unimaginable. Knowing how high the stakes were, he was damn sure this would *not* be the first mission he would lose. Mateo was on the hunt, and he intended to destroy the Kraken Elite once and for all.

When a lead points to Lainey Simpson, his mind tells him he has to do whatever is necessary to squeeze her for info, but his gut tells him something else entirely. Mateo is left trying to figure out if Lainey needs his protection, or if his team needs protection from Lainey and the people she might be working with.

This is an action, adventure, romantic, stand-alone novel.

PROLOGUE

THIS WAS THE FIRST TIME HE'D EVER BEEN IN A HOSPITAL. Scratch that. The first time he'd ever been in a hospice center, which was probably worse. He hated it. There hadn't been a hospital when Luis had died in a car crash, so they just identified him at the morgue. Just the morgue.

His boots didn't make any sound as he walked over the linoleum floor toward the nurse's station. He cleared his throat so that the middle-aged lady looked up.

"I'm here to see Graciella Aranda."

She scowled at him.

"She doesn't get visitors. Who are you?"

Yeah, because she never told me she was sick!

"I'm her son. Mateo Aranda."

He kept his calm, just like his mom and the Navy had taught him.

"Let me check my list."

She flipped through a sheaf of papers. Didn't they have things like this automated?

"Yes, I found you. You'll have to wear a badge."

"Really?"

"It's protocol."

He watched as she took out a 'Hello My Name Is' sticker and looked back and forth between the name on her list and the sticker to spell his name correctly. She still got it wrong, spelling his name with two T's.

"Here you go. The elevators are behind me on the left. Go to the second floor and then turn right to the nurses station. Someone will take you to your mother's room."

Mateo pressed the sticker to his bright white t-shirt and followed her instructions. The elevator seemed to take forever to get to him. He spotted the door to the stairs, but it was locked.

"You need to use the elevator."

Mateo looked over his shoulder at the woman manning the front desk. She was smiling with satisfaction. He had seen that look many times before on people bloated with their petty little pockets of authority.

"Yes, ma'am."

He went back and stood in front of the elevator and tried to will it to go faster. Hospice. His mom was in hospice. A place where people went to die. Why had she only contacted him two days ago?

The elevator was empty when he stepped in, but it smelled. It took a moment for him to discern the scent. It smelled like the time in the desert when his

Cascade Blue SEAL team had carried two dead Marines back to their outpost. The elevator smelled like death.

When he got to the nurses station, he found a much friendlier woman behind the desk. She glanced swiftly at his nametag and smiled.

"You're here to see Graciella. Are you her son?"

Mateo nodded.

She waved a big black man over to her. "This is Rodney. He'll take you to your mother's room. She'll be happy to see you. But I have to warn you, she tires easily and she might be asleep when you go in. I suggest you just take a seat and read one of the books she has at her bedside. But it's also okay to talk to her. Even if she's asleep, some patients wake up and say they heard their loved ones."

Mateo nodded again.

"Rodney, Mr. Aranda is Graciella's son. Can you take him to her room?"

"I'd be happy to." He grinned. "She's a pleasure to have here," he told Mateo. "She's pretty well-medicated, so she's not in pain."

"Mom didn't tell me much on the phone. What's her diagnosis?"

"Stage four pancreatic cancer. It's my understanding it came on fast." He stopped in front of an open door. Mateo looked in and saw his mother was in a private room. He knew that her benefits from DuPont, where she was a scientist, were top-notch.

Rodney knocked on the doorjamb. "Gracie, are you up for a visitor?"

Mateo winced. He knew his mother hated the Americanized version of her name.

There was no answer.

"Why don't I just go in? The nurse told me the drill. If she's not awake, I'll just sit beside her. How is she doing?"

It pissed him the fuck off that he had to ask a stranger about his mother's condition.

"Pancreatic cancer is one of the worst. It comes on fast, and the pain is unimaginable."

He should have been the one who knew that. He should have been here as soon as she got the diagnosis. His Lieutenant would have given him the time off, he knew it.

Mateo nodded once and marched past Rodney. He was done talking. He wanted to see his mother, and he wanted to see her *now!*

There weren't any drapes on the windows, just thin metal slats that sent stripes of light streaming across his mother's frail body like she was behind prison bars. Her head was turned away from the sun, and he went to the shades and shut them closed with an emphatic *snap*. She had enough pain going on; she didn't need the sun hurting her eyes.

When he turned back to look at her, he saw that her face had relaxed. That was good. It was the only thing that was good. The last time he'd seen his mom was at Thanksgiving ten months ago. She must have lost half of her body weight since then.

A large recliner was in the corner of the room, so he

picked it up and brought it close to her so that he could hold her hand.

The hands that had once guided him, and sheltered him, and sometimes whooped him, were now feather-light. These were not her hands. He looked at her face and his heart stuttered. This was not his mother.

He sucked in a deep breath, making sure he could hold it together.

"Ma, I got here as quick as I could. Come on and open your pretty brown eyes for me, huh?"

He stroked his thumb across the back of her hand and she slowly turned her head in his direction.

"Luis?" she whispered.

"No, Ma. It's me, Mateo," he corrected her gently. She was always looking for his brother Luis. Her pride and joy.

He felt her hand tremble as she tried to squeeze his, then her face spasmed in pain and she whimpered. The IV drip that had to be pumping her full of narcotics wasn't doing its job. He brought her hand up to his lips and kissed it.

"Just a moment, Ma. I'll get help."

He shot out of the chair and ran down to the nurses station. It was the same friendly nurse as before. She was talking to another visitor. Mateo didn't care, and he interrupted.

"My mother is waking up and she's whimpering in pain. She needs something."

She nodded. "I'll send somebody as soon as they're available."

"She needs something now."

"Mr. Aranda, let me just finish up here and I'll go there personally, all right?"

He realized it was as good as he was going to get, so he nodded, then hustled back to his mother's room. Now she wasn't just whimpering, she was moaning.

"Ma, it's going to be all right. Somebody is going to come in and help you, I promise," he said in Spanish.

"English. We're in America, we speak English," she corrected him. Just like she always had.

"A nurse is going to be here soon," he promised her in English.

Her eyes squeezed tightly, then opened. "Luis?"

"No, Ma. I told you, it's me, Mateo."

Now he could see her emotional pain as her lip trembled. "I remember. Luis died."

"Yeah, Ma. He did. It tore us up, remember?"

He watched as she tried to lift up her hand.

"What, Ma? What are you trying to do?"

"I want to touch your face, my son."

He wasn't sure if she wanted to touch him, or if she was thinking he was Luis. But he bent forward, picked up her hand, and brought it to his cheek.

"Thank you for coming."

He cleared his throat, trying to hold back all of his pain and anger. "Why didn't you call me sooner?"

"This is a hard way to die. I didn't want you to have to watch me suffer. I know my warrior son, you would want to fix this, and you can't."

She *did* know who she was talking to. She only ever referred to him as her warrior.

"I might have wanted to fix this, Ma, but I would

have set that aside. More than anything I would have wanted to share this with you. Maybe if you weren't feeling well, I could have finally beaten you at Truco."

She started to laugh, and it turned into a cough. He hated that. He looked over at the door. Where in the hell was that nurse?

When his mother stopped coughing, she gave a hoarse laugh. "Even on my worst day, you couldn't have beat me at Truco." For just a moment he saw a sparkle in her eye. He'd have to go find a deck of Spanish playing cards so he could bring them in tomorrow.

"Challenge accepted," he teased.

Her eyes drifted shut and she whimpered.

"Sorry, Mr. Aranda, can you move out of the way?" the nurse asked as she bustled in.

Mateo realized he and the recliner were blocking her way to the IV. He stood up and then moved the recliner back to the corner. He watched carefully as she fiddled with the drip.

"There, that should help," she reassured him. "But she's probably going to sleep for the rest of the day and on into the night."

"I want to just sit here a little longer, if that's okay."

The nurse nodded. "Of course." She glanced at Ma and lowered her voice. "I want to tell you. She's talked about you a lot, Luis. She bragged about the scholarship you got and how you were a straight-A student in high school."

Mateo sighed. "That's my older brother. He died in a car accident seven years ago."

"Oh." He could see she was embarrassed, but she

tried to cover. "That must be the reason she talks so much about him. A lot of patients near the end talk about their loved ones that they've lost."

He nodded. There was no point telling her that Luis had always been the apple of her eye.

"Where are you staying?"

"In a little hotel down the street. It has a fridge and a hotplate, so I'm covered. I'm in the Navy so my Lieutenant gave me time to stay with her."

She stood a little straighter. "Thank you for your service."

He nodded. He never had any idea how else to respond. She left and he sat back down. He moved the chair closer again and picked up his mother's hand.

"Mateo?"

"Yes, Mom, I'm here."

She smiled, then drifted off to sleep.

———

HE WALKED DOWN THE HALLWAY, holding the deck of cards in his hands, anxious to get to his mother. Hopefully, he was arriving early enough like the nurse had suggested, so that his mom would be able to play a game of Truco.

He got to the first hurdle and it wasn't the same woman as yesterday. If he had to guess, it was a temp.

"Who are you here to see?" the young woman asked.

"I know where I'm going. My name is Mateo

Aranda. Just give me my nametag and I'll go upstairs to see my mother, Graciella Aranda."

The girl typed his mother's name into her computer and stared.

"Hold on a minute."

She picked up the phone, then turned around and bent over, obviously trying to not let him hear something. It was at that moment that he knew something was wrong. But it couldn't be. The nurses told him that she would be stronger in the morning.

The young woman turned around and gave him a wobbly smile.

"Hold on for just a minute. Someone will be right down."

"Has something happened to my mother?"

"You need to wait for just a moment."

Mateo took a deep breath. The girl didn't even look twenty. She was just a temp. But, she knew something, and she wasn't telling him.

"Tell me," he barked.

"Sir, please." She was practically in tears.

The elevator dinged and they both turned to look at it. The big guy named Rodney came striding over to them.

"Tell me," Mateo barked again.

Rodney put his hands on Mateo's shoulders.

"I'm so sorry for your loss."

So sorry for your loss.

Always.

Always.

They were always so sorry for my loss.

1

MATEO ROLLED HIS SHOULDERS AS HE STEPPED OUT OF his truck. He had to slam the door shut twice to get it to take, but he was beginning to love the damn thing anyway. Gonna take a lot of work to get her fixed up. A lot of work and a lot of money, but it would be worth it.

The tan and cream fifty-year-old Dodge looked out of place on Gideon's fancy-assed circular drive in front of his brick colonial-style house. Too bad his teammate had such a long private drive so his neighbors couldn't see the type of redneck friends Gideon hung around with.

Seeing all the mommy SUVs and vans, he lifted his face into the pouring rain, savoring the peace, until he heard a crack of thunder. The birthday party that started at putt-putt golf and games must have shut down a little early and they all ended up here.

He'd really been hoping to get here half an hour before the rugrats so he could get some peace and quiet but the traffic had been a bitch. Damn, he'd really wanted to sit back and chill with one of Gideon's good beers before the chaos ensued. Oh well, it wasn't meant to be.

Of course, none of his teammates' cars or trucks were around. They were all watching the game out at the pub that was having two-for-one drinks out near Norfolk, instead of the local watering hole. He hadn't been able to join them because today was his mom's birthday, and he always lit a candle at church in her honor.

Always.

So, he'd told his friends he'd meet them at Gideon's house and help the moms run roughshod over the herd.

Jogging over to the garage door, he flipped up the panel and keyed in the nine-digit code and grinned. Only Gideon would have a nine-digit security code. The garage door started to rise and Mateo shook his head like a dog to get the water out of his curly hair.

"Jase!"

He looked up to see who had called his name, but it was anyone's guess. There were four little kids huddled around the door leading from the kitchen to the garage.

"It's Mr. Mateo. Can't you see?"

Now that was Amber, Bonnie's daughter, and she was definitely chastising her twin brother.

"Who's Mr. Mateo?"

Mateo squinted and saw a dark-haired boy asking the question.

"He's on Jase's SEAL team. Jase is our new dad," Amber's twin brother, Lachlan, said proudly.

Mateo winced. He didn't recognize the little boy that Lachlan Drakos was telling about the SEAL team. Mateo needed to let Jase know he needed to have another talk with his adopted son about discretion.

Lach jumped off the top step from the kitchen, straight onto the garage floor, bypassing four steps, and launched toward him. Mateo braced when the boy tried to take him out at his knees.

"I thought we agreed to call Jase, Dad. And Mom says you need to stop doing that and use the stairs," Amber Drakos said. The seven-year-old sounded thirty as she admonished her twin again.

"So, don't tell her," Lachlan called over his shoulder as he clung to Mateo, then he started talking at a rapid-fire pace.

"We can't play in the yard, cause of the rain. That's a bummer. His yard is humongous, and it has a pool! But Gideon has cool video games, even ones mom won't let us play. But we can play them with you, right?" Lachlan peered around Mateo's leg to see outside. "Do you think the lightning will knock down a tree or hit the house? I heard about that happening to Tina's best friend's older brother's girlfriend's dad. That'd be cool, wouldn't it? Lightning hitting a tree, I mean."

Bright blue eyes, partnered with a gap-toothed grin, stared up at him. Mateo shook his head as he looked down at the kid. "What have you been eating?"

"There's cake," Amber said.

"And because the putt-putt park closed down on account of rain, they gave us each a candy bar." The dark-haired boy scrounged an empty wrapper that was smeared with chocolate out of the front pocket of his jeans.

Well, that explained all the hyperactivity.

The boom of thunder was so close it reminded Mateo of a howitzer.

"Cool!" Lachlan yelled out.

"Who all is here?" Mateo asked Lachlan.

"Everybody."

"Not everybody," Amber answered as she sidled closer to Mateo and shook her head at her brother. "Some girls from my softball team are here, and a bunch of Lachlan's friends from his Tae Kwon Do class. So are Mom and Mrs. O'Rourke with her baby Iris, an' Mrs. Ericson, she's Sasha's mom. Oh yeah, and Miss Amy is teaching us kitchen stuff. I heard Mr. Ryker tell my mom that Miss Amy was his woman. My mom and Miss Amy growled at him." Amber took a deep breath, then continued. "This house is so cool, Mr. Mateo!" Amber was practically jumping up and down. "The backyard is bigger than our school's playground. Do you think Mr. Gideon would let us practice softball here?"

Mateo held back a laugh. The idea of little girls throwing balls through Gideon's windows wouldn't go over well.

"Let's get inside. I'm all wet. Maybe one of the five ladies can get me a towel."

Amber held out her hand. "Come with me, I know where the towels are."

He looked down at Amber and noted her attire. "Why are you wearing your bathing suit? You're not going to go swim in the pool, are you?" None of the women could have thought that was a good idea.

"Nope," she said as she popped the 'P.' Then she giggled. "We had to change into our swimsuits so Mom could put our wet clothes in the dryer. She can do the same thing for you." She paused and tilted her head. "Mom says it's going to be a madhouse once the game's over and everyone leaves the pub and comes back with the pizza."

It seems like a madhouse right now, and I haven't even made it into the house!

"Hey kids, I thought you wanted to learn how to make guacamole. If you do, you better come inside."

He looked up and saw Amy Linden standing in the doorway, looking mighty fine in a blue one-piece bathing suit. Ryker sure was a lucky man. Amy had worked in the restaurant industry forever, so it made sense that she was tempting the kids into the kitchen so they wouldn't be pestering everybody to play Gideon's PG video games.

"Hey Mateo," Amy waved, as the kids hustled on by her. "Come on inside. We've got plenty of towels, and I've got a load of clothes in the dryer. I bet Gideon wouldn't mind if you grabbed one of his t-shirts and wore that until yours was dry."

She was right, and the idea of getting dry sounded pretty good.

When he stepped into the house, it was the chaos he expected. The TV was turned on at mind-numbing decibels. He didn't need to look at all the seven-year-old girls dancing around the kitchen with their friendship bracelets, to know it was Taylor Swift singing. Hell, the youngest man on their SEAL team, Landon Kelly, was always playing and singing along to her songs. If he wasn't such a big bruiser, he probably would have had the shit knocked out of him by now.

"Mateo, I got a hole in one and came in second at putt-putt." Lachlan told him as Amber handed him a towel.

"You didn't come in second," a little, brown-skinned girl stomped over to him with a scowl. "We had to leave because of the rain before I could take my turn. If I would have made a hole-in-one in the clown's nose, I would have come in second, and you would have come in third."

Aw, shit.

Lachlan looked over at the girl, who was both mad and hurt. "You're right, Priya. I shouldn't have said that. Mom said that the game was called on account of rain. That means there's no winners or losers. I'm sorry."

It was like the sun came out with a rainbow the way Priya smiled at Lachlan. "You wanna go see my iPad? My mom let me download a new maze game. It's really hard."

"Sure. Let's go into Mr. Gideon's game room. Only Roy and Heather are in there. But let's ask Miss Amy for a soda first. She knows where the grape and orange ones are."

Now they were both smiling.

He felt someone taller than a kid coming up behind him before he heard Bonnie's laugh. "Looks like my son has made a friend."

"It was touch-and-go for a moment, but he pulled it out. He's a peacemaker at heart."

"That he is," Bonnie agreed.

He hadn't seen her since her and Jase's big wedding in Springfield, Missouri. Jase had sixteen brothers and sisters, and that was his hometown.

"Married life seems to have agreed with you." He grinned down at the grown-up version of Amber.

Bonnie blushed.

And isn't that cute as hell?

"It does. Every day seems to get better and better."

"Do you need to put me to work? I might not be in a command position at work, but I've watched Kostya often enough that I think I can help bring some order to this chaos."

She gave him an evil grin. "Oh, you do, do you?"

"Well, as long as there's hazard pay."

"I'll get back to you on that. First, I'm going to go get the girls to turn the volume down on the TV. I might be a Swiftie, but even I can only take so much."

He grinned down at her. "You'll have my undying gratitude."

Bonnie winked at him as she headed to the TV room.

"Want some chips and guacamole?" Amy asked as he walked toward the kitchen. Another roll of thunder rumbled, and he saw two girls move closer to the kind woman who was teaching them how to make the dip.

"When is my mom going to come and get me?" A pale little girl wearing a tutu asked him as Amy handed him a plate of chips and guac. He was surprised that such a tiny girl felt comfortable addressing him; usually they shied away because of his size. Maybe her dad was really big. Mateo crouched down, so he was at her eye level.

"What's your name?"

"I'm Leslie, what's yours?"

"I'm Mateo." He held out his empty hand. She put her small hand in his and he gently closed his fingers around it and shook it. "I'll find out where your mom is, but Leslie, I think with all this rain it would be safer if she didn't drive for a little bit. It's really slippery and we want her to be careful, don't we?"

"But I want her. I don't like the thunder and lightning," she whispered. "It's scary."

"Honey," Amy crouched down on the other side of Leslie. "Mrs. Ericson is going to take you home, remember? She planned to do that after you had pizza. But if you want us to call your mom before that, we can."

Mateo watched as the little girl's brow crinkled as she considered her dilemma. "Will there be the pineapple kind of pizza?"

"I'm sure there will be," Amy nodded.

"Then I'll stay," Leslie smiled shyly.

Mateo looked at the other girl, who was now trying to hide behind Amy. She was a little taller and looked just as pale and scared.

"Are you scared too?" Mateo asked her.

She nodded and put her arm around Amy's leg. Now *that* was the reaction he was used to.

"Where I come from in Argentina, we had thunder

and lightning storms all the time. When I was a little boy, my mama would have me and my little brother sing so that we could tease the sun to come out and play again. Do you want to try that?"

Leslie nodded her head and gave him a sweet smile, whereas the other girl looked skeptical. "What do you think, Amy? Does that sound good to you?" Mateo asked.

"Absolutely. Maybe we could go into the TV room now that it's quieter. By the way, this beautiful girl is Laura. Her daddy is supposed to be here pretty soon to come and get her."

"But not if the roads are slippery. Can we call him, Miss Amy?"

"How about if we get Mrs. Ericson to call him? She has his number on her phone. Would that be okay?"

Laura nodded.

Amy turned to Mateo. "Laura and I are going to find Mrs. Ericson. In the meantime, why don't you and Leslie go teach everybody the sun song?" Amy smiled at Mateo as she took the little girl's hand and left the kitchen.

"Lachlan said you're Mexican. Are you going to sing the song in Spanish?"

"I'm Argentinian," Mateo explained. "Argentina is in South America. I'll teach you all the song in English and then in Spanish. How about that?"

"That's so cool." She was missing two front teeth, the same as Lachlan. As they started down the hall to the TV room, he heard the faint sound of a dog barking over the sound of Taylor Swift singing and the washer and dryer running.

"Leslie, why don't you go sit down and keep watching the Taylor movie with everybody? I'll teach you the song in a few minutes. I have to go check on something."

"Okay. She plopped down on the other side of Lachlan.

He was a popular boy.

Gideon's dog Lucy hardly ever barked. The big black Russian terrier was too well trained. This was not good. Mateo felt a prickle on the back of his neck. He hurried to the back of the house to see if someone had put her outside, which didn't seem possible. Not if there was thunder and lightning. He stepped out into the great room that encompassed the dining room and also allowed him to see into the kitchen and gave him great views over James Lake, Gideon's pool, the back lawn, the patio and as far back to the neighbor's metal fence. Amber hadn't been kidding. They could play a softball game out back.

Lucy had to be in the mudroom. That's where Gideon would sometimes pen her up. He strode past the back window of the great room, then noticed that Gideon's leather couch had claw marks on the back. Shit, the prickle now felt like cactus spines.

What the fuck?

"Hey Mateo, that's a great idea on the song," Bonnie said as she passed him with a big bowl of potato chips.

"Is Lucy in the mud room? Why is she barking?" he asked Bonnie instead of replying to her question.

"Lucy was barking up a storm when we got here. She was scratching at the sliding glass door, so I let her out to do her thing, but nothing. When I finally got her back in, she kept barking and she was scaring the kids. It took some doing, but I was finally able to wrangle her into the mudroom. It was so out of character for her, but luckily I'm used to big dogs," Bonnie said.

"Did you call Gideon?"

"I didn't want to ruin their good time. I figured he'd be home soon enough. She probably saw a squirrel or something."

And there was the reason for the prickle. Mateo had his phone out of his back pocket in an instant as he double-timed past the laundry room to the mudroom.

"Mateo, you should have come. We're in overtime. Ryker owes me money." Gideon was laughing.

"I'm at your place, and Lucy is acting strange."

"What the hell do you mean, strange?" Gideon's voice was instantly sharp. "Describe it to me. It's important."

"Putt putt got rained out. The women and kids got here before I did. When they got here, Lucy was barking up a storm and scratching at the sliding glass door. She's even clawed your leather sofa._When Bonnie let her out, she didn't take a dump. Bonnie called her back in, and she was still barking. Bonnie said it was tough, but she managed to wrangle her into the mudroom."

"Fuck! She's on alert. Shit, man, I need to be there."

"What would she be on alert for?" Mateo started

counting how many kids he'd seen in the TV room, the game room, the kitchen, and the dining room.

Fuck.

Too fucking many.

"I don't like this. I don't like this at all. I left her inside. She must have seen someone fucking with the backyard. I want everybody out of the house. I know I'm over-the-top right now, but these are kids, Mateo. Get them the fuck out of there. Dammit, I need to be there!"

Mateo thought of Lachlan, Amber, and Nolan's baby girl. "That makes two of us who are losing their shit. I'll get them out of here."

Gideon had disconnected and Mateo slid his phone in his back pocket as his hand hit the door knob of the mud room.

"Mr. Mateo, are you getting Lucy out of time out? I want to play with her." Mateo looked behind him and saw Lachlan had followed him and winced. Pray God he had heard nothing that scared him.

"Where's your mom?"

"She's making everybody sing, since you weren't there."

Mateo let go of the doorknob. "Well, I'm headed there now." He didn't go as fast as he would have liked, because he wanted Lachlan to keep up. Damn, he wished he knew the headcount of all the kids here at Gideon's house. As soon as he stepped into the room, Bonnie looked up at him and quit singing.

"Hey kids. Now that you know the song, why don't

you sing it on your own? Mr. Mateo would love to hear you sing."

She got up off the couch and rushed over to him. "Lachlan, go back to the couch."

The kid didn't whine, he just did what she said. It must have been her tone of voice. "What's wrong, Mateo?"

"Gideon wants us to get everyone out of the house. I want you out and down the drive to the street. Lucy doesn't bark that way unless something is wrong. Since she was clawing at the door to the yard, he thinks she saw somebody doing something, and she was trying to alert you."

Bonnie's face paled, but she nodded her head. "I'll get everybody outside," she promised.

"Do you know the headcount?"

"Yeah. Besides Lachlan and Amber, we have eleven little girls, six boys, Amy, Maggie, and her two-year-old daughter, then there is Fern Ericson, she's one of the boys' mothers. Laura's dad is due to pick her up soon. I'll ask Fern what Laura's dad's ETA is. Laura and one boy went upstairs to go look out a window to wait for him to show up."

"You tag all the women and round up the kids and load them into the cars and go down the drive until you hit the street. Wait for me there."

She stared up into Mateo's face for a brief moment. She must have seen something, God knew what, but she nodded. "Time for coats?"

Mateo shook his head.

"Got it."

She turned back to the room full of children.

"Hey kids, we've got another game we're going to play. You know the grown-ups are going to come here with pizza, right?"

"Yay!" one girl yelled out with a fist pump.

"Well, we're going to go outside right now, and go hide in our cars so we can make them think we're gone. Won't that be funny?"

"That'll be great!" the same girl yelled again.

"That'll be fun," a young boy piped up.

Seeing that Bonnie had everything in hand, Mateo headed back to the mudroom, taking his phone out of his pocket on the way.

"Status?" Gideon asked when he picked up.

"The kids are being rounded up to go out to the cars right now. I don't want to add chaos to the mix. Where's Lucy's leash?"

"She doesn't need one. She'll head straight to the patio door."

Mateo eased open the door to the mudroom, and Lucy tried to lunge past him. Mateo shoved her back as he looked behind him.

"Down, girl. You head straight for the door, got it?" He opened the door wider, and Lucy bounded out of the room. Mateo ran after her. She skidded to a stop in front of the sliding glass door, then clawed at the glass. Mateo unlocked and opened the door and Lucy shot onto the patio like a bullet from a gun, then ran toward the pool as lightning flashed.

"What's your ETA?" he asked Gideon.

"We were already getting ready to head home. Now

we're heading east on the expressway, but there's a wreck that has traffic stopped. I'd say we're fucked..."

"But?"

Mateo looked over his shoulder and didn't see anyone in the great room, dining room, or kitchen, which was good.

"I've already put an SOS out to the rest of the team to head to my house to help you figure out what's going on. I sent out a text to Kane McNamara of Night Storm to get the word out and see if anyone can head west on the expressway two miles west of Rosemont. But Mateo, unless one of the team members gets to you fast, you're on your own. I'll have them text you when they're close. Are the women and kids safe?"

"Bonnie took care of that."

"Good."

"What should I do with Lucy?"

"Trust her. If she's fired up, then she saw someone or something. Let her take the lead, just like we have with our mission dogs."

"Gotcha."

2

_____

THE PRICKLE WAS GONE. NOW FIRE ANTS HAD DECIDED TO build a colony on Mateo's neck. After all the barking and lunging, Lucy was dead still in front of a three-foot-high cinder block enclosure close to the pool. Mateo ignored the rain and the roar of thunder as he stepped over the wall and found that it housed the pool pump and heating unit.

He looked over at Lucy. He'd gotten the same look before from dogs in the field. It was the "hurry up, dumbfuck, we don't have all day" look.

"I'm hurrying, I'm hurrying," he assured the big dog.

Lucy growled.

Great. Now he had ants on the back of his neck and low-pitched grumbles in his ear. He shut his eyes, wiped the rain away, and took a moment to block out everything. Then he opened them to concentrate on the machinery in front of him.

It had to be a bomb.

He eyed what he figured was the pump and looked all around it, then carefully ran his fingers around the bottom.

Nothing.

He did the same with the heater.

Nothing.

Now for the electrical panel. There was a simple latch on it and he hesitated before opening it. Trying to think like whatever asshole might have planted a bomb.

Would he or she have set a trap for it to go off when the panel was opened?

He wouldn't have.

This whole thing felt like it was planned to cause casualties, otherwise it would have gone off as soon as the perps had left the house.

Nope. This was a remote signal or a timer. A remote meant they had a chance to catch the asshole. A timer was scarier. That meant that someone knew the comings and goings of Gideon and the rest of the team.

Mateo looked at his watch. It'd been four and a half minutes since Gideon had sent the text to their teammates, and nobody had texted him to say they were close to the house to help him out.

Dammit!

He thumbed off the latch of the tall electrical panel and there it was.

A bomb.

Not just any bomb.

A timer connected to three bricks of C-4.

Three bricks.

Someone wanted to annihilate Gideon's house.

It was set to go off in eighteen minutes. Mateo did the calculations in his head and realized it would have been fifteen minutes after the kids were actually due to arrive from the games center, but an hour before the men would have arrived from the pub. Somebody was keeping track of the members of Omega Sky, and they were aiming for their families.

He needed Nolan O'Rourke; he was the guy who knew demolitions inside and out, forwards and backwards. Linc and Braxton weren't far behind in their skills, but he'd prefer Nolan, and if Maggie had been with the girls, then Nolan couldn't be far away.

"It's gotta be Nolan," he muttered.

Mateo pulled his phone out of his back pocket and hit Gideon's number.

"Found a bomb. Eighteen. Nope, scratch that. Seventeen minutes and nineteen seconds before it goes off." He ignored the clap of thunder. "It's connected to the electrical housing for the pool pump. Shit, man, I can't tell which wires are for the pool and which wires are for the bomb. I need Nolan."

"Nolan's with Lark and Ryker. We've hopped the meridian. We're flagging down drivers heading west on the expressway. So far, no takers. I'll call Brax for his ETA. Linc and Leila are up in Maine for the weekend.

"Tell Brax to get here fast."

The timer now said sixteen minutes and fifty-one seconds. Mateo set the timer on his watch to coordinate with the timer on the bomb while Lucy growled at him, then she ran off.

What the ever-loving fuck?

"I found the bomb, girl. It's okay, now." Mateo yelled after her as he climbed over the wall enclosing the pump. Lucy had run around to the other side of the house, but now she came running back to him. She butted her huge head against his thigh.

"What, girl?"

She gave him that same look again. The look that told him he was being a dumbfuck.

"Show me."

Lucy streaked off and Mateo ran after her.

The dog careened around past the patio to the other side of the house and ground to a dead halt in front of the air conditioning unit. She looked up at Mateo.

Fuck, I have another bomb.

Looking at the unit, he didn't see shit, then he spotted the connection point to the house's electrical box. That was it. He yanked open the door, expecting to see the C-4. There was nothing. There weren't a lot of electrical wires like he'd seen on the pool pump, and there was no sign of a bomb. He looked down again and examined the hose connecting the unit to the house. Every bolt looked shiny and new. There was no way to know if somebody had recently unscrewed them and shoved C-4 inside with a timer.

He looked all around the bottom of the unit, and it was the same thing. None of the bolts connecting the unit to the concrete pad looked like they had recently been turned, but he couldn't really tell with the rain pouring down. Lucy began to whine.

"Quiet. I need to think."

Mateo peered down into the unit. It was too dark to see anything but the fan at the top. The grill and screens on the sides wouldn't let him look into the unit either.

Mateo looked sideways at Lucy. "Are you sure about this?"

Again with her look of superiority.

Mateo looked down at his watch. They now had thirteen minutes and ten seconds on the bomb. He pulled his phone out of his back pocket and pressed in his voice recognition button and yelled at it to call Braxton.

"I'm on my way," Braxton answered.

"What's your ETA?"

"Eight minutes."

"Make it three and bring your flashlight and wire cutters. I'm in the backyard. I'll leave the gate open."

Mateo rushed to the back gate, unlocked it, and flung it open. Then he yelled at his phone again, this time to call Gideon. Before the man had a chance to answer, he demanded to know where he kept his tools.

"In my garage. What kind of tools do you need?"

"I need a screwdriver. Phillips."

"My electric tools are in the cupboard beside the red Stanley tool chest. You'll find the cordless screwdriver in its black case. I have it labeled so you can tell which one it is."

"Are you shitting me?" Mateo was already running back through the sliding glass door that he'd left open.

"You don't have time to criticize, just get the job done." Gideon hung up.

Mateo damn near skidded on the wet tile in the kitchen and grabbed the doorknob to the garage, shoving it open. He zeroed in on the red tool chest in the corner and saw the white cupboards beside it. He flung open the cupboard and was confronted with at least eight black cases of power tools.

Who in the hell needs this many?

As he read the labels and didn't find what he was looking for, he tossed the case over his shoulder until he came up with the case with the cordless screwdriver. He followed Lucy's barking to the backyard. Why was she barking if there was a bomb? That wasn't protocol.

Hallelujah, Braxton must have arrived!

No such luck. Two dogs who looked just like Lucy were at the adjoining six-foot steel fence and were barking at her. A teenage girl came running out of the house yelling at the dogs. Shit, if a bomb did go off, she'd be hurt too. Mateo took out his phone again.

"Gideon, the girl next door is in her yard. Call the—"

"On it." The line went dead.

Shoving his cell back into his pocket, he dropped the case beside the air conditioner and opened it up. He pulled out the Phillips head he needed, then shoved it into the head of the battery-operated screwdriver and released the first screw, then did the next one and next one and next one. He was halfway through when he heard a man yelling for the dogs and the girl to come into the house next door.

At least that was taken care of.

For one brief moment he looked at his watch and his sphincter tightened when he saw he had ten minutes and twenty-four seconds on the clock.

"Mateo! Where do you need me?" Braxton shouted.

Thank fuck!

"Cinder block enclosure next to the pool," Mateo yelled. "Bomb's in the pool pump electrical panel. Do it fast, we have another one. I haven't found it yet, but it's in the HVAC unit."

"Aye, aye."

Braxton would be on that like flies on shit.

Mateo went back to working on the screws in the unit, trying to make the process go faster. Trying and failing.

This bomb would be the worst. Having it so close to the house meant the flying debris would be catastrophic.

"Mateo! Where are you?" he heard a woman yell out.

Bonnie?

"At the side of the house."

What in the ever-loving-fuck was Bonnie doing back in the house? He dropped everything and stood, horrified, as he saw her racing around the corner of the house towards him.

"Goddammit, Bonnie, get back to the cars!"

"One girl is still in the house," she screamed as she slammed into his chest.

"How—?"

It didn't matter.

"Braxton," he yelled. "One kid is still in the house."

"Fuck!" Braxton yelled back at him. He might not be able to see the man, but at least Mateo could hear him from where he was.

"Work faster," Mateo hollered as he glanced at him on the way back to the patio and the sliding glass door. "Then go to the AC unit. I've got to go help find the girl." Mateo yelled, hoping he would be heard over the rain.

"Gotcha," Braxton yelled back.

Good, he heard him.

As soon as they got inside the great room, Bonnie careened to a halt. "It's bad, right?" She was trembling, her face the color of parchment.

"There are two bombs. I don't know if we can diffuse them in time," Mateo burst out. "We've got to get her out of here. What's her name?"

Bonnie didn't bother to answer him, just turned around and shouted, "Laura!" at the top of her lungs. "Laura, honey, you need to stop hiding. Your dad is worried about you."

The house was two stories, and massive. There were at least four bedrooms upstairs and one bedroom downstairs.

"You take downstairs, I'll take upstairs." He didn't wait for Bonnie's response; he just ran to the staircase and took the steps three at a time as he pulled his phone out of his back pocket.

"We're in a car and on our way," Gideon said as he answered his phone.

"You'll be too late." Mateo looked at his watch. "We

have six minutes and fifty-five seconds. Two bombs and one girl hiding in your house. Are there any hiding places we should know about?"

Mateo hit the first bedroom on the right. "Laura, I need you to come out and stop playing. The other kids are worried about you."

He scanned the room. Just a bed, dresser, chair, and closet. She was little, but she wasn't behind the curtains or the chair. Not under the bed, and not in the bathroom or the glassed-in shower. Next door was a closet with towels and sheets. He yanked out the folded sheets at the bottom of the closet and found nothing.

He hit the next room; it was another guest room. He checked the closet first. It was piled high with shoeboxes. He tore through them, seeing if the girl was behind them.

"Mateo!"

Shit, he'd forgotten that Gideon was still on the line.

"What?"

"Don't forget to check the deck off the master. Jada washed out the planters. They're empty. She could be there."

"Got it." Mateo shoved his phone back into his pocket and raced to the room at the end of the hall, hoping it was Gideon and Jada's room. As soon as he opened it, he struck gold. The size of the bed told the story. He glanced at his watch.

Three minutes, seven seconds.

"Laura?" Mateo called out in a normal tone, trying not to scare the girl so she'd come to him. "I need you to come here. Bonnie's worried about you, honey. Your dad is worried. I need you to quit hiding."

With the storm outside, he was pretty damn sure little Laura wouldn't be hiding out on the deck, but he checked out the potting containers, anyway. They were empty. He checked under the bed. Nothing.

He went to the bathroom and didn't see her. Then he flung open the door to the toilet and saw a tiny huddled little girl staring up at him with wide, terrified eyes as she tried to jam her body between the wall and the back of the toilet bowl. But she couldn't. He would have loved to have coaxed her out of hiding and soothed her fear, but there was no damned time.

No damned time.

He grabbed the little girl underneath her armpits and she whimpered. Then he grabbed her around her waist.

"I want my Daddy," she pleaded.

"Hang on, we're going to go fast." He glanced at his watch.

One minute, twenty-eight seconds.

"I've got her, Bonnie!" he yelled as he raced for the stairs. "Bonnie? I've got her."

When he got to the first floor he saw that the front door was wide open.

Bonnie came from down the hall and almost bumped into them. "Let's go!" he yelled.

He took a millisecond to turn toward the open sliding glass door that felt miles away.

"Braxton, stop what you're doing. I've got the girl," he roared at the top of his lungs. He turned back and ran out the front door, thankful that there were no steps leading up to the house. Instead he just hit the circular drive, making sure that Bonnie kept up with him.

He couldn't check his watch, not with Laura in his arms.

Then he was at Bonnie's side when she stopped at the open door of a minivan. He put his arm around her and forced her to run beside him. There was no time to drive, only run.

He didn't have time to look behind him to find Braxton, not while helping Bonnie run.

If the bomb in the HVAC unit was anything like the pool pump, Braxton wasn't going to survive the blast, not with three bricks of C-4. But he had to get Bonnie and Laura to the end of the drive. He counted in his head. He knew he was down to seconds.

He knew it.

They were halfway down the drive. He looked over his shoulder.

He had to.

No Brax.

Bonnie slipped on the wet drive and fell to the ground.

It was a done deal.

He dropped down on top of her, making sure to cradle Laura's head and little body so she wasn't hurt.

The noise pummeled his eardrums as Laura shrieked, and then his body jolted so hard that he was lifted up then dropped back down onto the two bodies underneath him.

"Fuck!"

Before he could agonize over hurting Bonnie and Laura he was punched in the ribs. He took another shot in his ass. Then he was battered over and over again by hot rain. He gritted his teeth, trying not to scare Laura as he took the beating. The fiery hammer that hit his head forced a cry from his lips.

"Mateo?"

Something was shoving at him. He groaned as his back hit concrete. He peered up into the sky. It was wet and ashy. Ashy?

Smoke.

He tried to sit up. Mateo rolled over and pushed himself up onto his knees. Everything was coming together. He squinted and saw Laura and Bonnie. Both standing. That was good.

Real good.

Laura was sobbing, but she didn't look hurt.

"Braxton? Did you see Braxton?"

Bonnie's mouth was moving, but he couldn't hear her.

"What? Did you see Braxton?"

Her mouth moved again.

"I can't hear you!" he yelled.

She finally shook her head. That was when he realized that besides the rain, she was crying.

"No! That can't be right," he yelled.

Mateo turned to look at Gideon's demolished house. He didn't hear anything.

Nothing.

"Braxton!" he yelled at the top of his lungs. At least he thought he did; he couldn't hear shit. He started to run forward, but his knees gave out and he fell on his face.

He lifted his head. "Braxton!" he yelled again.

Was he hearing sirens? Who the fuck knew.

"Braxton!" Over and over and over again, he yelled for his friend.

He felt something touch his head. A hand. He looked up. It was Bonnie.

"Lucy?" he croaked out her name.

Bonnie slowly shook her head.

The smoke seemed to swirl around him, turning everything gray. He watched the tears drip down her face, leaving clean tracks through the ash. Then his world went black.

3

MATEO GAGGED AND ROLLED OVER ON HIS SIDE, SURE HE was going to vomit, but nothing came out. Was there anything worse than dry heaves?

Where was he?

He tried to push up, but he fell back down again, but at least he landed on something soft.

He took a deep breath and the sharp scent of alcohol-based disinfectants and latex assaulted his senses, and he gagged again.

He was in a hospital. There was something worse than dry heaving.

"Yo, drink some water. It'll help."

He squinted but couldn't make out a face.

"Why am I—" he croaked out the question in a voice that sounded like a rocky landslide.

Fuck, like the explosion itself, everything came roaring back to him. The party, the kids, the singing, and the goddamned rainstorm. And Brax. He slammed the back of his head against the pancake-thin pillow, wishing it was a brick. Wishing it would knock him out and he could go back in time.

"Yo, Mateo, you need to watch it. If your blood pressure goes up anymore, those machines will start going off and they'll kick me out of here."

"Braxton?"

Brax gripped Mateo's hand. The one that wasn't connected to an IV. "I'd turn on the light so you could see me, but you've got a severe concussion, my friend, so I'll just say yes instead."

"But how?"

"Heard you yell. Almost had that bomb disarmed but couldn't get 'er done. Knew I couldn't go through the house, there wasn't time. Yelled at Lucy to follow me to the back metal fence. I hoisted both our asses over and ran like hell. Lucy's fine. I got hit by a brick on my thigh. I asked to be let out of tomorrow's obstacle course. Kostya denied it, the bastard."

Mateo's laugh turned into a cough.

"So, everybody's all right?"

"I wouldn't say that. Right now, the team is pretty goddamned pissed. Those two bombs were set to blow when the kids would be in full birthday party mode. But Kostya, being the paranoid bastard he is, thinks that whoever did it, knew that our team members would still be at the pub watching the game."

Mateo thought about what Brax was telling him. But he wasn't connecting the dots. Instead, his head was pounding. He didn't have a marching band in his head; he had Metallica playing with The Lord of the Dance stepdancing to it. It was a wonder his ears weren't bleeding.

"I'm not tracking."

"Between your injuries and the drugs, it's not surprising. Kostya is thinking that whoever set the bombs planned to kill the women and children. Some of *our* women and some of *our* children, but keep us alive to grieve."

"That's pretty fucking stupid. Have a bunch of enraged SEALs on their ass?"

"Think it through, Mateo. Just how effective would some of us be?"

The idea of Nolan O'Rourke losing Maggie and his daughter Iris knotted his gut like a snake constricting around his throat. And Jase losing Bonnie and the twins? Jesus, the man would burn down the world.

"The Kraken," he breathed out. "They'd do this."

"Yeah, that's what the rest of us have been thinking. They've gone to ground since Dubai. We might have killed off the latest head with Ely dead, but that soul sucker Amanda is still around."

"I thought she was your new girlfriend," Mateo tried to tease, but then coughed again.

"You know, I don't give a shit if you cough so hard you break a rib, after that comment. That Aussie bitch is a stone-cold killer. I don't know if she was really into Ely or not, not with her coming onto me the way she did. I can't decide if she would be behind this kind of retribution or not."

Mateo finally got his coughing under control and squinted so he could see Braxton clearly.

"According to Ryker, she was a psycho."

"She was that, for sure. It made my skin crawl when she called Ely 'Daddy.'"

Mateo cringed. "It would have made my skin crawl, too. Are you sure she wouldn't want revenge for Kostya killing her sugar daddy?"

Brax slowly shook his head. "I really think she was in it for the money. And they were out over fifty million dollars."

Mateo grinned, then so did Braxton. Everybody on the Omega Sky team grinned when they thought about one certain part of the mission: everybody but Landon, Tanner, and Keegan. Those were the three men assigned to stay in the basement of the Burj Khalifa tower where all the shit and sewage was gathered each day and then pumped into over a hundred trucks. Their job had been to check all the supposedly empty trucks that came back from the desert to see which ones contained the C-4.

The three SEALs found the C-4 and forced the driver to take them to Ephram Brady, who was going to use all the explosives to blow up the US Consulate and the British Embassy. Ephram was taken into custody by the United Arab Emirates. While discussions were going on between the US and the UAE about extraditing Ephram back to the US for trial, he was unfortunately killed in a prison fight in the UAE prison. It was curious, since he was supposed to be in solitary confinement. All in all, Mateo and the rest of his team were happy with that particular outcome.

"If you think she was in it for the money, what would be the point of coming after our families?" Mateo asked. "I mean us? Yeah. There are always bounties on Navy SEALs, but not the kind of money she's used to."

"I've been thinking about that," Braxton muttered. "We haven't heard word one about the Kraken since Dubai. That's been five months. Absolutely nothing, and you know Gideon has had his ear to the ground. What if this is the way for the Snow Queen to prove that her organization is still relevant? What if showing that she is busy taking down an entire Navy SEAL team does that?"

"I go back to my last statement. She had the opportunity to set those bombs for when we would be there, not when only the women and kids would be there. How would that be a show of strength to potential customers?"

Braxton clenched his fists and his jaw tightened. "That's the part that I haven't been able to work out. The bitch is all about money, not retribution. I know it in my bones. But Gideon and Kostya keep saying that this has to be revenge, and for all intents and purposes, it looks like it."

Mateo's head was killing him. He was trying to keep up with Braxton, but it was difficult. Just how hard of a hit had he taken? He struggled to hold back a yawn as he asked, "Recruitment?"

Braxton gave him a funny look. "I don't understand."

"Remember when Ryker told us about the Kraken killing his brother's friend's parents? That was after the guy tried to quit the Kraken Elite. Then they said they'd kill his wife and kids. Maybe this was their way of making us fall into line so we'd do what they'd say."

"There is no way that would happen. No way," Braxton shook his head vehemently.

"Are you sure about that?"

"Mateo, you've been out of it for the last couple of days. The team's rage is palpable. Kostya is having a damn hard time keeping everybody under control. There's no way any of us would turn."

"Okay, it was a stupid idea," Mateo agreed as he tried to rub the back of his neck but found his hand trapped since he was tethered to an IV pole. He grunted in frustration and used his other hand.

"Maybe it's not. I haven't had much sleep since Gideon's house blew up, but you have. Maybe you're on to something. I'll bring it up to the rest of the team. Now that you're awake, expect visitors. Bonnie's been chomping at the bit to see you, but Jase is even worse."

Mateo frowned. "What's up with that?"

"You're a hero."

"Shit, I was just the guy who showed up at the right place at the right time. Any one of us would have made the same moves, and you know it."

Braxton tilted his head and gave him a long look. "I'd like to think so, but I'm not so sure. Your instincts have always been on point. I don't know if you've noticed, but when you talk, the Lieutenant pays special attention."

"Humph. Are you sure you weren't hit in the head?"

Braxton shrugged. "Whatever. Just glad to see you awake. You were out for twenty-four hours. We were getting worried. I'll let the team know you're awake now."

"Why were you here?"

"Bonnie told me that all the way into the ambulance, you kept calling for me. Well, me and the dog," Braxton grinned. "They wouldn't let me bring Lucy in, but I figured that seeing my ugly mug when you woke up would be a good thing." Braxton smirked.

"Ahhhh, you love me. Admit it."

"It's true. I've been lusting after you since you were transferred from Blue Cascade four years ago. And here I've thought I've kept it under wraps."

Mateo let out a whoop of laughter. "Hmm, hmm, I believe that. But seriously, Brax, thanks for sticking around. I was sure the bomb got you."

"It's going to take more than a few pounds of C-4 to take me out," Braxton winked at him. "Now I'm going home. That recliner," he pointed to a chair in the corner in the room, "leaves a lot to be desired. I'll let the nurse on duty know that you're awake."

"Don't. I'd like to sleep instead of being poked and prodded, okay?"

Braxton gave him a chin lift. "You've got it."

THE DAY after he'd woken up, Mateo had assured the doctors that he'd have someone at home to stay with him and monitor him if he could be discharged, so they'd released him after having his prescriptions filled at the hospital pharmacy.

It was the Uber driver who had signed the release paper and wheeled him out to his car. Mateo had tipped him huge. Brax had clued him in that Bonnie was going to want to say thank you, and the last thing he wanted was for her to be hovering over him while he was lying in a hospital bed, looking all helpless and shit.

He'd been right, too, because that night after he'd checked himself out, there was a knock on his door. When he opened it up, it wasn't Bonnie and Jase, though. It was his Lieutenant.

"Are you out of your fucking mind or just stupid?" Kostya roared and Mateo winced. "Oh, did my yelling hurt your tiny little brain? Perhaps if you'd stayed in the hospital where you belonged, I wouldn't be yelling at your sorry ass."

"Kostya, you promised you wouldn't do this," a woman's voice said. Mateo looked past one of the two men on his team who was his size, and saw Kostya's beautiful blonde wife, Lark.

"That was before I saw what pathetic shape he was in." Kostya scowled at his wife. "We saw him in the hospital when he was unconscious. I had a hope and a half that he might be looking a little better if he'd checked himself out. Instead, he looks worse. Look at the bruises on his face and the road rash on his chin. He looks like he was hit by a ton of bricks!"

"Will you at least keep your voice down? Every time you yell, he winces. The man has a concussion and you're not helping." Lark shoved Kostya to the side and pushed past Mateo to get into his home.

"Mateo, we need to open a window in here. All I can smell is pizza."

"Just don't open the blinds, yeah?"

She squeezed his upper arm and nodded as she moved toward one of his windows and opened it, ensuring that the blind remained closed.

"Go sit down before you fall down," Kostya ordered, as he pointed to Mateo's couch. "And to think I depend on you when we're out in the field," he muttered. Mateo watched as he stalked into his kitchen and opened the fridge.

"Who hauled your ass home?" Kostya called over the door of the fridge.

"Some nice Uber driver. He stopped at the store and loaded me up."

Kostya rolled his eyes and pulled out a liter of Gatorade and brought it to Mateo. Lark shook her head at her husband as she passed him on the way to the kitchen.

"When was the last time you ate?" she asked.

"Last night. I ate a couple of slices of pizza."

This time, *she* shook her head at him. She opened the box lid of the pizza he hadn't remembered to put in the fridge last night.

"Seriously, Mateo? Meat lover's pizza with

concussion and pain killers? It's a wonder you didn't spend most of the night yacking it up." She looked over her shoulder at him and must have read the guilty look on his face. "Men," she said derisively.

She opened up his fridge and pawed through it, then started opening up his cupboards. "You need something that would soothe your stomach, not spicy sausage and pepperoni." She went over to her purse and fished her phone out. She turned away from him, leaving him stuck with Kostya.

"Drink the Gatorade."

"Is that an order?"

"Yes. If you don't drink it, I'm hauling your ass back to the hospital."

Kostya sat down on Mateo's sturdy coffee table so he could watch his subordinate drink. Mateo rolled his eyes but drank down the beverage. It tasted really sweet and he was surprised at how thirsty he was. Shit, he should have realized he was dehydrated.

Lark slipped her phone back into her purse and went back into the kitchen. She opened up his freezer. "Ah-ha. At last."

Mateo watched as she pulled out a carton of frozen custard. It was his favorite from Blue Cow, mint chocolate chip. She looked in his cupboards and found a bowl. She dished out three scoops and brought it out to him.

"Here you go. This should help soothe your tummy."

"Tummy?" he and Kostya said at the same time. They both laughed.

"You've been talking to Romy too long if you're using words like tummy," Kostya said with a warm smile.

"Can it, buddy. You're just as bad when it comes to our daughter."

Now Mateo was laughing on his own. Married life and motherhood hadn't mellowed Lark Sorenson-Barona, that was for damn sure.

"Now you," she pointed at him. "Quit your laughing and start eating. When are you due for your next pain pill?"

"I hate those things. I can't think straight, and I already can't think straight with the damned concussion. I just need some Tylenol."

"You damned Navy SEALs. Okay, where do you keep it?"

He started to get up.

"Just keep your ass planted and tell me where the bottle is." This time Kostya chuckled.

"You better listen to her."

"And start eating your ice cream." She jabbed her finger at him before darting down the hall.

"The bottle is next to my bed," Mateo yelled after her.

When she left the living room, he turned his attention to his boss. "Braxton filled me in. What have you all come up with?"

"I'll tell you about it, the day after tomorrow. Like you just said, you can't think straight."

"I said I couldn't think straight on the meds. I'm fine with Tylenol. Now tell me what the fuck is going on.

We know it's the Kraken. Do we think the Aussie bitch is in charge now?"

"Braxton's take is that she could take charge after Roberts and Brady were killed."

"Yeah, he told me how she was fucking him and calling him 'Daddy' but his take was that she would have slit his throat during the night so she could take over if she thought she could get away with it."

"Nice." Kostya grimaced. "Women can be ruthless."

"And don't you forget it," Lark said as she came back with the Tylenol bottle. She stopped and opened it up and shook out a couple of tablets.

"Make it three," Mateo said as he kept his hand held out.

This time it was her turn to grimace. "Fine." She shook out one more. "Drink it down with the Gatorade, then eat all of your ice cream. You need the milk to coat your stomach. What in the hell did your Uber driver get at the store for you anyway?"

"Gatorade, protein bars, Doritos, protein shakes, cheese puffs and ice cream."

Lark started to say something when his doorbell rang.

God. In the name of all that was holy, that sure as hell hurt. He needed to get that damn thing disconnected.

Lark opened the door and let Amy Linden in. She was holding a crockpot with oven mitts. Where in the hell was Ryker?

Kostya was off the coffee table before Mateo could blink and had the crockpot out of her hands and on the kitchen counter. Ryker came in loaded for bear. He had at least seven grocery totes.

"What in the hell?" Mateo demanded to know as he got up off his couch.

Lark looked over at him and winced. "I really should have known better than to have called Amy. I should have called Jada. She wouldn't have bought out half of Teeter's Grocery."

"You called while we were grocery shopping. It was no problem," Amy said with a smile. She was already starting to unload everything and put it away. She'd plugged in the crockpot and a heavenly smell was wafting through the air.

"And the crockpot?" Lark asked.

"We just stopped by our house and picked that up. Since it's our dinner, we figured we'd make it our lunch instead and come on over here and share. And check up on the idiot who checked himself out of the hospital three days early."

Shit, he'd forgotten that Amy was Lark's best friend and she didn't pull any punches either.

"That smells really good," Mateo admitted.

"Too bad you don't get any." Amy smiled at him. "It's spicy chili. I brought yogurt and I'm going to whip up some homemade chicken noodle soup and grilled cheese sandwiches for you."

"But I love chili," Mateo heard himself whine.

"And in three days I'll give you some." She handed Ryker the half full pizza box and pulled out the trash can from under his sink. "Here, honey, take out the trash. This is stinking up the house."

Ryker looked over his shoulder at Mateo. "You owe me."

Mateo got the feeling he was going to be owing half his team before the next two days were over. He'd been out of the game for seventy-two hours being held hostage at the hospital and lying around here in his condo, and it was two more days until he'd be in a meeting. It was five days too long to be out of things, as far as he was concerned.

4

———

NIGHT STORM HAD JUST BEEN DEPLOYED ON A MISSION. So had Black Dawn. Midnight Delta, out of Coronado was the next team up to bat, so it looked like Omega Sky had a breather. It didn't matter; if necessary, Kostya would have gone over their new commander's head and talked to Captain Hale about the situation, and why they couldn't be deployed.

If their commander was still Lt Commander Simon Clark it wouldn't have been a problem, but they couldn't take a chance with the new guy. Not with their families being targeted. It was possible this new commander, Theo Nash, might bring in the FBI, because the military wasn't supposed to operate on US soil, but there wasn't a chance in hell that the men of Omega Sky were going to let anybody but themselves care for their friends and families.

Not a chance in fucking hell.

Today everybody but Gideon and Mateo put in a full day's training at Little Creek SEAL center. Gideon was still handling the 'faulty gas furnace' that had destroyed his house. Jonas Wolff's brother was a Battalion Fire Chief in Norfolk. He had enough pull with the Virginia Beach Fire Investigator to get them to go along with that story after a long weekend fishing together and him explaining the circumstances. Jonas was going to owe his brother.

Now they were all assembled at Kostya's house. Gideon's fiancé Jada was with them, and so was Lark Barona, their lieutenant's wife. Jada was almost as good, if not better than Gideon, when it came to cyber shit. Lark was there because, as an award-winning journalist, she had sources around the world, and could often uncover things that would help the team when they were at a loss.

"It's got to be Amanda," Ryker said. "Come on, Braxton. She was all over you in Dubai. She recruited you to be part of the Kraken Elite. Don't you agree?"

Mateo knew Braxton had worked undercover on that mission, and Ryker was correct. Braxton had the best chance of knowing whether Amanda Melton would have taken over the corrupt private military consulting company. Their methods were brutal. In the beginning, they were known to torture and kill whoever was necessary in order to get their finder's fees. As time went on, they became the 'go-to' company to handle assassinations and whatever dirty work that people were willing to pay for. On their last mission in Dubai, they found out that a zealot in the CIA had hired them, but the CIA director assigned the Omega

Sky SEAL team to stop the Kraken while he worked to discover the traitor in his organization.

Braxton got up from the ottoman where he'd been sitting and started pacing the living room. "Look, I agree Amanda would throw her own kids into a volcano to take over that operation, but I'm not so sure that all-male outfit would let her. That's all I'm saying."

Mateo thought about his mother. They'd come to America when she was recruited to work for DuPont. She had received her PhD in chemistry and had authored a white paper about cutting-edge polymers for her dissertation in Argentina when DuPont sponsored her to come to work for them in the United States. She'd struggled to work in an all-male laboratory, and that was a little over twenty-five years ago, but she'd succeeded.

"I think the right woman could take over the Kraken. Especially if she was cruel and brutal enough, and everything you've said about her tells me she is," Mateo said to the group in general. "Tell me, Braxton, would she be willing to kill a couple of people, arbitrarily, just to instill fear in the others?"

"In a second," Braxton nodded slowly. "You're right, Mateo. She would. She has an ice-encrusted dollar sign where her heart should be."

"Okay, so we go with the supposition that Amanda Melton is in charge. We agree she showed up from nowhere, and she's Australian," Jada said as her fingers flew over her laptop keyboard. "It's likely that's not her real name, but do you really think that was a real Australian accent?" She looked up at Braxton.

"Sure," Braxton said. "She wasn't faking. It was a stressful situation. She would have slipped if it wasn't."

"Wait a minute," Gideon stopped his fiancé before she started typing again. "It wasn't Australian. It was Kiwi."

Braxton asked, "What's Kiwi?" before Mateo had a chance to ask.

"New Zealand. They kind of sound alike, but not really. I should have picked up on it before." He looked over to Jada. "We're going to need a sketch, then do facial recognition of women coming from New Zealand to Dubai. It's pretty much a straight shot. She might have had to make a stop in Australia, but it would have been a connection only."

"Yeah, but if she'd been part of the Kraken for a while, why are you assuming she came from her home? She could have been operating anywhere in the world before going to Dubai." Ryker said.

Gideon rubbed the top of his head.

"He's got you there," Kostya muttered.

"You're forgetting the first rule in all of this," Mateo spoke up. Everybody turned to him.

"Okay, Big Guy," Gideon said. "Spit it out." Then he sighed, and Mateo could see that he realized what he missed and he was pissed at himself.

Mateo grinned.

"Follow the money," they said in unison.

Jada hit Gideon's arm. "Are you telling me you haven't been doing searches on how they're getting paid?"

"Cut me some slack, Sweets. They haven't had a

successful mission that I've been able to track in ages, so how could I possibly follow the money?"

She pursed her lips and gave a sad shake of her head.

He held his head in shame. "Okay. Let me get you the names of the men who paid them when we were in Türkiye," he said to Jada.

"Finding the Kraken is half of the equation, now tell me about your families. I want to make sure everybody is covered," Kostya said as he looked around the room. "You first, Drakos, since your family is the size of a small town."

Jase was leaning against a wall. It was the first time Mateo had seen him be anything but in full alert mode since the explosion.

"Bonnie and the kids and Grandma are with my folks. They're not staying anyplace that is familiar. They're at a friend's bed-and-breakfast. She's shut it down for the duration and went on vacation. My brother Bruno, who used to be with Homeland Security, is there with a couple of his buddies. I trust him. Things are tight."

"What about your brother and sister-in-law?" Lark asked.

"They both decided to take their families to Hawaii. My sister Angelica set them up at some hot shot director's beach house for a month. Malik told me he'd pay me to get into this kind of trouble every other year."

Mateo was happy to see the left side of Jase's mouth curl up just a little.

"And the others?" Gideon asked.

"I've made calls to all of them. Five are out of the country, so I'm assuming they're safe. Three families went to Florida, that included Elani and her brood, and my other two brothers have taken jobs where they're on site. The one I'm most worried about is Angelica. But Bruno insisted on two bodyguards while she's on location. I vetted these guys. They're good. The filming ends in two weeks. If we're not done by then, Renzo is taking her to Jasper Creek."

"What about Renzo?" Kostya asked. "Aren't he and Millie sitting ducks on her farm?"

"She's gotten a little better. Somehow, he got her to agree to sit things out in a cabin up in the Smoky Mountains. I don't know how he did it, but my brother has always been a bit of a miracle worker. My guess is, he made her think he was in danger."

The men chuckled.

"Asshats." Jada muttered to Lark.

Kostya turned to look at everyone else. He went through the same drill. He wanted to know about parents, sisters, brothers, or any long-term relationships. Truly, Mateo didn't know why in the hell he was asking—like any of his teammates would leave anything to chance.

"Mateo, what about you? You haven't said anything," Kostya asked.

"There's nobody I need to worry about," he assured him.

"Are you sure? I would have thought there would have been two or three," Braxton teased, and Jase laughed.

"Hey, watch it," Mateo glowered. "There might have been a few women in my life, but there was never crossover. When I was with someone, I was with them exclusively."

"So, aren't you with somebody exclusively at the moment? After all, the weekend is coming up." Braxton's eyes were positively dancing.

"You're an asshole, Braxton. Trudie and I went our separate ways two months ago, and no, I'm not seeing anyone at the moment."

"Are you okay? Did they thoroughly check you out at the hospital?" Jase asked.

"Enough already," Kostya broke in. He turned to Gideon. "So, that's eighty-seven. Is that the count you got?"

"Yep."

"I want each and every one of these people to have some type of life alert that comes to each one of you. I don't want to take any chances."

"Wait a minute. My grandmother thinks she won a trip to Branson, Missouri. She's going to know something is up if I tell her she has to wear a life alert," Landon said.

"How old is your grandmother?" Jonas asked.

"Grandma Kathleen is sixty-eight, and she can probably out-shoot most of you. She still goes duck hunting every season, and if necessary, she'll fill in as a bartender in town when a waitress is sick. But mostly she's a church-going lady who works at the food pantry, and she deserves time watching Elvis impersonators and playing poker at Branson. If I tell her to wear a life alert, she'll tan my hide for sure."

"Landon," Gideon started. Mateo clearly heard the exasperation in his voice. "These will not be typical life alerts. Most of these will be concealed in wrist watches or jewelry. For the kids, they'll be in those kinds of braided—"

"Friendship bracelets. Yeah, my girlfriend has dozens. A lot of them are Swiftie bracelets. She tries to get me to wear them, but I can't hang with that."

"Thank everloving fuck," Braxton called out. "But yeah, I can see how the little kids could wear them. We can ask Bonnie if some of the boys would wear them."

"Yeah, I saw the little boys at Lachlan and Amber's birthday party wearing some. It'll depend on their age," Mateo stated.

"So, we'll get your grandmother a necklace or a watch. It'll be fine, Landon," Lark assured him. Kostya squeezed her shoulder from where he was seated on the arm of the couch, right next to his wife. "I'm going to talk to each of you about who we're getting the alerts for, and we'll make sure to get the right thing for them to wear. Trust me," Lark said seriously.

Mateo saw every man in the room relax. They trusted Lark, and it wasn't just because she was married to their lieutenant. She'd proven herself on that mission in Pakistan. She was a warrior, the same as they were.

"Now for the enemy. You're right." Kostya nodded his head at him. "Gideon and Jada can work on the money angle, but what else do we have?"

"I say we dig deep on Ely Roberts and Ephram Brady," Jonas spoke up. "Yeah, they're both dead, but I wouldn't be surprised if they weren't training other men to take over for them. Also, if we find family members of either of them, maybe they'll know of other folks who are part of the Kraken."

Everybody in the room smiled and Kostya turned to Lark. "Seems to me we need an investigative journalist digging up those kinds of answers."

Lark gave an evil grin. "Let me at it."

"Don't forget Frank Sykes," Ryker said. "He was the original leader of the Kraken."

"Good point." Kostya nodded. He turned to Lark. "So, you're off making up the alerts. Who wants to take that over?"

"I do. I want to make sure Grandma will wear it," Landon said with his hand raised.

Kostya nodded. "I'll put you in touch with the woman who will make these up."

"Linc, you, Braxton and Nolan do demolitions. Track down where that C-4 came from."

"The rest of you are going to be with me at the base. We're going to make a big show of being everywhere the Commander can see us, so it doesn't look like we're short men."

"And when we hear something?" Jase asked.

"Then there will be more assignments, trust me," Kostya said as he looked him in the eye. "Right now we're focusing on the right things. We stick with the old leader of the Kraken, Frank Sykes and his two dead lieutenants, Ephram, and Ely, while keeping an eye out for Amanda. That's more than enough to start on."

Mateo looked around the room. Every single man had something in common with one another. They had people who were depending on them, people they loved and who loved them back. Everybody but him. If he had one damn word to say about things, he was going to take point on whatever popped up first. He was going to make damn sure all of his brothers got home to their families.

5

<hr>

"How are you doing?" Mateo asked Jase, after he let him into his condo. He really didn't have to ask his friend; Jase was clearly wound up tighter than an eight-day clock.

"How do you think I'm doing?" Jase growled.

"Probably—"

Jase held up his hand to halt Mateo's words as he stalked over to Mateo's refrigerator, pulled out two beers, and handed one to Mateo before he yanked the cap off his. "Wait a minute, you can have one of these, can't you?" Jase suddenly thought to ask.

"Or for God's sake, it's been a week now. Of course I can. If one more person worries about me and my head, I'm going to punch them in *their* head."

"Great, now we're both going to be out of sorts. Tell you what, let's both of us agree that your place is a neutral zone? How about it? Anyway, I'm still not over my debt of gratitude."

Mateo squinted his eyes and glared at his friend.

"You know, I had to take all that gratitude shit from your wife, but you and I both know that what I did was the job. It's exactly what you would have done. So not only will I punch you in the head for worrying about my head, I'll punch you in the throat for saying thank you...again. What's more, it's fucking understood, got it?"

Jase started to laugh. "We're sure a pair, aren't we?" He settled down in the chair across from where Mateo was now lounging on his couch in gray sweatpants and a Rush t-shirt.

"You've got that right," Mateo said as he took a pull of his beer. Damn, it tasted good. Almost as good as having someone to talk to. "When is the Lieutenant pulling us together again?"

"Speak for yourself," Jase muttered. "He's pulling us sad saps together every day at the base and working us over like new recruits. My muscles haven't ached this bad since BUD/S."

Mateo laughed. "You know what I mean."

"That's why I came over. Kostya was going to call you, but I said I'd come and pick you up. We're heading back to his house. Which is a bummer. Liked it better going to Gideon's. A lot more room."

Mateo did his best not to shudder. Jase must have caught it, though.

"Sorry, man. I wasn't thinking. Shouldn't have brought it up." He stood up and paced across the room to Mateo's window and looked out. After a minute he turned back to look at Mateo. "Are you having nightmares?"

"I've had one or two. Just imagining I didn't get Bonnie and Laura down the drive. But none for the last four nights."

"Bonnie is still having them. She took a room at the Springfield B&B far away from the twins in case she screamed in the night. She finally went to a doctor for sleeping pills." Jase ran his hand through his hair, then pulled at it. He turned around and gave Mateo a long, considering look. "She needs a counselor."

Mateo nodded.

"She said now's not the time."

Mateo nodded again.

"This is so fucked up. I'm going to kill these motherfuckers!"

"Stand in line," Mateo said as he got up and took his half empty beer to the kitchen. "You done?" He asked Jase.

The man nodded. He brought his half empty bottle to the kitchen, and they left Mateo's condo to head over to Kostya's home.

"WE'VE HAD a couple of breaks in the case. Nothing we can totally sink our teeth into yet." Kostya turned to Lark, who was sitting in the couch's corner with him sitting on the arm—not hovering over her exactly, more like he didn't want to be far from her. Mateo had noticed the same thing with all of his teammates who'd paired up.

"Why don't you tell them what you found, Lark?"

"Brady wasn't Ephram's last name. It was his middle name. His last name was Hicks. He was born in Peacetime, Oregon.

The 'oh shits' and 'what the fucks' went flying around the room.

"Let her finish," Kostya said quietly.

Mateo hadn't been living in the States when the showdown at Peacetime took place, but he'd heard about it. Mateo had run into the type of men in the military who came down on the side of the men of Peacetime who called themselves the Peacekeepers. They had wanted no government interference in how they operated their society, taught their children, or governed their town. They especially didn't want anyone involved in how they handled any problems within their group. They lived in a compound out in the mountains in the Wallowa-Whitman National Forest in the Northeast Oregon border. They did their best to stay off everybody's radar, and it worked. Mostly. Occasionally, some camper would come out of the woods and bitch about the maniacs with guns who threatened to kill them if they didn't get off their property, but mostly, they just went about their business.

That all changed when two women escaped with five children in the dead of winter. One woman was beat to hell, but she helped carry the youngest kid out of there, and they were spotted close to a campground. Turned out there was a flu going round at the Peacekeeper compound, and these kids now had pneumonia, so the women were desperate to get them to a hospital, no matter what they had to do. The husband of the one who wasn't beaten-up had helped them escape and stayed behind to buy them time.

When they were finally brought to the hospital, authorities questioned them. Olive, the woman who hadn't been hurt, told them what was going on. She explained that some of the women wanted to leave, but they couldn't. She said the men had amassed guns and explosives, and they were determined to defend themselves if anyone from the government ever came onto their land.

The raid hadn't been as bad as Ruby Ridge or Waco, but it had been bad. The leader of the Peacekeepers was Ezariah Hicks. He had three wives and fourteen children. The woman who had been beaten so badly and escaped was one of his wives, and she taken three of his children. One of them died at the hospital from complications of the pneumonia.

"Ephram was one of his younger sons. He was in the compound when it was raided. He saw his dad and two of his older brothers killed that day," Lark explained.

Mateo winced.

"How old was he?" Jase asked. Of course, he asked. He might be a big guy who you wouldn't want to get on the wrong side of, but he had a gentle heart.

"He was seven," Lark answered.

"What happened to him?" Jonas asked. "Did he go with his mother?"

"His actual mother wasn't the woman who escaped. His real mother was a zealot, just like her husband.

When she saw her husband die, she slit her throat in front of her children."

Great, it just kept getting better and better.

"So this is how Ephram started out. No wonder he was a psychopath." Braxton shook his head. "He never stood a chance."

"Did he ever check in with his other brothers and sisters?" Mateo asked.

"I'm still working on that," Lark said. "Ephram and one brother and one sister were sent to live with a family in Bend, Oregon. The mother was a child psychologist. The social workers thought that would give them the best chance at a normal life. I'm going to fly out tomorrow to talk to her."

"You didn't tell me that. I thought you were just going to call her." Kostya frowned at his wife.

"This is the best way to get the information I need. A phone call just won't cut it."

Mateo could see the frustration on his lieutenant's face. He knew both Kostya and Gideon had wanted to send their women into hiding, but their help was too valuable. And now, Mateo would bet his bottom dollar that Kostya wanted to go along with Lark to keep her safe, but Kostya, missing from the base, would be too noticeable. Mateo thought about volunteering to go with her, but he didn't. He wanted in on the action. He wanted to play an offensive position.

"I can go with her," Keegan volunteered. "Nolan and Linc can work on the C-4 angle, I'll make sure Mrs. Barona is covered."

"You're sure as hell not coming with me if you call

me Mrs. Barona," Lark said as she rolled her eyes. "My name is Mrs. Lieutenant."

Everybody laughed, breaking some of the tension.

"Do you have anything on Ely Roberts?" Jase asked Lark.

"My God, man, I give you all this good data, and you want more? What do you think I am, a magician?"

"Yes," pretty much everyone said at once.

Lark laughed again. "I've got some feelers out on Ely, but I think Jada is further along than I am. We should have something solid in forty-eight to seventy-two hours."

"But I have something," Gideon chimed in from where he was sitting at the dining room table beside Jada. They were both behind their laptops.

"Spill it."

It was clear Kostya was losing patience. Mateo knew he didn't like the idea of someone besides himself having to do protection duty on Lark when she went to Oregon.

"Franklin Talbot's hedge fund wired out a substantial sum the same week we were in Turkey trying to rescue his son."

"So?" Mateo tilted his head as he looked at Gideon. "Their hedge fund is one of the biggest in the country. They must take in and send out money thousands of times a week. How could you pinpoint something that would be related to the Kraken?"

"Well, my smart friend who told me to follow the money." Gideon flashed his blindingly white smile.

"One thing the hedge fund does not do is handle cryptocurrency, but—"

"But every bad actor in the world is using cryptocurrency to handle their transactions," Mateo finished for him.

Gideon and Jada both nodded.

"Where did they send the money?"

"To a smallish bank that has its headquarters in Annapolis. It's called Lionel Security and Trust Bank. The money sat in an account there for over a month, before it was converted to cryptocurrency and half of it was transferred to the Cayman Islands and then smaller amounts to banks here in the States and overseas. Jada and I are still working on who those accounts belonged to."

"There are a shit-ton of government regulatory and compliance issues when dealing with large cryptocurrency transfers. How much did the hedge fund deposit?" Lark asked.

"One hundred million dollars. The hedge fund paid in cash. It was the bank that converted it, so they were the ones who did the currency exchange. It's not unheard of, as long as they follow the rules," Jada responded.

Landon whistled. "I can't imagine that much money. Imagine paying any company that kind of money."

"It was for his son's life," Jada pointed out.

Landon shrugged. "I guess if you're a billionaire..."

"Who handled that transaction?" Mateo wanted to know.

"They're no longer with the bank, and no longer living in the US. They took their payoff and ran, is my guess." Jada grimaced. "But another big deposit was made to the same account two weeks ago, and it was converted to cryptocurrency and deposited to a different account in the Cayman Islands. It was handled by MacLaine Taylor Simpson. Jada and I are looking to find more information on him. He's our target. What we do know is that he started within two weeks of the other guy leaving."

Before anyone could say anything, Mateo spoke up. "I'm on it."

"You don't even know what that means," Kostya looked over at him.

"It means while Gideon and Jada backtrack the money, I get close to MacLaine and find out what he can tell us about the depositor and what he can tell us about the account he transferred money into. Better yet, he can also tell us about the transfer that was made a couple of months ago."

"Just how do you intend to get close?" Lark arched an eyebrow at him.

Mateo laughed. "I'll wing it."

"Not good enough," Lark said, shaking her head.

"Yes, it is, *Solncè*. Let it go," Kostya murmured.

Mateo had heard Kostya call Lark that Russian word a few times, so he'd looked it up. It meant Little Sun. It fit. Kostya turned to him.

"Mateo, are you sure your head is—"

"Lieutenant, I wouldn't volunteer if I wasn't one-hundred percent good to go."

Kostya nodded. "All right then. Is your truck one-hundred percent good to make it up to Maryland?"

Mateo glowered at his team as they all laughed at Kostya's question.

"She sustained some injuries during the blast. I'm still working on her," Mateo sighed. "I'm having to drive the Challenger."

The chuckles continued. "My question still stands."

"I've worked out the bugs," Mateo promised. "She's road-trip worthy. I just want to give her a rest, that's why I'm taking the Challenger."

Gideon looked up from his computer. "Email me with your expenses. I've got you covered."

"I can cover my own damn self. Anyway, what do I need an expense report for? Annapolis is only four-and-a-half hours away."

"Gas and food," Gideon answered. "Keep track and expense it."

"I want this done right. I want Mateo to get housing up there, and ID to go with his cover. Got it?" Kostya looked at Gideon.

"I'm on it."

"I can cover my expenses," Mateo ground out.

Everyone in the room knew that Gideon Smith had made himself a vast amount of money when he sold off most of his company stock when he left a Silicon Valley start-up company to join the Navy. But just because he could afford to cover the cost of his adventure up in Maryland, didn't mean he should.

"Mateo," Kostya shook his head sadly. "If you don't submit an expense report, Gideon's just going to buy you a new truck or somehow put money into your account. Just deal with it and submit an expense report."

A sudden memory of one of the closets in Gideon's house popped into his brain.

"Gideon, aren't you going to need all that money to replace Jada's shoes?"

Lark barked out a laugh.

"I buy my own shoes, thank you very much," Jada said as she looked up from her computer. "Submit an expense report."

"Fine." It was no skin off his nose if cancer research got a bigger check from him this year.

"When are you leaving?" Kostya asked.

"First thing tomorrow morning, since the bank is closed now."

Kostya turned to Gideon. "Work fast."

6

_____

As she opened her car door, Lainey was pummeled by the moist heat of a Maryland July. Who would have guessed it would be this humid in Maryland? She thought she had left that behind in South Carolina. But at least her dress was lined, so it would keep it from sticking to her, so there was that to be thankful for. Lainey grinned. Her mother would hate the fact that she wasn't wearing the obligatory size-two, sweater twin-set, even on a day that was over ninety degrees. Cucumber sandwiches during charity teas were never her thing. Leaving that life behind was the best thing she ever did.

She liked having a donut from time to time. And a cheeseburger. A bacon-cheeseburger. Food made Lainey happy. She bet if her mom and her sister actually ate a cookie once in a while, they wouldn't look like they were perpetually sucking lemons.

Lainey pictured her mother and Bennett in their

little Chanel suits as they sat at their garden table where they hosted their lunches at the country club, waiting for the women of the Historical Society to come to their table and pay their homage.

Ick.

That had never been her scene. She liked the idea of working and using her brain. Maybe not this exactly, but eventually she'd have the background she needed to do what she really wanted to do.

"One step at a time, Lainey. One step at a time."

She checked her make-up in the rearview mirror. Of course, she had bitten almost all of her lipstick off. She needed to stop biting her lip. She'd had that habit all of her life, but the more her mother and sister harped at her, the more she did it. She pulled out the pale pink lipstick that was office appropriate and reapplied it.

She opened the door and gracefully stepped out. That was easily done in three-inch heels. It was when she wore five-inch heels she had to take a bit more care. Luckily, up here in Maryland, there weren't any parties, balls, and cotillions that her mother could drag her to, and what's more, she hadn't found anyone she wanted to impress. Yep, three-inch heels were just fine by her.

She shut her car door and marched toward the bank. Maurice was on security duty this morning, and she gave him a bright smile. Whenever she baked scones, she brought a Tupperware container just for him.

"Well, aren't you a sight for sore eyes?" He smiled back.

"You sure know how to bolster a girl's confidence. How are your grandbabies? Isn't Todd about to turn three soon?"

"My yes." The guard grinned. He pulled out his phone and pulled up a picture with five children gathered around him.

"Those are some good-looking kids, Maurice. It looks like they adore you."

"Seem to. I go to all of their ball games and recitals. Wouldn't miss them for the world."

"You're a good grandfather, Maurice."

"Thank you. You have a good day, Miss Lainey."

"You too, Maurice."

He opened the door for her, and she walked into the main branch of Lionel Security and Trust Bank. It had opened in Annapolis in 1852 to service the Naval Academy graduates. It survived the great depression and the mortgage crisis that began in 2007. It was the reason that Lainey had applied to this bank. She liked that it only had eleven branches, and that they had a higher percentage of liquidity than most banks. If she was going to work at a bank, she was going to work for a good one.

She smiled at the tellers who weren't assisting customers as she made her way through the spacious lobby. The building was built the year the bank opened, and it was gorgeous. She walked up the winding staircase to the second floor to the small office of the Compliance and Regulatory Adherence Department. It was her fourth week in this department. So far, in her management training program, this department was the most complicated. Her one co-worker was Janice, who didn't have the time of day for her, and her boss. Arnie Pine had started a two-week vacation last Friday. Lainey hated to admit it, but she was in over her head.

When she voiced her concerns to Mr. Pine before he left, he told her that Janice or his boss would help. "But you won't need them. You're a smart girl, Lainey. It'll be fine." Unfortunately, he had said that loud enough for Janice to hear.

When Lainey had gone to Mr. Pine's superior, she found out she was prepping for a bank wide audit and had no time for Lainey, which meant she needed Janice's help. The problem was, Janice had applied for the one spot available in the management trainee program, and instead, it was given to Lainey. An outsider. In the beginning she'd been just spiteful, but after hearing Mr. Pine praise Lainey, she'd turned downright malicious. So, anything Janice didn't want to do, she threw on Lainey's desk.

"Here's another crypto transfer," Janice said as soon as Lainey sat down. "I can't make heads or tails of it, but you being such a *smart girl*, I'm sure you can figure it out," Janice said as she flounced back to her desk.

Dag nab it!

The last transfer had taken three days to work through, and she still was working on pulling down and reading through the latest set of anti-money-laundering regulations posted on the FBI website, and updating the bank's regulations. After working the cryptocurrency transaction right after Mr. Pine left for vacation, Lainey was going to suggest to Mr. Pine that they add another person to his department, one who was well-versed in cybersecurity. That person could have a dual purpose of updating the company's internal website so that every employee could access the latest regulations, and then set up ways of flagging suspicious activities that were out of compliance.

She looked down at the cryptocurrency transfer in front of her and started pulling up all of the government websites that cited the regulations and compliance issues, just in case she forgot anything from two weeks ago. Then she got to work.

Before leaving in the morning, Mateo did a quick search on the bank's website. MacLaine's name was mentioned on the company's website, but there wasn't a title or a picture. It was almost like he was a teller or something, but that didn't make sense if he was handling crypto deposits. Maybe he had just been promoted recently.

Mateo made the ultimate sacrifice and dressed in a pair of chinos and a button-down shirt instead of his normal summer uniform of cargo shorts and a T-shirt. Even leaving at oh-four-hundred, he knew it was going to get hot quick.

He prayed his car's temperamental air conditioning would work today. Truly, it was time for him to start working on his car, but the condo association frowned on anybody working on their car on the premises and his buddy Rocco had work coming out of his ears at his auto repair shop right now. Until things slowed down for Rocco, Mateo didn't have a place to work on either of his vehicles.

He poured his travel mug to the brim with black coffee and hustled down to his Challenger. It might be a hot day, but there was no way he was going to ruin good coffee with ice. He stretched his shoulders as he opened up his trunk and threw in some things he thought he might need for today's reconnaissance. Even after a week, he was still pretty sore where one of the fiery bricks had hit him on his shoulder blade. He'd been doing exercises to improve his mobility, but they did nothing to negate the pain.

He chuckled. Yeah, like he was going to need to worry about a physical confrontation with Banker Boy.

Mateo got behind the wheel of his car and he threaded through all the small streets that led out of his community and pulled onto Virginia Beach Blvd. There wasn't a chance in hell he was going to take the 64 to the 95 and go through DC to get to Annapolis. Hell, rush hour traffic in the nation's capital? He'd prefer to do another day at BUD/S. Therefore, he headed toward the Chesapeake Bay Bridge Tunnel that would take him up the peninsula. Instead of appalling traffic, he'd get to see the sun rise over some farm or another. That should help him figure out a way to approach MacLaine.

This deposit and transfer request was worse than the last, and who even knew that was possible?

"Janice, you wouldn't happen to know if—"

"You sure do have a lot of questions for such a smart girl," Janice said as she got up from her desk. "I'm going to lunch."

"Look, you're the one who peppered these documents with sticky notes. I can't read half of them. I need your help deciphering them before I can do my job."

"NMP." Janice said as she pulled her compact out of her purse to check her lipstick.

"What?"

"Not. My. Problem."

"Are you for real?" Lainey could swear her eyes were about to bug out of her head. This woman could give her mother and sister pointers in being a witch.

"What are you talking about? You applied for the management training program, and you got it. It's not my problem that you can't cut it." Janice draped the strap of her knock-off Prada bag over her shoulder and tossed her fake red hair over her other shoulder. "Don't fuck things up too badly, or you could get fired," she smiled sweetly.

Lainey stood up and blocked her way out of the office. "Look here, you feckless woman. I don't care for your language, your churlish manner or the perverse way you've been 'assisting me' since Mr. Pine has been on vacation." Lainey put air quotes around the words 'assisting me.'

Janice took a step toward Lainey and shoved out her chin. "Who are you calling a pervert?"

"Listen to me carefully, you ignorant ingrate. I said you were perverse. That means you're being deliberately unreasonable."

"Just because you went to college, don't try to rub it in my face. I've worked here seven years—"

"And I know that. That's why I'm coming to you for help. I value your input."

"You should have thought of that before you took my job." Janice hip checked her as she flounced out the door.

"Good God!"

Lainey sat back down at her desk. That woman was a menace. Lainey didn't even know who Janice was when she applied for this program. Lainey had applied when she couldn't stand another cucumber sandwich and had to leave South Carolina and her family or commit murder. Thank God she'd had the good sense to fight for a college education like her older brothers, instead of following in her big sister's footsteps. Her dad was hard pressed not to support her after she got accepted into Clemson University. Heck, none of her brothers had managed to get accepted there.

Her sister, Bennett, had married a real go-getter in their dad's law firm, a man named Frederick Laughton III, otherwise known as Trey. Of course, his name was Trey. As soon as Bennet and Trey came back from their honeymoon, Trey had a corner office in her father's law firm. They currently had a house in the swankiest area outside of Charleston, that her father gave them the down payment for. Her sister currently had two daughters that she dressed like her and was now pregnant with the obligatory son.

Lainey had tried to fit into her family's ideal of a Simpson woman, but when she had choked down her last dry scone at the monthly Historical Society tea, she couldn't take it anymore. She decided to take the bull by the horns and get the heck out of town. Her dad and mom were against her leaving South Carolina. After all, her duty was to get married to a lawyer and propagate the next generation of lawyers and hostesses.

But she'd had enough, so she started sending out resumes. Her dad and mom thought she couldn't leave since she didn't have a job and was living with them. They had no idea what Gran had really left her, when Lainey was left with the contents of Gran's safe deposit box. Gran had always said she liked Lainey's moxie, and when Lainey had opened up the box, she'd been stunned. Stunned and elated. Gold. Who kept gold in this day and age? Her grandmother. This was her key to getting out. But it really was a way for her grandmother to screw over her father. He received nothing in the will. Gran never thought her father had moxie.

When she was accepted for the management training program with Lionel, she jumped at it. And for the first time ever, she used some contents of the box to buy herself a small house in Eastport.

"Enough down memory lane. Get to work, MacLaine," Laine ordered herself. She opened up the file on her desk, then clicked into the massive set of documents on the secure server.

Yep, this was going to take much more than a minute.

MATEO LOOKED UP AT THE STATELY BUILDING FROM A bygone era. It was out of place against all the new construction in downtown Annapolis, but that made it all the more impressive. He walked across the street to a coffee shop and sighed when the clerk seemed confused when he ordered just black coffee.

"You know, we have a lot of different coffee drinks, right?" the kid, who couldn't be more than eighteen, asked him.

"Yep, I see your menu." Mateo pointed to the menu on the wall. "I just want a coffee."

"Cream or sugar."

Mateo remained patient. "Black means no cream or sugar."

The kid frowned as he looked down at his register. "Oh, yeah." He pressed a bunch of buttons. Seriously, why did a plain cup of coffee require that many buttons?

"What's your name?"

"Mateo."

"Ma-What?"

"Matt."

The clerk wrote his name and order on a cup.

"Okay, Matt. Go wait over by the barista. Your order will be up in a few minutes."

He looked at the empty area over by the barista.

Really? A few minutes?

He wandered over to the barista. By the time he got there, his coffee was waiting for him. He looked over at the barista and saw a young girl who smiled at him.

"We give free refills for coffee. Come back whenever."

Now that was how it should be. He tipped his head at her. "Thanks." He walked back to the register and threw in a couple of bucks to the tip jar, then found a comfortable seat to sit down. He pulled out his smartphone to see if Gideon or Jada had any more info on MacLaine Simpson for him.

There it was, something from Jada and it came with all the opinions and humor he'd come to expect from her.

Apparently, MacLaine had started working for the bank in the management trainee program nine months ago. He had graduated from Clemson University with honors and was part of a well-respected, aka snooty, family in Charleston, South Carolina. The family had money. Lots of old money. Chances were, daddy pulled strings for MacLaine to get into this program, since over one hundred people had applied.

He's dirty, that's for sure, because within six months

of starting at the bank, he liquidated almost a quarter of a million worth of gold coins from Fredson's Gold and Antiquities which he then dumped into his bank account, and he bought himself a condo right in the heart of Annapolis.

He's our man, Mateo. You find a way to take him down and find out all his secrets.

Mateo grinned as he read the last two lines. He definitely intended to do just that. But he wasn't going to start with an all-out frontal attack. This required some reconnaissance, i.e., a phone call. Then some finesse.

He crossed his ankle over his knee and leaned back in the comfortable chair and dialed the number to the bank across the street. And wasn't it a pleasant surprise when a human answered, and not some fake computer-generated voice who tried to herd him toward one department or another?

"Hi," he said to the woman on the other end of the line. "I'm thinking about transferring some of my money from my current bank to Lionel. It's rather complicated, and a friend suggested I talk to Mr. Simpson." He was careful to keep all hint of his Spanish accent under wraps. He didn't want to be identified when he showed up later.

There was a pause on the line. "I'm sorry, sir. We don't have a Mr. Simpson who works here at the bank. I'm sure one of our personal bankers can assist you."

"No, my friend was pretty specific that MacLaine Simpson was the man who could help me."

The woman laughed. "Oh, you mean Lainey. She's

not working in the personal banking department anymore. Now she is in the Compliance and Regulatory department. I'm sure someone else could help you. Arthur Stevenson is great and he has availability today. Do you want me to make you an appointment with him?"

"Let me talk to my friend and see if there was somebody else he worked with at your bank. I really do like to work with recommendations. I'm sure you understand that."

"Oh, I do."

"Thank you for all of your help. What was your name again?"

"Penny Durby."

"Well, Penny, you have been extremely helpful. Thank you."

"You're welcome."

Mateo peered off into space as he considered how to approach MacLaine "Lainey" Simpson. It shouldn't put a different spin on things that she was a woman, but it did. Not that a woman wasn't capable of being a criminal, or a murderer for that matter, but it would definitely change his approach.

His mother had always been so fond of quoting Steven Hawking. "Intelligence is the ability to adapt to change."

So, he'd adapt.

"HELLO, THIS IS LAINEY SIMPSON," she said as she picked up her phone.

"Lainey, I have Cliff Ackerson from the FBI on the phone for you. He wanted to talk to Mr. Pine, but I told him you could help him."

Lainey looked over to where Janice was typing at her computer. She couldn't see her screen, but she'd bet next week's manicure that she was on her social media account.

"Penny, I think that—"

"Have a heart," Penny interrupted her. "He sounds nice. Don't make me send him to the piranha."

Lainey stifled her giggle. They were going to have to go to dinner soon. She missed her girl time with her friend. "Fine. Pass him through."

There was a click on the line.

"Hello, this is Lainey Simpson, with the Lionel Security and Trust Bank Compliance and Regulatory Department. How can I help you?"

"I think Penny might have told you. My name is Cliff Ackerson and I'm a Special Agent with the FBI."

"Yes, she did, Agent Ackerson." Janice's head jerked up, and she glared over to Lainey's desk. "How can I assist you?"

"This is just a routine check. I need to set up a meeting with someone in your department to go over some of the new AML reporting standards."

She frowned. "Why would you need to do that? If there is some new reporting standard, won't that just come through the FBI portal? Or is there something specific that our bank has done that has brought attention to the FBI?"

Janice was darn near shooting daggers at her with her eyes.

"No, it's nothing like that. Your bank was one of the twenty lucky banks in the Mid-Atlantic region that won this special attention," he chuckled. He had a friendly laugh.

"Oh, okay."

"I can't make it over there until late. I have an appointment in Richmond, then I'll be coming your way, but I'll have to make my way through DC traffic. What time do you leave?"

"I leave at six."

"I should be able to get there before then."

"I look forward to meeting you."

"Same."

He hung up and so did she.

"Who was that?" Janice demanded to know.

"An agent from the FBI."

"Why are you handling somebody from the FBI? If Mr. Pine isn't available, then I usually handle the Feds."

"I don't know what to tell you, the call came to me. Agent Ackerson didn't leave his number. He said he would arrive late. You'll probably have to stay late to meet him."

"Oh, hell to the no." Janice pointed one of her red talons in the air. "I have a date tonight, and I'm expecting good things from this guy. Like appetizers and everything."

"Well then, I guess I'll be handling the FBI."

"Well, don't blow it. The last thing Mr. Pine is going to want when he gets back is to have the Feds breathing down our neck."

"Thanks for the advice." Lainey looked back at her computer and the nightmare that was the cryptocurrency files. Would these ever end?

MATEO kind of felt like shit, just a little bit. Knowing that Cliff Ackerson would never show up for a meeting with a good Southern girl, Lainey Simpson. He'd been living in Virginia for almost ten years now, but he didn't think he'd ever heard such a sweet, honeyed Southern accent like Lainey's.

"Do you have what I need?" he growled at Gideon.

"I have almost everything. You'll be getting a download in fifteen minutes."

"Seems to me like this is coming eight hours too late."

"Quit busting Gideon's balls," Jada groused. Apparently, Gideon had his phone on speaker. "I'm the one who did the background check on MacLaine. I'm the one who missed that MacLaine was a woman. Seriously, who names their girls Bennett and MacLaine anyway?"

"Bennett?" Mateo asked.

"Yeah, that's her sister's name. Apparently, it's a deep South thing to give the girls first names that are family surnames. I'm going to have everything for you soon. Including her driver's license, all of her financials, her address, and her dress size."

"Will it include the make and model of her car?" he asked.

"Yep."

"Why do you want to know that?" Gideon asked.

"Now that we know our MacLaine is Lainey, I'm going to do the chivalrous thing and fix her flat tire tonight. And if my skills are still up to snuff, I'm going to take her out on a date."

"You know, this makes even more sense now," Jada said.

"What does?" Mateo wanted to know.

"Lainey was living with mommy and daddy down in South Carolina. She was living the high life. She had a Mercedes AMG that they bought her, but now she's driving around in a Toyota Corolla. Something tells me our little girl didn't like living under mommy and daddy's thumb, but she was missing the money."

"But how did she get involved with the Kraken?" Mateo asked.

"Well, that's your job to find out now, isn't it?" Gideon asked.

"Yes, it is. Send me the file. I'll talk to you two later."

He hung up and went over to the barista. "Can I get a refill to go?"

"Absolutely." She smiled.

8

"Flub-a-dub! Fudge-bonnet! Crap on a cracker!"

When was the last time she had been this out of sorts?

Oh yeah. When Bennett foisted Lifeless Luke on her because Trey needed to get him a date for the Country Club's annual charity ball. Even now, thinking about that could set her pulse rate skyrocketing. It was just one more reason she'd left Charleston.

Lainey sighed. Maybe the gold coins in Gram's safe deposit box would be worth a bunch of money, too. She really needed to get a better car than the one she'd been driving since college.

She was glad she was parked around the back of the building, near the seafood restaurant and the pet shop. Instead of watching her drive away, Maurice had just watched her from the corner and waved as soon as she'd opened her car door. He still had a lot to do before he could go home, and she knew he liked to get home to his wife's home cooked meal. If she'd been parked out front, Maurice would have wanted to help her with her flat tire, and with his arthritis, it wouldn't have been a good thing. She pulled out her phone and took her Triple A card out of her wallet and made a call. Three minutes later, she was back to thinking what a rotten day this had turned into.

First there was Janice, who from this day forward she would always think of as 'Janice the Pervert.'

Then there was the Invisible Agent Ackerson.

Now she had a flat tire and a three-hour wait from Triple A.

Maybe she should just go check out the bar of Home Port next door. Penny said it was hopping. That was the one area where she and Penny disagreed. She just didn't like the loud music, and the idea of being approached by a bunch of newly minted Naval officers held no appeal. It would be like meeting Dad's latest crop of attorneys that he brought into the firm each year. All of them knew that the surest way to a partnership was marrying into the family. She preferred it when she and Penny could go to a quiet bar and have a drink and talk.

At least it wasn't still ninety degrees—it was now a bearable eighty degrees with one hundred percent humidity. Lainey lifted her hair off the back of her neck and turned in a circle, trying to get a little bit of breeze going. It wasn't working all that well. She worried about sitting in her car and running the air conditioning. Wouldn't that run down the battery?

Google would know.

She pulled her phone out of her purse again and leaned against the car near the flat tire.

"Hello?"

Startled, she looked up from her internet search and saw a man standing thirty feet away from her. It looked like he had come from the bar, but he didn't have that fresh-faced look of a boy who had just graduated from the Naval Academy. Actually, there was nothing boyish about this man.

"Hi," Lainey smiled, secure in the knowledge that she had pepper spray and her phone.

"Is there a problem?"

He had a hint of a Spanish accent. It went with his dark, close-cropped hair that hinted at a curl.

"I have a flat tire, and I'm waiting for Triple-A."

"Ahhh. So, you're covered." He looked up, then over. Then he frowned at her. "How soon will they be here? It's getting dark soon, and there are only two lights here in the parking lot."

"I could call Maurice. He's the security guard at the bank, to come and wait with me if Triple-A takes too long."

The man didn't move closer to her, but he again looked all around. "Where is this Maurice? Why isn't he here already?" She heard just a hint of disapproval in his voice.

"I didn't want to bother him."

"Hmmm." Yep, definitely disapproval. "How long do you have to wait for Triple-A? If it's too long, maybe I can change your tire for you."

"They said I might have to wait two hours. But who are you?"

The man chuckled. "That is an excellent question. My name is Matt Aguilar. I'm a chemist for a pharmaceutical company in Baltimore. I was here to see an old friend of mine," he said, motioning to Home Port, "but he was more interested in meeting someone new tonight."

He gave a resigned shrug, so Lainey laughed.

"That's a bummer. I'm sorry about that," Lainey said. "If it makes you feel any better, I was stood up today, too."

"You were? I find that very hard to believe."

He was so giving off a good vibe. Not like the creepers at Clemson University or the lame-butt lawyers working for her dad. "Hey, I've got an idea. Instead of yelling across a parking lot, how about you come closer so we talk like normal people," Lainey suggested.

"I didn't want to make you uncomfortable, since you were out here alone."

"Now, sugar, that is the sweetest thought I've heard in ages. But please come closer. If I feel uncomfortable, I'll yell for Maurice and he'll come running."

As the man walked closer to her, she realized just how big he was. No wonder he hadn't gotten closer to her in the beginning.

"You're right, a man your size could have given me quite a jolt if I wasn't expecting you. Just how tall are you, Matt Aguilar?"

"Six foot three."

"My guess is you played offensive or defensive lineman."

"I did grow up in Texas, so there was a little bit of football in my past."

Lainey laughed. "I imagine so."

"And you know football? Why?" he asked as he smiled down at her.

"I went to Clemson in South Carolina. You can't attend that university without becoming indoctrinated."

"Southern football, there's nothing like it. Except for maybe Argentine fútbol."

"Soccer right?"

He nodded.

"Is that where you're from? Argentina?"

"Yes, I came here when I was five years old. My mom got a job here as a chemist for DuPont."

"That's impressive. So you're following in her footsteps?"

Matt nodded. "Do you want to pop your trunk so I can see what I'm working with?"

Lainey bit her lower lip. Why did that question sound so dirty? Why did she like it so much?

Lainey hit the trunk icon on her key fob and watched as Matt looked inside. Since she had recently cleaned out the garage, she'd also cleaned out her trunk, so she knew he'd only find the tire and some tools.

"It looks like we're good to go." He unbuttoned his cuffs, then rolled up his sleeves on his buttoned shirt. Lainey's eyes widened. Under the lights of the parking lot, she saw just how muscled his forearms were under his bronzed skin. Outside of an action star in a movie, she'd never seen a man's arms look so strong. Matt swung the tire out of her trunk with one hand and a wrench and some other thing with his other hand.

"What's that?" she asked, pointing to the thing she didn't recognize.

"It's the jack," he answered as he moved past her to squat down in front of her flat tire. "It will allow me to jack up the car and remove the tire."

In the time he used to answer her question, he had removed her hubcap and had loosened the bolts on her car's wheels.

"Aren't you going to take off the bolts?"

He grinned up at her. "They're lug nuts. And no. If I do that, the whole thing will fall off while I'm jacking up the car, and we don't want that to happen," he explained.

She liked it that he didn't seem to mind her questions. She watched as he finished loosening the lug nuts, then he looked under her car and set up the jack and began pumping it so that the car lifted up.

It was when her bottom lip started to hurt that she realized she was biting it. But who could blame her? Watching his shirt strain across his back muscles and watching his pants pull tight against his butt was positively mouth-watering.

Gah! I need to be hosed down! And it's not because of the humidity.

But it didn't stop her from admiring the view.

Matt made quick work of loosening the lug nuts

and carefully placing them in a pile, then removing the flat tire. He had the spare tire on the car far too soon, in her opinion. She tried to think of another question to ask him so she could hear his sexy Spanish accent.

"You're good at this. Have you changed many flat tires?"

Great, that could go into the most stupid question hall of fame.

Matt looked up at her. "This is my second, but it's not a tough process."

He slid the spare tire on and put the lug nuts in place, then used the wrench to tighten them.

"Oh, I didn't tell you my name," Lainey said. "I'm Lainey. Lainey Simpson. I work here at the bank."

Stupid, stupid, stupid.

Like he hadn't already figured out she worked at the bank.

Matt stood up. She had to lean her head back to look up at him.

"I'd shake your hand, but mine are all greasy." His grin was mesmerizing.

"Wait a moment." She turned to open the car door and dove in for her purse. She pulled out a packet of Kleenex and grabbed the water bottle from the front seat. She pulled out a couple of tissues and poured water on them, dousing her dress at the same time.

Of course I did.

Lainey powered through like it hadn't happened, and handed the damp tissues to Matt.

"Here you go. That way you can have clean hands when you drive home."

"I appreciate it. Let me put all of this back in your trunk first."

I'm an idiot. Lainey mentally slapped her forehead.

When he came back, he took the proffered tissues.

"Thank you, Lainey Simpson."

Was it her imagination, or was his accent even more pronounced when he said her name? She watched as he wiped the grime off his hands.

"I'll be back in a moment." Matt sauntered off to the trash can near the street next to the restaurant, dumped the tissues, then came back.

Lainey was happy to have that time so that she could arrange for her hormones to no longer be in control of her brain and her mouth. As soon as he was within a few feet of her, she thrust out her hand.

"I can't thank you enough."

His lips curved up into a smile as he took her hand. "You're welcome. Glad to be of service." He paused. "You know, that spare tire of yours has seen better days. I think all of the auto shops are closed at this time, so I'd really feel better if someone followed you home, to make sure you don't get stuck with another flat, only this time on the side of the road."

"I'm sure it'll be fine." Lainey tried to convince herself.

"Do you have a friend you could call who could come and follow you home?"

Lainey thought about Penny, but she knew she was at dinner with her parents.

"I'll wait here until Triple A comes."

"For over two hours?"

She bit her lip. "I'll call an Uber."

"Would you feel comfortable if I followed you home, so I could make sure that your spare tire doesn't blow out?"

She shook her head. But at the same time, the Triple A guy would be a stranger, the Uber driver would be a stranger.

Crap on a cracker.

"Lainey, I'm not asking to come into your house. I just want to follow you to make sure the spare tire holds. How about this? You take a picture of my license plate and my driver's license and text a picture of both of those to someone you trust. Tell them when you expect to be in your apartment, and should expect a call back. If they don't hear back from you in a timely manner, they can send those pictures to the cops."

For God's sake, Janice had gone back to men's apartments after meeting them that same night at a bar!

Lainey bit her lip.

"Okay. Let me grab my phone."

"There's really no need." Lainey bit her lip and tried again, but stopped when she saw the frown on his face.

"Thank you, Lainey. I feel much better about this. Let me bring my car over, so you can take a picture of the license and send it to your friend."

He took out his wallet and pulled out his Virginia driver's license.

"You live in Virginia?"

"I did. I'm living here now. I got a job at Reduxler."

"Oh." Lainey took the picture.

"I'll be right back. I'm driving a black Dodge Challenger."

She watched as he hurried off.

Lainey nodded. "I'll wait." She sent Penny a quick text telling her what was going on. She immediately replied back and told her to be safe, and then asked if Matt was cute.

> Lainey: I WILL and YES, he's twice as hot as his driver's license picture.

> Penny: SWEET! Text me as soon as you get home! Don't forget.

> Lainey: I WON'T.

He was really nice. And not one of her dad's toadies, or some fresh-faced kid. Even in college, all of the boys had seemed too young. Yeah, Matt was pushing all of her buttons.

9

Mateo laughed as he followed MacLaine Sinclair through the streets of Annapolis. He couldn't be more surprised than if Godzilla had popped up and stepped out in front of him. Not only was Lainey all woman, she was about the prettiest Southern lady he had ever met. Mateo didn't think he'd ever had a woman give him such shy admiring glances before.

He'd already loved her accent before meeting her in person, and having her words drip sunshine on him while he worked on changing her tire had been staggering. Even her clumsiness was cute.

Down, boy.

She's a target.

She's done transfers for the Kraken.

She had a quarter of a million in gold to buy a house, obviously a payment from the Kraken.

As he followed the brunette in the flowery dress who was driving like a retiree from Boca Raton, Mateo was having a hard time imagining her in cahoots with the Kraken. A dupe, maybe? Maybe she didn't know what was going on, but not a willing participant with a terrorist organization.

"Then explain the gold coins," he muttered to himself.

He looked out his car window, waiting for Godzilla to pop out and answer his question. No such luck. When he didn't get any answers, he went back to concentrating on the red Toyota in front of him.

Seriously? Could she drive any slower? She was three miles below the speed limit as they drove through Annapolis' Historic District. They were almost to Church Circle when she took a right and started crawling down one street and then the next. Finally, she went down an alley and stopped. Mateo got out of the car and went up to hers, where she had rolled down her window.

"I'm good, Matt. Thanks for watching out for me."

"What do you mean you're good?" Mateo looked at where they were, and it was behind a tavern. "You can't live here."

She laughed. "Of course I don't. We just passed where I live. Did you see that big brick building that took up the entire block?"

He nodded.

"That's where I live. It used to be where a hospital was, now it's a condominium. It has an underground garage, and you couldn't get in, so I figured I'd go here and say my thanks now. I don't suppose you'd let me bake you some scones, would you?"

He felt his eyebrows lift. "Scones?"

"Or maybe something with chocolate? Do you like chocolate?" she quickly asked. "Chocolate chip cookies?"

"I like chocolate," he admitted. He remembered his mother's chocotorta that she continued to make even after they came to America and she was working long hours.

"Then it's a deal. When can we meet again so I can give you some cookies?"

It couldn't be this easy, could it?

"I'll let you bake me cookies on one condition." He looked down into her hopeful blue eyes.

"What's that?"

"You let me take you to dinner."

"Uh-uh. I buy you dinner," she said, shaking her head. Even just with the light of the moon, her hair still shined.

"Nope, you bake cookies. I buy dinner. Trust me, I'm getting the better end of the deal." And he meant it. "I have to work late tomorrow and Friday. Will Saturday work?"

"That would be perfect."

Mateo reached to pull his mobile out of his cargo shorts pocket, then cursed the chino pants he was wearing. He'd left his phone in his car.

"My phone is in my car. Let me give you the number, and you call it. That way, you'll have mine, and I'll have yours."

She reached over and grabbed hers out of her

purse. He rattled off his number and heard the faint sound of his cell phone ringing in his car.

"What do you like to eat?"

"I'm not particular. I just like food. So anyplace is fine."

He liked her attitude and her smile.

"How about I pick you up at eighteen—six-thirty," he quickly corrected himself.

"Eighteen six-thirty? That's kind of an odd time." She teased him gently. There was no snark involved. She was kind. Didn't she understand what the Kraken did?

"I changed my mind to six-thirty. I'd like more time to get to know you. I can come pick you up."

"Can we meet at the restaurant? I don't really know you."

Mateo smiled and nodded. "Smart." Luckily, Gideon and Jada—but he was pretty sure it was Jada—had taken this into account. He pulled his wallet out of his back pocket and pulled out a fake business card. "This is me. This is where I work. If you call this number and ask for Jada Harlow, she's my boss, she can give you a reference. Would that work?"

He watched as a smile blossomed across Lainey's face. "That would be great."

"So, if I pass muster, you can call me, and I'll pick you up at six-thirty." He smiled in return.

He watched as her lips parted and her eyes drooped just a little.

"I'd like to get to know you better, too, Matt. It's not often I meet a knight in shining armor."

Mateo tensed and squeezed the back of his neck. "Don't let me fool you. If I had armor, which I don't, it would be dirty and dented."

"That just means you've been through the fires. Shiny armor is for those boys who just graduated from the Naval Academy, and they never caught my attention. But let's meet at the restaurant. I really don't know you."

Mateo squeezed his neck harder. He needed to get his shit sorted. He didn't need her complimenting him, and him beginning to like her. She was a target. Everything pointed to her working for the Kraken. The same people who tried to kill Amber, Lachlan, and baby Iris. He backed away from her car.

"Well, I'll see you on Saturday," he promised. "I'll call you to firm things up on Friday. Don't forget to get that tire replaced as soon as possible."

He watched as she frowned. "Is everything okay?"

"I just remembered, I'm Ken's ride. I need to get back to Home Port."

She grinned big. "Oh. Well then, I probably owe Ken some cookies too."

"Nah, he's already had more sweets than he needs. Don't forget, I'll call you on Friday. And be careful on that tire."

"I will."

THINGS HAD BEEN LOOKING up by the time Friday afternoon rolled around. Janice had left early because of a non-existent dentist's appointment. The cryptocurrency transfer had been vetted and had gone through without her having to call the Grand Cayman Islands Bank like last time. And, she'd gotten all the ingredients for *alfajores*. She'd looked up the Argentine layer cookie that had *dulce de leche* in the middle and were then coated with a layer of chocolate. The only problem was she couldn't figure out if she should go dark or milk chocolate, but with the sweet caramel center, which was kind of what *dulce de leche* was, she went dark chocolate. Now all she had to do was a trial run tonight, and hopefully work out the kinks so that tomorrow's batch would be perfect!

"Lainey?" She looked up and saw Penny knocking on her open office door.

"Hi Penny, what's up?" Lainey sat back in her chair and motioned for Penny to sit down at Janice's vacant desk.

Penny shook her head. "I've got a problem." She sat down on the corner of Lainey's desk.

"How can I help?"

"Your mother is on hold, and it's the third time she's called in twenty minutes. This time, she's being out-and-out ugly. You know the rules: we don't transfer personal calls through the main switchboard to employees. That's why we all have direct lines. I told her to call you directly, but she said she lost your number and demanded to be put through. I told her I would take a message. She wanted to talk to my supervisor, but I knew if I got Rita involved, you might get in trouble."

Lainey wanted the floor to open up and swallow her.

"I think you need to take the call and get a handle on things before they escalate. I know you've never talked about your family, and now I see why." Penny reached down and touched Lainey's forearm. "After you talk to her, you tell me if there's anything I can do to help. I know you've told me she can be a bit of a pill, but if you need a shoulder to cry on, I'm here. You know that don't you?"

Lainey nodded. She would have said something, but she didn't know what to say.

"I'll go down and put her through to your number, okay?"

"Absolutely. I'm so sorry about this."

"There's nothing to be sorry about. We all have some wack-a-doodles in our family tree. I'll tell you about my twin cousins sometime."

Penny popped off her desk. "Just give me a minute. In the meantime, I'll close your door to give you a bit of privacy."

"Thanks," Lainey said in a weak voice. As soon as the door was closed, she dropped her head down into her hands.

"Crap, Mom. Why are you doing this?"

She rubbed her temples, already feeling the start of a tension headache. She needed to stop with this. She no longer lived with her mother. Her mother couldn't pull her strings, and she would not let her cause her physical pain.

Lainey jerked when the phone rang.

"Go time," she muttered.

"Hello, Mother," she said in a clipped tone of voice. "I'm working. Why are you calling me during my workday?"

"It's an emergency," her mother wailed. "I told that twit downstairs that I must speak to you immediately. I told her it was of utmost urgency."

"Is someone sick? Is someone in the hospital?" They were the same questions she always asked when her mother said something was urgent.

"Of course not," her mother sniffed. Once again, they were saying their same old tired lines. "If it was something like that, your brother Bartholomew would have called you. I would be at whoever's bedside, ministering to them."

Lainey rolled her eyes.

"So now that we've established this isn't an emergency, tell me why you're calling me during a workday." She didn't give a darn if her mother could hear the impatience in her tone.

"Bennett has decided that she needs to be on bedrest for the rest of her pregnancy."

What the heck?

"I thought you said it wasn't an emergency. What's wrong with her? What did the doctor say?"

She might not like her sister much, but she loved her. Lainey calculated how much accrued vacation she had. She started up a search engine on her computer so she could check flights to Charleston.

"Her doctor said she was perfectly fine, but Bennett decided she needed to check into Charleston Place and

Spa for the rest of her pregnancy. Daddy and I were able to get her a club suite for the duration."

"What did you say?"

Lainey was appalled. That place cost an arm and a leg, not that her family couldn't afford it, but still. "Bennett's not due for another four months, Mom. What about the girls? Are they going with her?"

"Of course not. They'll stay with the nanny."

"But they're only four and six, Bennett can't leave them for so long."

"It's okay, they'll visit her. The nanny will take care of them just fine. This will help them grow a backbone. That's what she's paid for. Francine did quite well for you children."

Lainey shuddered just hearing Francine's name. "But I thought Bennett fired the girl's nanny."

"That was two months ago. They found a darling girl last month. The girls love her. She's from France. She just graduated from the Sorbonne. Bennett was lucky to get her."

"Wonderful. So, Bennett is basically abdicating all responsibility for four months."

Trey had always had a wandering eye. He'd even made a pass at her once. Bennett was going to leave him with some darling Parisian girl for four months? Just how stupid was her sister?

"That is exactly my point. I need you to come home and take your place by my side. I can't possibly run these charity events without one of my daughters by my side. The whole situation is untenable."

Lainey snorted.

"MacLaine, you need to stop that disgusting habit. You're never going to catch any man of worth when you make such ugly noises. I suppose you're still biting your bottom lip?"

"Yes, I am."

"What size are you?"

"None of your business."

Her mother sighed. "We'll just have to have a seamstress come in to help tailor a wardrobe for you and put you on a diet. Please tell me you're not wearing things from off the rack."

Lainey covered her nose and mouth to stop from snorting again. This woman wasn't for real, but after twenty-four years, she knew she was.

"Mother, I'm not coming back to Charleston. I have a job, and I can't leave it."

"And it's not just charity lunch functions. There is also your Daddy's and my fortieth wedding anniversary. I've already selected two eligible bachelors who will be perfect to escort you. And you can't complain this time because I've given you a choice."

Darn it, she'd forgotten about her parents' anniversary.

"Mother, this isn't a good time right now. I'll call you back on Sunday."

"Don't you dare hang up on me, MacLaine Taylor Simpson, I must have answers, now!"

"My boss is giving me the evil eye for being on a personal call so long. I have to hang up. I'll call you on Sunday, I promise."

She could hear her mother squawking as she hung up.

Lainey called Penny and told her to do the same thing if she got a call from her mother again. *Hang the fudgesicle up!*

10

LARK WAS SITTING IN HER NORMAL POSITION, ON THE corner of the couch, but this time Kostya wasn't sitting on the arm. He was beside the fireplace at the front of the living room, with his arms crossed over his chest.

"It's not good, or it's good. It depends on how you want to take it," Lark said.

"Spit it out," Jase demanded.

Kostya cleared his throat, but it came out like a growl as he glared at Jase.

"Sorry, Lark," Jase said. "But please don't keep us in suspense."

"This is what I found out from the people who took in Ephram and his siblings. Ephram was the middle child at seven years old. He had an older sister who was eight and a younger brother who was five. All three of the children were traumatized after witnessing their father and older brothers being shot, and their mother killing herself in front of them."

"She slit her throat, right?" Mateo asked.

Lark nodded. "According to Rusty, she's the woman who took them in. The sister was the one who was most indoctrinated into the zealot's way of life. Constance only went to school when they threatened her with being separated from Ephram and Lloyd. The boys seemed to adore and fear Constance. Rusty would often find the boys with bruises that they swore came about because of falls. Rusty never saw Constance hit the boys, but she was sure she did."

Lark needed to speed things up. He needed to get to Maryland.

"So did Ephram recruit either Constance or Lloyd to be part of the Kraken?" Mateo asked.

"Constance died of a drug overdose when she was fifteen. According to Rusty, Lloyd thought Ephram walked on water, and the two of them were thick as thieves. When Ephram left, as far as she could tell, there was no contact between the brothers. Lloyd joined the Army when he was eighteen. He never responded to any of Rusty's overtures while he was enlisted. She has no idea where he is today."

"I hear an 'and' coming up," Mateo said.

"Yep, I gave all this information to Gideon. Lloyd Hicks became a Green Beret. He was coming up for a promotion when he took his retirement. Nobody knows where he went." She nodded toward Gideon.

"Lloyd Hicks ceased to exist. And I mean, ceased to exist. The home address, email, and phone number he gave the Army when he mustered out were phony. There is no record of his social security number being used anywhere. No record of his name being used. The

Army did a cursory search when he dropped off the grid, but gave up after three months. I'd say he joined big brother."

"So, you've got nothing?" Nolan O'Rourke asked.

"I've got nothing," Gideon admitted. "At least when it comes to Lloyd." He turned to Jada who was sitting on the floor beside Gideon. Both of them had their laptops on their thighs. "Your turn to report."

"I found something about Frank Sykes, the former leader that Ryker killed."

"And wasn't that a beautiful day," Ryker said as he leaned back in his chair and rested his linked hands on his belly. Everybody chuckled.

"Yeah, yeah." Jada waved her hand dismissively. "You did good. Huzzah, accolades, and compliments. Anyway, my lead on Sykes, I'm pretty sure, is solid. I found where his ex-wife filed three different restraining orders against him in three different states when they were both in their early twenties. The last one was in Pennsylvania. They had two children, a boy and a girl. In Pennsylvania, her nine-year-old boy went missing. She, local and state law enforcement, were convinced that Frank took him. Frank popped up again nine years later. Two years after that, Ivan Sykes popped up when he joined the Navy. He swore up and down that he had run away from home. Frank was never prosecuted."

"And their relationship?" Kostya asked.

"Ivan only spent four years in the Navy, then he cut his teeth with Decker Worldwide. His dad was already working there. They were both involved with some high-profile hostage rescue ops with Decker, which taught them just what they needed to know to work on the other side when Daddy got the Kraken Elite up and running," Jada explained.

"How come we haven't heard about Ivan before this?" Mateo wanted to know.

"He was badly injured during the last op with Decker. He was out of the game. But when I checked out where he was supposed to be living, and the in-home care he was supposed to be receiving, there was nothing. According to the nurse's agency, he fired them five years ago. But he's still collecting benefits from Decker."

"So, he's an all-around asshole," Braxton muttered.

"Sounds like," Keegan agreed.

"If he's collecting benefits from Decker, you must have some kind of line on him," Kostya growled. "What is it?"

"Yeah, what?" Mateo demanded to know.

"He's having his benefits deposited into the same bank he always did. It's in Oklahoma, but surprise, surprise, it then routes to Lionel Security and Trust Bank in Annapolis." Jada and Gideon both gave Mateo pointed glances.

"How long ago did that start happening?"

"Five years ago."

"So long before Lainey started working there," he pointed out.

Kostya swung his head around to stare at Mateo. "Are you defending her? Are you thinking that she's not involved with the Kraken?"

"I'm not saying that at all," Mateo said with his

palms up. "I'm just saying that's before her time, so there must have been someone working with them at the bank before she got there. It's just one more piece of information I'm going to need to get from her."

Kostya nodded. "Gotcha."

———

MATEO OPENED the door to his condo after the fourth doorbell ring, the third knock, and the second pounding. He flung it open.

"Oh, it's you. I was expecting Jase."

"So, are you going to let me in or not?" Braxton asked.

Mateo let out a long-suffering sigh. "Come on in."

He watched Braxton take in his duffel and one suitcase.

"Interesting. I can't remember when I needed to go somewhere that required more than a duffel bag," he said as he looked over at Mateo.

"Yeah, well. I'm going to be living in a furnished apartment in Baltimore for a little while. I need more than just a change of clothes to make this look legit."

"Yeah, I heard that our guy MacLaine turned into a Lainey. Gideon showed me her picture. Not surprised to hear that you're going to park your ass in Maryland for a bit," Braxton said as he headed over to Mateo's fridge and pulled out one of his IPAs. He knew exactly which drawer to open to find the bottle opener. Shit, he needed to buy a small fridge for his deck and store his beer there. Maybe then he'd have some of the shit he bought instead of it all being drunk up by his friends.

Mateo watched as Brax came back into the living room and sat his happy ass down in Mateo's favorite chair and took a long pull from his beer. "This is good. You and Gideon always have the best beer. I hope he gets his place rebuilt soon."

"Cut the shit and tell me why you're here."

"Can't a friend just stop by and shoot the shit with his buddy?"

"Sure, except when said friend pounds on the door loud enough to wake my neighbors. You've got something to say, so say it."

"I asked Gideon and Jada to send me the workup on our girl Lainey. She seems lovely. I read the part where she adopted her dog from a kill shelter when she was twenty-four hours away from being put down. The pup only has three legs."

Mateo nodded. "Yep, read the same file. What are you getting at?"

"I'm saying that you're not the love-them-and-leave-them type like everybody thinks. Yeah, you leave them, but you're always careful to choose the type who knows the score. You keep up your walls and never let any woman in. You would never date a woman like this."

"Again, what's your point?"

"You're getting a furnished apartment in Baltimore. Just how do you plan to get your information from MacLaine?"

"I'm going to become friends with her. That's what I

would have done if MacLaine was a MacLaine, and it's no different if MacLaine is a Lainey."

"Bullshit. I read up on her. Besides having a soft heart and being a looker, she has a brain. She graduated with honors from Clemson University. Don't lie to me, these are all things that ring your bell."

"What are you talking about? That's not the kind of woman I date."

"Exactly. You date women who have as much depth as a mud puddle, with an IQ to match. Lainey's going to do it for you, and just being friends is going to be tough. I had it easy when I was in Dubai dealing with that piranha, Amanda. No matter how hot she looked, there was not one redeeming quality about her. As a matter of fact, kissing her was damn near impossible."

"Who said I'll end up kissing Lainey?"

Braxton lifted his left eyebrow.

How did he do that? Mateo's brother Luis could do that too, but try as he might, Mateo never could master the art of the one eyebrow lift.

"Seriously Brax, that's not my plan. Yeah, I asked her to dinner, but I plan on keeping this platonic."

"And if that doesn't work? If you aren't getting the info we need? Right now, MacLaine Simpson is our best shot at tracking down the Kraken. What then?"

"I'll cross that bridge when I come to it."

"All I'm saying—"

"You've made your point. Finish your beer. I need to get a move on." And he didn't need to hear anymore of Brax's warnings.

Brax got up and meandered to the kitchen. He

poured the rest of the beer down the sink, rinsed out the bottle, then put it into Mateo's recycling.

"Mateo, if things get sticky, just know you can give me a call, okay?"

Time to change the subject. "How's your sister doing?"

Braxton lit up. "She's doing a lot better. The latest treatment is working wonders."

"That's great to hear." And it was. "When will she be up for visitors?"

Braxton grimaced. "Not quite yet. But soon. Dad and I are working on her. So, soon."

"Let me know the day, and I'll be there with bells on."

"I know, and I can't tell you how much that means to me. To all of us." Braxton headed for the door. Then turned around. "By the way, I'll give you that little bit of deflection, but I mean it. Call me if you need to talk. You're going into the emotional lion's den."

That's what he was afraid of.

11

LAINEY LOOKED IN THE MIRROR FOR THE SIXTH TIME. DID she have lipstick on her teeth? Hadn't she blotted? She leaned in closer. Nope, no lipstick.

Dang it, calm down.

The problem was, she hadn't been on a date that she had been looking forward to since college. She'd been on too many dates to count that her dad, mother, and sister had set up, and not once had she given even a little bit of a boonswoggle if she looked good. Okay, she did care that her breath didn't smell, but that was the low bar she'd set for all those pompous country club idiots. And as for the college boys? Well, there had been two. One was named Randy, and that had been apropos. Then there was Rob. Both of them had been boys, and neither of them had lasted too long.

She'd been beginning to think there was something really wrong with her, and then boom. Suddenly, lust had hit her like a freight train. And even more, there was a healthy dose of 'like.' So yeah, not only did she want her breath to be minty fresh, but she also wanted to look really, really good.

She jumped when she heard the doorbell ring, and her dog whined.

Darn it.

She'd left Xena all snuggled up in her safety bed and here she was nosing her way into the bathroom.

"Xena, it's going to be okay."

Dagnabbit!

She should have told Matt to knock on the door, quietly. Anytime she called for maintenance to come to her house, she coaxed Xena into her closet and had her lie down in the comfy bed Lainey had bought for her. There was water and food and chew toys. She was debating whether to put a TV in there, but maintenance didn't come over there all that often.

Lainey crouched down and cupped the black and white border collie's muzzle and petted her head. Xena relaxed into her touch and some of her trembling stopped. Lainey prayed Matt wouldn't ring the bell again. She prayed he was patient.

"Everything's good." She stroked the silky hair of her friend's back, then Lainey stood up. "Follow me, okay?"

Xena had no problem walking as she followed Lainey down the hallway to her bedroom. She'd been surprised that having three legs wasn't a problem for the little girl, when she'd put a leash around her and took her from the kill shelter to her car.

The doorbell rang again after Lainey got Xena settled. She gave her the little Elsa doll that was her favorite chew toy and got up to answer the door. On the way, she stopped and looked in the bathroom mirror.

"Drat." She still hadn't put on her earrings. And they were pretty. Maybe he could have a cookie while she put in her earrings and put on her lip gloss.

Yay. A plan.

She scooped up her garnet earrings and hustled out of the bathroom and down the hall, through her living room to the door. She stopped before unlocking the door and took a deep breath, then slowly let it out.

There. She was ready. She smiled, then opened the door.

Oh no.

He was wearing a white dress shirt with the top two buttons undone and some kind of slacks, but who cared? The white against his bronze throat was...

Lainey looked up and up and took in his square jaw and pronounced cheekbones and then was caught up in dark brown amused eyes.

Holy heck, had he realized I was staring?

Say something.

"You look beautiful."

Lainey slapped her hand over her mouth. She couldn't believe she'd said that. He grinned at her. She needed to invite him in, but her hand was still over her mouth.

I'm such an idiot.

"Come on inside," she mumbled as she took her hand away from her mouth and opened the door wider. She glanced up at him through her lashes and saw his mouth was fighting a smile.

"I think you're the beautiful one," he whispered.

She tried not to frown, but as she assessed his face, she saw nothing but truth, so she smiled back at him, relieved.

"Do we have time for you to have a cookie while I put on my earrings?" she asked. Good, she sounded like an adult.

"Yeah, we have time, but I don't need a cookie," he chuckled.

Lainey blushed. She totally sounded like she was offering a five-year-old a cookie. She looked toward the kitchen where his treats were waiting.

"You don't understand. I promised to bake you cookies. So, I've got a container of *alfajores* for you to take home and I just thought—"

"*Alfajores*?"

She jerked her head back to him at his sharp tone and slowly nodded.

"You baked me *alfajores*? Those were my favorite thing that my mom baked for me and my brother."

Lainey felt some of the tension draining out of her shoulders. "Oh, so you like them. That's good. Does your mom make them with dark chocolate or milk chocolate on the outside?"

"She used to make them with dark chocolate."

"Used to?"

"She passed away a while back."

"So, it's just you and your brother?"

Matt said nothing for a moment, then finally he shook his head. "No, he died in his early twenties. It's just me."

Shoot!

He must have seen her look of dismay because he started talking again.

"I can't wait to taste your baking. I hope you have more jewelry to put on than just earrings," he teased.

"Why don't you sit up on the barstool at the island, and I'll serve you up two cookies. What would you like to drink with them?"

"Do you have milk?"

Lainey bit her lip. He looked all muscley and fit. He probably drank some milk substitute or non-fat milk. "I only have whole milk."

"Perfect. That's the only thing you should drink with *alfajores* as far as I'm concerned. Are you going to join me?"

"I'll have half of one. I did a taste test on two earlier." She grinned. "I had to make sure I wasn't poisoning you. But first, let me finish getting ready."

"Take your time."

HE WATCHED as she walked down the hall. She looked damn fine.

He hadn't been giving her a line when he told her that she looked beautiful, because she definitely did.

Mateo looked at the Argentine cookie on his plate. It looked good, but he didn't have high hopes. Rarely did people in America get it right. He was glad that Lainey was down the hall when he took his first bite. That way he didn't have to mask his reaction.

As the cookie got close to his mouth, the smell of the dark chocolate hit his nose and he smiled. But he kept his glass of milk close at hand and took a small bite. The two soft, buttery cookies covered in chocolate crumbled in his mouth and brought back memories of his childhood. He put his hand under his chin, so that he didn't make a mess, then the dulce de leche layered between the cookies burst across his tastebuds, and he groaned.

So good.

So, fucking good.

He chewed slowly, savoring the flavors that mirrored his childhood, but the experience was over far too fast. He took a bigger bite, downing half the cookie, and forced down another moan of pleasure, but this was right on up there with an orgasm.

Again, he chewed slowly, his eyes closed. He didn't set down the cookie, instead he finished off that last bite, content knowing there was another on his plate and more to take home.

He heard a soft laugh beside him. It had a hint of music in it.

He looked sideways. "You caught me."

"You're looking like I imagined I looked yesterday and today. Those things are addictive. I had to get them out of my house yesterday really fast."

He tilted his head, and she answered his unasked question.

"I did a trial run yesterday. They were eighty-five percent right. Not like today's batch. Today is at about ninety-five percent. Yesterday's cookie wasn't as crumbly. But it didn't stop me from sampling a few. After all, I had to figure out what was wrong, didn't I?"

Her eyes were sparkling.

"So, what did you do with the rest?"

"I gave them away to my neighbors. There's Lars next door. Normally, his body is his temple, but he made an exception. Then there is Mr. and Mrs. Lyles. They're older. He probably shouldn't be eating them, but he said at ninety, he isn't going to have some doctor taking away the joys in his life."

"Sounds like a smart man," Mateo smiled.

"I was hoping today's batch would come out perfect, but you were going to be the ultimate judge. By the look on your face, it seems like I came close."

"You didn't come close. These are beyond perfect. I think I'm going to have to start puncturing your tire once a week so I can come and rescue you, just so you'll make these for me again."

"I don't think you'll need to do something that drastic."

"We'll see," he muttered.

She laughed. "I'm ready."

He eyed her from head to toe. "You certainly are. I'm going to have quite a time keeping you all to myself."

Lainey laughed again. Pretty. He was right, it did sound a little like music. "Keep talking me up like that and you'll for sure get more cookies. But I was also thinking of making chocotorta."

Mateo's chin lifted and he stared at her.

Is she for real?

He was the one who was supposed to be doing things to pry information from her, not the other way around.

"No? You don't like that dessert?"

"Oh. No. That's not it. I love that dessert. I even remember getting it for my birthday. It was for special occasions."

"Is that something else that your mother made for you?" She picked up her raincoat and he took it from her so he could help her put it on.

"Mom did make the chocotorta, but she said she didn't do it as well as her mother did, so she found a bakery close to us in Wilmington."

"Delaware?"

"Yeah, like I said. She was a silicone research scientist for DuPont." It was always best to keep his cover as close to the truth as possible. And that was the truth.

"Hmmm. That sounds impressive," she said as Mateo opened the door for her.

"It was, especially for a woman coming from a South American country in the late nineties."

He waited for her to lock her door, then he walked with her to the elevator.

"You sound very proud of your mom."

"I am."

They made their way to the lobby, and he ushered her out the front door to the visitors' parking.

"Can I tell you a secret?" Lainey asked as he opened the passenger door.

"I would love to know all of your secrets," Mateo said in a teasing tone, but deep down he was serious.

"I have been wanting to ride in this car as soon as I saw it. I love old muscle cars."

"Then you're in for a treat." He shut her door, walked around to the driver's side, and folded into the car. He watched as Lainey grinned when the car rumbled to life.

"Yep, I'm loving this already. I hope the reservation isn't really close."

"Consider your wish granted."

12

LAINEY WAS GLAD THEY CHOSE TO EAT OUT ON THE DECK here at the Severn Inn. It was her night to try new things, and with the heat lamps and umbrella, it made their table seem extremely intimate as they gazed over the river. Okay, they might have spent more time gazing at one another. She didn't think she had ever laughed more. Mateo's friends on his soccer team were a hoot.

"So how long have you been playing together?" she asked.

"They've been a team for seven years. I transferred from another team four years ago, and I have to tell you, I'm glad I made the change."

"I would say so. Just the stories about Jase are enough to keep me entertained all evening. Sixteen brothers and sisters? Are you sure you're not pulling my leg?"

They were sitting kitty-corner from one another, and as Lainey leaned in, Mateo's leg settled against hers under the table. She liked it.

"I swear, I'm not. His mother and father are remarkable people. I've met them twice. Once when they came to visit them here, and once when I went to his and Bonnie's wedding. For the wedding, every single one of the siblings showed up. Then there were all of his nieces and nephews, and Jace knew every one of them by name."

"It sounds like you have some great friends. It almost sounds like you've created a family of your own."

"You're right, in a sense I have."

"What about you? Tell me about your friends and family."

"Mine is boring compared to yours. I'm the youngest. I have two older brothers and an older sister. I come from a long line of prominent Southern families. The Simpsons and Winstons. That's a big deal down in Charleston. I'm considered the rebel because I wanted to go to college."

"Why would that be rebellious?"

She liked how Mateo leaned in as she was talking. He was really listening.

"My job, as a female, was to marry one of the young men from Dad's law firm and produce three children, and one would have to be a son. College was only supposed to be for my brothers."

Mateo frowned. "That sounds like the thinking my mom was up against in Argentina forty years ago. It doesn't make sense."

"That's what I thought. But then again, who names their girls Bennett and MacLaine?"

Mateo grinned. It was a glamorous smile, and she saw his lips move, but she didn't hear his question.

"What?"

"That's your name? MacLaine?"

"MacLaine Taylor Simpson. At least these days, girls are named Taylor, so not that big of a deal. But Taylor was another family name. My sister Bennett has it worse. Her full name is Bennett Parker Simpson. I blame that name for her being the way she is."

"How is she?"

Lainey bit her lip. She didn't want to air all of her family's dirty laundry. But she could give him a small little slice. After all, her mother would be haranguing her for the next two to three months to return to the fold.

"Bennett married Frederick Laughton III, and of course he goes by the name of Trey. She hosts all the charity luncheons and galas with my mom. These are the approved ones. Things like sponsoring the symphony, or getting money for the arboretum. God forbid we earn money for a homeless shelter or for kids going hungry. Anyway, Bennett is pregnant with her third child. The first two were girls, and after she found out that this baby was a boy, she told me Trey had to get a vasectomy. Which I think is a good thing, considering what a player he is."

Lainey sighed.

So much for only telling him a slice.

"And your brothers?"

"They all became lawyers. They work with my dad. They're all married. One of them happily."

Lainey shook her head. "I'm really talking far too much. I blame the lemon drop martinis."

"I hate to tell you this, but you only had one and you didn't have any wine with dinner. I think you needed to vent."

Mateo's voice was gentle. It matched the look in his eyes. "Is that why you don't live in Charleston?"

"Yeah. It's why I want to be a banker. Lionel Security and Trust Bank does a lot of loans for small start-up businesses. They do strenuous evaluations and I would really like to learn everything I could from this side of the business on what they require."

"Why?"

"I checked it out. I would only need fourteen more credits to earn an MBA in nonprofit leadership. If I knew what banks needed for start-up businesses from their side of the table, and I had a firm foundation of nonprofit education, then I should be able to help people."

"So, no Charleston charity luncheons for you, huh?"

"God, no," she laughed. "I'd have to diet. That's a four-letter word I abhor."

He frowned. "I can't imagine why anyone would think you would need to go on a diet. Your body looks perfect to me."

Lainey blushed.

"Okay," she finally said. "That's nice. In that case you won't mind when I say that I want to see the dessert menu."

"You can have dessert. I'm saving my appetite for

more *alfajores* and milk when we get back to your home."

———————

"I'M GLAD YOU LIKED THEM." Lainey looked down to where their forearms were touching and Mateo did what he'd wanted to do all night. He took her hand and laced his fingers through hers.

"Like is too lackluster of a word to describe how I feel about those cookies. Instead of me just liking them, how about I lust after them, I'm in love with them, and long for them?"

This time, she didn't just laugh. She threw back her head and *really* laughed. As she tried to control herself, she snorted, and she turned beet red.

"Well, there you go. You're never going to want to go out with me again. I snort when I really laugh out loud."

"Yeah, and it's adorable," Mateo said, as he gave her hand a comforting squeeze.

"Hmm hm. I believe you. I've got your number now. You're just after me for my treats."

He brushed his thumb over the top of her hand. He watched how her pupils got bigger and she shivered. "I definitely want a treat from you."

"I don't give out the kinds of treats I think you're talking about on the first date."

She didn't pull her hand away from his, which was a good sign in his book. "How about a kiss? Do you give those away on the first date?"

Lainey's gaze dropped to his lips and Mateo felt it in his groin. God, what was he thinking? He just wanted information; he didn't want to seduce this woman. She was the enemy.

Supposedly.

"Why don't you take me home and find out?"

"How about we take your dessert to go?" Mateo suggested.

Lainey blushed and nodded.

MATEO GRINNED when Lainey didn't move to open her car door. She had definitely been brought up in the South. It worked out well, because he liked opening doors and doing all the gentlemanly things for ladies. It was how his mother raised him and Luis. The Argentine way. The rare times that his mother would go out on a date, she would often come home disgusted with the lack of manners that American men displayed.

Mateo held out a hand for Lainey to grasp as she unfolded out of his Dodge Challenger.

"You know how you feel about the *alfajores*?" she asked as he brushed the small of her back and guided her toward the entrance of her building.

"Yes."

"That's how I feel about your car."

He laughed. "Good. Then maybe I can talk you into another date if I promise you another ride."

"I thought I was bribing you for another date with the *chocotorta*," she corrected as she nodded to the older man who was behind the large desk in front of the elevators.

"I think this could be the start of something beautiful," he said as he pressed the up button. "We continue to tempt one another with small treats to continue to see one another for an entire year, and then we realize that the ultimate enticement is just seeing one another."

As he expected, Lainey blushed, but she didn't just nod. Nope, she gave as good as she got.

"Fine, but you can only use your muscle car twice as an enticement. After that, you'll have to come up with something else. After all, I'm going to have to up my game after the cookies and cake."

"I'm not sure you can. But I'm going to love to see you try." He ushered her into the empty elevator and then held out the hand that wasn't holding her dessert box. She immediately took it and they held hands all the way up the elevator, down the hall, and to her door.

"Why don't you have an alarm system?" he asked as he came in and helped her out of her coat.

"Why would I? There hasn't been any kind of break-in here in this building in years. The only thing we've had is the occasional domestic dispute."

Mateo put her lemon tart down on the kitchen island while Lainey got out plates, forks, and glasses of milk. She opened up her tart and the cookies container.

"I meant to ask you. Why do you take your glasses off when we eat?"

"I'm near-sighted. When I want to see you or my food clearly, I have to take off my glasses, but if we're walking through the restaurant, I need to put them back on."

He nodded.

"Why? Do they bother you?" she asked.

"I think you're just as beautiful when you're wearing them, or when you're not."

"You sure are full of compliments." She looked down at her tart.

"Lainey. I don't say things I don't mean. If I didn't find you beautiful, then I wouldn't say it."

She frowned, then bit her lip. "Okay. Thank you."

She passed over a plate of cookies and the glass of milk, then came over to sit beside him. "Would you prefer to eat at the dining room table?"

He'd noted that she had paperwork and her computer set up on one end of the table, so he figured she normally ate here at the island. "I like it here."

She blew her bangs out of her face, then smiled. "Good. So do I."

Then she bit into a piece of her tart and hummed. "Dang, this is good."

Would she hum with pleasure when he kissed her?

He stopped his wayward thoughts and tried to think of something else. "Dang?"

She grinned. "I have nieces and nephews. I try to keep my language to a 'G' rating. If I don't do it all the time, then it will spill over when I'm with them."

"Makes sense."

"What about you? I haven't heard you swear. Are you around kids much?"

Mateo thought back to the birthday horror show.

"Sometimes," he mumbled. He hated thinking about that day. Those bastards had targeted kids. Amber and Lachlan could have died that day.

He remembered the first time that Nolan had introduced him to Iris, who had just turned two years old. She was all fussy and determined to get put down so she could crawl.

Then there was Laura, who had been huddled next to the toilet bowl, seconds away from being killed.

All of these moments flashed before his eyes as he stared at Lainey.

Lainey who had deposited a quarter of a million dollars of gold bars lying around to sell and deposit into her bank account. Lainey who'd done the cryptocurrency bank transfer.

"Are you okay?" Her voice was soft and concerned.

Mateo realized he had zoned out for just a moment. "I'm fine," he clipped out. "Look, I have to go. I have a lot of work I have to get done tomorrow. I have a presentation I need to do for the team first thing on Monday morning. It's important."

"Oh." She set her fork down on the plate of her half-eaten tart. "Well, I had a lovely time."

"So did I, Lainey." He forced a smile.

Mateo stood up and Lainey turned her stool so her knees brushed his thighs, causing a current of electricity to race through his body.

Nope, time to shut this shit down.

He headed for the door.

"Wait a minute." Lainey rushed after him. He

looked over his shoulder and saw she was holding the container of cookies. "Don't you want these?"

"Oh yeah," he muttered. This way, he'd have a reason to see her again. He'd need to return the container. No dates. No kisses. Just returning the container and getting his questions answered.

"Thanks again, Lainey." He took the container from her and turned to the door. She touched his bicep.

"Matt. Did I do something wrong?" Her voice was soft and confused.

He was glad she couldn't see him wince. He turned around. Her eyes were wide, and she looked hurt. God, if she wasn't with the Kraken, he'd done something he'd never done before. He'd hurt the feelings of a good woman by being an asshole.

"Lainey, I'm sorry. I really am. When it comes to my job, I have myopic focus on certain tasks, and I can be a bit of an asshole to others."

"Oh." Yeah, she sure was agreeing about that.

He reached out and stroked the back of his knuckles against the soft skin of her cheek and she took a step back.

Shit, that wasn't good.

"I'd really like to take you out again next week. I promise I don't have any other tasks coming up, and I can focus entirely on you."

"Okay, sure."

He knew what that meant. There wasn't a chance in hell she would pick up his call. Hell, she'd probably block his number.

"I really am sorry."

She nodded.

Mateo was too conflicted to kiss her, so he pushed back a lock of her hair behind her ear. "I'll call you on Wednesday. That will give me time to have received feedback and change the presentation."

She nodded again.

He hated the vulnerable look in her eyes, but there was nothing he could do about it. Not now. Not after thinking about Amber and Lachlan and that gold deposit. He took one last look at her, but he couldn't shake it. He just had to go.

"Don't forget to lock the door after I leave." He kept his voice soft.

"I won't," she replied just as softly. Then she straightened her shoulders and there was a glint in her eye. "Goodbye, Matt."

He could almost hear her saying; *don't let the door hit you on your ass on the way out.*

Man, he needed a beer.

13

It took the entire weekend for her to get her head on straight.

Sure, he had a presentation. I believe him. Just like I believe I'm a supermodel!

One minute Matt was sitting there dunking cookies in his milk, and then she asked him about kids and he couldn't bail fast enough. It was like he had a bottle rocket up his butt.

Lainey giggled.

"What's so funny?"

She didn't bother to turn her head, instead she just gave Janice the side eye. "Nothing that you would think was funny. How was your dentist appointment? Are they doing hair extensions these days?"

Janice whipped the extensions that didn't match her other hair color over her shoulder. "My dentist appointment went just fine. He said I had perfect teeth."

There were still four more months left on this

particular banking intern rotation, and she didn't know if Janice was going to survive. Of course, she'd never killed or maimed Bennett so Janice should survive. Her type of annoying was really just grade school compared to Lainey's sister.

"So, why were you laughing?"

"Just thinking about my hot date on Saturday."

"Yeah, sure. Like a stick in the mud like you would have a hot date. They talk about you around here. Every time somebody has invited you to go over to Home Port for a drink, you've said no. There isn't a chance in hell you had a hot date...unless."

Janice got up from her desk and planted one butt cheek on the corner of Lainey's desk. She was going to have to use Lysol before she went home tonight.

"Did you set up a profile on Tinder? Did somebody finally swipe right on your picture? Come on, you can tell your good pal Janice. I won't tell anyone. Was he like fifty or something? Looking for someone to stay home and bake cookies and raise his rugrats from his other three marriages? Is that who you dated this weekend?"

Janice leaned in. Lainey could hardly breathe, what with all the perfume that Janice was wearing.

"Or maybe it was something like this. It was somebody who was using a different picture, and you showed up at the restaurant and he was some bald, fat guy, who ate with his mouth open. Was that your hot date? It's got to be something like that. Give me your phone. I want to see your profile. I can help make it better so you don't attract those kinds of losers."

"For goodness sakes, Janice. I don't have an on-line dating profile. Those things scare me. I don't want to go out with a total stranger."

"Like hooking up with some guy in a bar and going home with him isn't the same thing."

Lainey shuddered. "Janice. You don't do that sort of thing, do you?"

"Sure, I do. Everybody does. Get with the times."

She thought about the conversation she had with Jada Harlow. The woman couldn't say enough nice things about Matt. Of course, she didn't know that he would turn into a butthead as soon as they started talking about kids. Heck, it wasn't like she was asking him how many kids he would like to have when he got married. It was just plain weird.

"Janice, it's not safe. You have to be careful."

"Don't sound like a granny."

God give me patience.

"Haven't you read any statistics about what could happen to a woman if she's not careful?"

"I'm careful. I talk to them. I'm a really good judge of character. For instance, I know that the stick up your ass has been up there since grade school and needs to be surgically removed. I bet I'm not the only one who's told you that, right?"

Lainey sighed. "Janice, why don't you go back to your desk, and just concentrate on your work, and I'll concentrate on mine? Don't we want everything cleaned up and taken care of when Mr. Pine comes back from vacation?"

"Arnie won't care. You just show him a little cleavage, and he lets things slide. Trust me."

Janice slid off her desk, and Lainey waved her hand in front of her face, trying to dissipate whatever strong perfume the woman had been wearing.

"Oh yeah." Janice turned back to her after she had sat down in her chair. "I got a weird phone call from some foreigner. He wanted to talk to the person in charge of cryptocurrency transfers. I told him that was you. I explained you were at lunch and you'd call him back. Here's his number."

She stretched across the aisle between their two desks and Lainey got up from her seat so she could snag the piece of paper that was actually a napkin. When she sat back down and looked at the message she let out a loud sigh that blew her bangs up from her forehead.

"Janice, I can't read the phone number."

"Do I have to do everything?" The woman squawked.

She got up from her seat and stalked the four steps over to Lainey's desk.

"This is the country code. I don't know what the country is. And these are the numbers." She jammed her fingers against the mayonnaise-stained napkin.

"Read the numbers to me." Lainey took out her pen and a sticky note.

Janice started to rattle off numbers, then stopped. "I'm pretty sure this is a five, and then next one is a one or a seven. I can't read this next one, but if you just try all nine numbers, you'll eventually get the right number, right?"

"Crap on a cracker, Janice. Are you kidding me? This is important."

"Well, look in the crypto file. There has to be a phone number with this country code in there."

"I've handled five cryptocurrency transfers this week alone. Each one of them contains at least ten phone numbers. Not only can't I read the number, but you also didn't write the name of the person."

"Sure, I did." Janice peered down at the napkin. "Ah shit. It's covered with mustard." She looked over at Lainey and winced. "I'm sorry. Okay, let me think a minute."

This should be interesting.

"Okay, the guy didn't sound Middle Eastern or Chinese or anything. More like those funny European countries. You know?"

Lainey could feel her muscles tightening and the pulse in her temples pounding. It was the precursor to a headache. She needed to breathe deeply then roll her shoulders and neck, then drink an enormous glass of water, then she might stop the headache from coming.

Might.

"Okay. I'll go look at the last five transfers I did and see if there are any with a telephone number with this country code attached to it."

"I knew you could figure it out. You're really good at this. Arnie was right about you."

Yeesh, she didn't need to lay it on so thick.

"OKAY, HOW DID THE DATE GO?" Kostya asked.

Mateo was at the Little Creek base in his lieutenant's office. They were supposed to be talking about when he was coming back to work. Instead, they were talking about his off-the-books mission.

"I blew it," Mateo bit out the words.

Kostya said nothing. He just raised one eyebrow.

What the hell? Can everybody but me do that?

"I talked to Jada. Lainey called her for a reference before allowing me to come over to her house to pick her up."

"That was smart," Kostya smiled.

"That's what I told her. Hell, Lieutenant, she found a recipe for one of Argentina's most popular cookies and she made a homemade batch for me. They were just like, or maybe even better, than the ones my mom used to make."

Kostya scratched the bristles under his chin. "Doesn't sound like a terrorist, but there is a shit ton of evidence pointing against her."

"It gets worse. She told me why she took the job with Lionel Security and Trust Bank. She wants to understand the ins and outs of the banking industry, especially what they require for providing small business loans. She intends to go back to school and get her master's in Non-Profit Management so that she can help the people who really need help getting loans. And she uses phrases like fudge-bonnet and frack-cracker instead of really swearing because she doesn't want to swear around her nieces and nephews."

Mateo sat back in his chair and crossed his arms. He knew his posture basically told Kostya that he would not listen to anything negative about Lainey Simpson. Or was he? Shit, he didn't know, she had him confused as hell.

Dammit, get your head in the game, Aranda!

"Mateo, I understand where you're coming from. But if she is innocent, you're not doing her any favors by basing her innocence on your gut. We currently have facts that point to her. And we'll need actual facts to clear her, and when you do clear her, we need to get her on our side so we can trace those transfers."

Mateo uncrossed his arms and leaned forward in his chair. "Shit, Kostya. She's such a straight arrow, I don't think she would help us. Not if it means disclosing confidential information."

Kostya leaned forward and rested his forearms on his desk. "If she's everything you're telling me, she'll help us. There is no way this woman will be any kind of unwitting accomplice to an organization like the Kraken."

"I agree with you. I just think she'll go to the FBI. Especially after she figures out that I've lied to her."

"Then it's your job to see that she doesn't."

Fuck!

"Now tell me how you blew it."

"We were on a friendly date. Everything was going well. I was in her apartment at the end of the date, and I was going to kiss her, when I remembered how Iris,

Lachlan, Amber, and the rest of those kids could have been killed. I couldn't get away from her fast enough." Mateo shook his head. "Kostya, she looked at me like I had two heads. First, I was all into her, then I was heading for the door. I doubt she'll take my next call."

"What kind of excuse did you use to leave?"

Mateo sighed. "I told her I had to get a presentation written and ready to deliver first thing Monday morning. I could tell she didn't believe me. Hell, I told my mom better lies when I was five."

"How did you leave things?" Kostya asked. He didn't sound mad or disgusted, just curious.

"I told her I would call her on Wednesday. I explained that I would have to gather everybody's feedback then update the presentation, so I'd be busy until then."

Kostya shook his head. "You really are a shit liar. We should have sent Ryker, except Amy would have had my balls for breakfast. You're going to have to grovel."

"Don't I know it."

"Huh, so you're probably not going to see her until this weekend," Kostya said as he scratched his whiskered jaw.

"That's only if I can do a good job groveling."

"Call Lark. She'll have good ideas. She'll tell you which of my groveling attempts has been most effective."

Mateo barked out a laugh. "Should I call Jada too?"

"Fuck, like Gideon has ever made a mistake."

"Good point."

"But you can help me out. I've got to keep as many

of the team running around here as possible. Commander Nash is sharp. He notices things. However, you have a reason to not be around, and we need someone to track down a lead we have on somebody Ely Roberts was tight with when he grew up in a small town in Pennsylvania. Lark wants to go, but Mateo, I just don't have it in me to let her go again. I want to send Lark to the same island where her mother has taken Romy, but she'd have my balls for breakfast if I sent her away. So right now, when I'm not home, Gideon and Jada are over at my house with her, along with Lucy. *That* I feel comfortable with."

"Makes sense to me," Mateo nodded. "So, who's the target?"

Kostya pushed a slim file over to him. "His name is Pepper Higgins. Here's the basics. I'll have Gideon or Jada send the rest in an encrypted file."

Mateo opened up the file and glanced over it.

"Shit, Kostya, this guy seems like kind of a loser. I'm not sure the Kraken would want him. The minute his parents named him Pepper, he was bound to be a little psycho. He was kicked off the police force and hell, he was even fired as a mall cop."

"He and Ely both did time in juvie for trying to steal a car. According to Jada, they stayed in touch, even after Ely joined the Kraken."

"Not only was he not at the caliber of lieutenant level of the Kraken, I don't think they would let him polish his shoes." Mateo shook his head in disgust.

"That's for damn sure." Kostya chuckled. "Hell, it sounded like his own son Ivan could run circles around everybody, unless he really was injured, which I bet my bottom dollar he wasn't. I have no idea why Frank Sykes didn't make him one of his lieutenants."

Mateo looked up at his boss with a half grin. "You're an exception, Kostya. A lot of men don't want to promote people who could be their competition. They're too insecure. Meanwhile, you just want to build the best team possible."

"Shit yeah. I've met fools like you're describing, and Captain Hale never puts up with them long. That's why I have hope for this new commander, Theo Nash. But still, he's coming from Strategic Command, not Spec Ops, and it has me a little worried."

Mateo nodded. He and the rest of the team had talked about this at length, but this was the first time he'd ever heard Kostya talk about his concerns. Strategic Command was known for being a little more prissy, whereas Spec Ops knew what it was like to be in the field making split second, life-and-death decisions.

"Well, Lieutenant, you can count on me. I can definitely get to Pennsylvania and check this guy out."

"One of the other things you'll find out in the file is that he lives on a farm upstate, and he raises pit bulls. He's been arrested three times for animal cruelty."

"Is he training them to fight?"

Kostya nodded. "You're going to have to assume he's armed and dangerous, and you're going to have to deal with a bunch of fighting dogs."

"Wonderful." Mateo said sarcastically.

"Kostya grinned. Aw, admit it, you love animals."

"I might like dogs, but not when they want to eat me."

Kostya laughed. "Get to your house, read the encrypted file, and call Gideon if you have questions. I want you to be on the road before nightfall."

Mateo stood up. "Aye, aye."

Kostya nodded, and Mateo felt great. It was good to feel like a solid member of the team again. Yeah, checking out Lainey was necessary, but questioning an actual target like Pepper Higgins? That was a real mission that he could sink his teeth into.

MATEO PULLED out his M2010 sniper rifle from the false bottom of his tool chest in the back of his truck, as well as his pistol. Now that he and Rocco had fixed the exhaust leak, his truck purred like a kitten, letting him get within a mile of Pepper's place on one of the many logging roads.

He slowly made it to the perimeter of Pepper's place that was covered by enormous trees and put his rifle up to his shoulder. The scope was better than any set of binoculars, if you asked him. What he saw about broke his heart.

He counted eight pit bulls at the front of the fenced-in property. Four of them were chained up, but why Pepper even bothered was a mystery to him. They were so emaciated, their ribs were protruding, and they were just lying there, panting for their next labored breath. He saw abscesses all over their bodies that hadn't been tended to. These must have been the fight losers. He saw a couple of bowls near them, but they were empty. Why that vile fuck just tortured them like this and didn't put them out of their misery was a mystery to Mateo. Then he took a closer look, and realized every one of those dogs were female and pregnant.

He's breeding them?! What the fuck?!

The biggest of the male pits was roaming around the females, and it looked like he was standing guard. Mateo watched as he growled, then barked, and then swiped at one of the other three males who tried to get at one female. A bit of a fight ensued, which the big pit easily won. That big one had recent wounds that had been stitched up. Apparently, Pepper Higgins made money when he brought that pit bull to the fights. Pepper didn't come out to see what was going on. That was a good sign.

Mateo had never planned to use lethal force on the pits when Kostya had told him about them. After watching his mother literally die in front of him, he was very judicious on who he tapped, and innocent animals weren't on his list of targets.

He'd talked to his mechanic friend Rocco's sister. She was a vet. She set him up with a tranq gun and enough darts to take out the rhinoceros and tigers at the Virginia zoo. She'd told him that each full-grown pit would only need one dart to put them to sleep, and it would take about fifteen minutes to take effect and it would last for no more than thirty minutes.

The pregnant dogs were a different case altogether. There was no way Mateo was going to tranq them.

They looked so ill, he was afraid that a couple of them might never wake up. But would they bark a warning that would alert Pepper? That was the real question.

Gideon's file had been very thorough. He saw the rusted-out Buick Skyhawk up on blocks beside the house, and the shell of a Ford Elite that he was obviously parting out. He also saw a Datsun truck circa 1970 that was on its side, which was no big loss. But there was no sign of the 2003 Jeep Wrangler, which had to be Pepper's daily ride. He needed to do an entire perimeter check to see if that vehicle was anywhere on the premises. If it wasn't, he was going in and waiting for the man.

MATEO FINISHED WATERING and feeding the pregnant dogs. Two of them were so sick, he had to hand feed them before they could eat from the food bowl. Pepper had a lot to answer for. That was when Mateo heard a vehicle coming up the rutted road, music blaring. Mateo let himself back into the filthy house. The whole place stank to high heaven. It wasn't just the cigarette smoke; it was the dirty dishes lying all over every surface that had attracted ants and cockroaches. How could someone live like this?

He'd planned to just sit down and wait for Pepper, but he was thinking he would need to have his boots sprayed with Lysol when he got home. There wasn't a chance in hell he was resting the seat of his pants against any of the furniture. It had been bad enough searching for dog food and something to hold the water for the sick females.

The four other pits were going to wake up soon, but the fence only extended to the sides and front of the house. The back, where there had once been a probably nice patio with decent furniture and a barbeque, didn't have the fence enclosing it. Whoever lived here once took care of this place, and Pepper Higgins let it all fall to shit.

He listened as the Jeep pulled around to the back, came to a halt, and the blaring music stopped. Damn, the man was such an idiot. He was just leisurely walking to the same back door that Mateo had used, like he hadn't even noticed that his dogs weren't barking. Even so, Mateo positioned himself behind the door, his Sig Sauer in hand. It always paid to be careful. The scent of body odor overpowered the scent of the pizza that the man was holding as he shoved through the door. Mateo kept his gun trained on him as Pepper used both hands to carry pizza toward the debris-strewn coffee table in front of the wide screen TV.

Mateo took his opportunity, and as Pepper was bending down to place the pizza onto the coffee table, he silently came up behind him and shoved his gun into his neck.

Pepper twirled around, dropping the pizza. He had a knife in his hand and he lunged. Mateo feinted left, his boot coming out and kicking Pepper in the side of his left knee.

Pepper howled, but didn't let loose his knife. Instead, he swiped it around and caught Mateo's thigh.

There was no way Mateo was going to use deadly force on this fuck. He needed answers. Pepper re-gripped the knife and jabbed upward, and Mateo reared back, slipping in pizza sauce.

Pepper saw his advantage. He turned the knife around and aimed for Mateo's boot. His steel-toed boot.

Dumbass.

Mateo kicked up and caught Pepper in the chin. He went flying, the coffee table splitting in two under his massive weight. All the disgusting debris fell on top of him. He was out like a light, and Mateo watched as ants and cockroaches started crawling all over the man.

He shuddered.

With two fingers, he picked up Pepper's knife, then patted him down for other weapons. He shook off the bugs that had crawled on him as he finished his task. He didn't find any weapons. He pulled out zip-ties and bound Pepper's ankles and wrists, then went and rinsed his hands.

Of course, there was no soap.

He heard one dog start whining in the front of the house. He hoped it was the big dog who protected the pregnant bitches. He needed to get animal control out here immediately. That meant he needed information fast.

He found a moldy bowl that looked like it once contained Froot Loops, and he filled it up with water and swirled it around. He went into the living room and poured the mess onto Pepper's face.

"What the fuck?" Pepper slurred.

He tried to wipe his face, but then realized his hands were tied.

"What the fuck?" This time, he yelled his question.

"The fuck is, I need some answers," Mateo said calmly.

"Tell Cooter I'll get him his money next week. I've got a shipment coming in and I've got a buyer. I'm going to be flush. I'll even be able to pay the interest that I owe."

Mateo felt a little trickle of blood sliding down his leg, and he didn't want it to get infected from the dirty air, so he needed to get this done fast.

"I'm not here because of Cooter. I'm here because I want to know about your good friend Ely Roberts."

Pepper looked him straight in the eye. "I don't know anyone named Ely."

"Wrong answer." Mateo took the bowl back to the kitchen and threw it into the sink. He looked around and found something worse. God only knew what the dumbass had cooked in this saucepan, but it stank to high heaven, and the ants and cockroaches loved it. He poured a little bit of water into it and swirled it around, so that the paste at the bottom became liquified.

He went to the living room and started pouring this concoction over Pepper's mouth.

"Ahhhhhh. Enough." Then the man started to gurgle, and Mateo took pity on him and kicked him on his side so he could spit some of the goo out of his mouth.

"I can keep this up all day," Mateo said quietly.

"I give. I give. I saw Ely three months ago. He

needed a favor. He wanted me to get my sister to quit her job and start working at a different daycare. He gave me three thousand dollars to give to her."

"What daycare?"

"Shit, I don't remember. You'd have to ask her."

"I'm asking you, you worthless piece of shit."

"Some place in Virginia Beach." Pepper started coughing, and Mateo waited. "The fucking bastard lied to me. He promised that he'd give me another seven grand after she started working there, but he gave it to Shelly instead. Bitch wouldn't give me my cut, even after I worked her over...hard."

Mateo couldn't help it. He just couldn't. He kicked Pepper in his side. Twice. Then a third time for the pregnant dogs. He waited until Pepper stopped gasping for air before he asked his next question.

"Give me her number."

"I can't. Cooter's goons took my cell phone as part of my payment. I don't know what her number is."

Useless piece of shit.

"How about your mom, your dad?"

"Yeah. Yeah. Mom would know it. Mom's number is on the fridge."

Mateo stalked over to the fridge and saw a family photo. It was an average family. Smiling. The brother and sister couldn't be more than seven or eight. Mateo recognized the haircuts. The boy was holding his skateboard, and the girl was holding her cat. Dad had his arm around his wife. A happy family.

Damn shame.

He yanked the stained piece of paper off the fridge

that said mom with a number on it. Gideon should be able to trace the sister's number from the mother's number.

He headed to the back door.

"Please, man, you gotta untie me. The bugs are everywhere. Please. I told you what you wanted. Please untie me."

"Fuck no. I'm calling the police and animal control."

"I'll report you," Pepper threatened.

"Go for it. I wonder what all you'll be able to describe that the cops'll care about."

"Fuck you!"

"Word of advice. Keep your mouth and eyes closed."

Mateo hid himself back in the trees and waited until the cops and animal control came. He waited until he was satisfied that all of the pit bulls had been handled well, then he went home.

14

Lainey opened the door and burst out laughing. She couldn't even see Matt's face, what with the bouquet of pink, yellow, orange, red and white Gerber daisies in front of his face.

"I think you went a tad bit overboard," Lainey said when she could catch her breath.

Matt peeked around the bouquet. "It's just some daisies."

"Come on in. I'll see what kind of container I can find for the world's largest bouquet. You had to have paid some Annapolis florist's mortgage this month."

She hustled her way to the kitchen, trying to think of something big enough to house at least three dozen flowers. She couldn't help but take in the other six flower arrangements that graced her living and dining room. That didn't even count the beautiful stargazer lilies that she had by her bedside. Thank God she wasn't allergic!

She heard Matt chuckle as he walked behind her. "I think I might have gone a little overboard."

"Ya' think?"

Lainey fished out a pitcher that she used to serve iced tea and started filling it with water. She pulled out her vinegar from a cupboard and her sugar, then put a little of each into the pitcher.

"That's ingenious," Matt complimented. "The sugar will give the flowers nutrients and the vinegar is basically an antibacterial agent. How did you know to do that?"

Lainey shrugged. "It's just what our housekeeper always did at home. She said it kept the flowers fresh. You, being a chemist, would know all the details. I just know to do it." She set the daisies on the kitchen island.

"I love the smell around here. Thank you, Matt. But you didn't need to go to all this trouble."

She watched as his cheeks flushed.

"Yeah, I did. I acted like an ass. It wasn't just the presentation that had me leaving so abruptly."

Lainey leaned back against her kitchen counter and crossed her arms over her chest. "You don't say. Care to enlighten me?"

"I've never been on a date with a woman like you before. It was disconcerting."

She didn't respond. He was going to have to do better than that.

"You specifically made cookies I would like. You were easy to talk to about anything. I found you... I mean, I find you immensely attractive." He stopped talking.

Lainey waited a little longer, but he didn't continue. She knew men like Matt, but he had to be one of the worst cases she'd ever met. Talk about not being in touch with your feelings!

"Are you saying that last Saturday night when you bolted, you realized you liked me? I mean, really liked me?"

She watched as his eyes widened. "Yes. That's it exactly."

"And that scared you?"

He straightened up to his full height and his presence seemed to get larger. "No, I wasn't scared. I'm saying this all wrong. It was disconcerting," he said again.

Lainey struggled to keep a straight face.

"Is it because you're a scientist? Did you need to maybe take some time and analyze what was happening?"

At first, he frowned, then she watched as a slow grin spread across his face.

"Yes, that's it. And you're right, I needed time to think about what was happening."

"Did you figure it out?"

"I did. I realized I liked you more than other women. I realized I really wanted to date you again. But then I realized I had totally fucked up. So, I talked to my friend Kostya's wife. She suggested I send you flowers."

Lainey bit her lip. "Flowers, huh?"

Matt nodded.

"A bouquet?"

"She said, based on my level of fuck-up, I should send a big bouquet. So, I figured big and more would be best."

Lainey rolled her eyes. "When I studied to be a banker, I had to take a lot of math classes. Did you know that?"

"No, but that makes sense."

"Do you know who else takes math classes?" Lainey asked.

"Bankers?"

Lainey could barely keep a straight face.

"Engineers. I think scientists and engineers are a lot alike. You're going to have to loosen up, Matt." She pushed away from the island and took the four steps necessary to stand in front of him. "I think you need a hug."

"GOD, yes. I could really use a hug about now."

How in the hell was he channeling his brother Luis so well? Mateo was laid back. He was not a stick-up-his-ass engineer/scientist type of guy. He was a take risks kind of guy—well, that wasn't totally true. He would follow a plan down to the letter if necessary.

This whole thing was just plain weird.

But he sure as hell would take a hug. Especially from Lainey. When she didn't make a move toward him, his blood heated. He liked the idea of taking charge. He really liked that.

He reached out and lightly touched her waist. She

stood still, then he stroked down until his hand curled around her hip, and his other hand moved around her back and he took a step forward, so that his leg was between hers.

He pulled her in and brought her chest to breast.

God, she was soft, in all the right places.

Then she did something wonderful. Lainey wrapped her arms around him, then rested her cheek against his chest and sighed. He could read so many things into that sigh, and he did. Enjoyment, relaxation, but as she snuggled closer, he felt a wave of contentment coming from her that settled back to him. How long had it been since he had felt the beauty and comfort of a genuine hug?

Too long.

His arms spasmed and she let out a whimper. He immediately relaxed his hold, worried that he had held her too tight.

"No," she breathed out the word. "Don't let me go."

Where was this coming from?

He didn't care. All he knew was he needed this. Long moments went by. Then Lainey tipped her head back, and he looked into blue eyes that now seemed navy. Her lips were parted, and now he wanted that kiss they'd talked about the other night. He needed that kiss.

His hand drifted up and threaded through her lush hair as he cupped her head and tilted it so that she was at the perfect angle for his first taste. When his lips brushed against hers, once, then twice, his eyes closed and the essence of Lainey burst through his senses. He needed more. Slowly, he licked against the seam of her lips. She opened for his tongue and he entered the heated cavern of her mouth.

He groaned as he tasted something better than any dessert he'd ever experienced. Lainey's tongue tangled with his as his other hand drifted down to cup her bottom, loving the round, soft bounty of this sexy woman.

Lainey's whimper was masked by his mouth, but the way she rubbed herself against him, he knew she was just as lost in the kiss as he was. Mateo felt the bite of her nails on his sides and he broke off the kiss as he grinned.

"Mmmh mmmh," she protested. But he wasn't done. He was only starting. He peppered kisses down along her jaw, to the back of her neck, until he softly bit, then laved her earlobe. Lainey went lax in his arms.

"Oh God. Again."

He grinned, then moved to her other ear. Then moved back to the slick beauty of her lips. There was just so much to enjoy. He heard Lainey humming against his mouth. It was a constant buzz that just told him how much she was reveling — "Matt," she pushed at his chest, as she broke away from his kiss.

"Hmmm?"

"The timer."

He frowned. Then he heard it. How in the fuck had he missed it? Jesus! How had he missed the timer going off? What in the fuck was wrong with him?

"The empanadas are done. I don't want them to overcook."

"Empanadas?"

"Yeah, beef and cheese. Plus, I have *cabonada* in the crock pot. I didn't follow that recipe exactly. I didn't make it with beef since we were having the beef empanadas. But I did some taste testing, and I think it's okay."

Mateo felt his eyes widen. "I thought I was taking you out to dinner."

"After the fourth bouquet arrived, I decided to cook." Lainey laughed as he followed her into the kitchen. It smelled like heaven. Almost as good as having Lainey in his arms.

Almost.

She cooked, baked, wanted to help the disenfranchised, and graduated with honors. What the hell wasn't she good at?

He watched as she pulled the empanadas out of the oven. The crust was a perfect golden brown. She then fished out two hollowed-out small pumpkins and put them on plates.

"I was supposed to heat these up, but I figured that with the heat of the stew, that they'll heat up just fine. I also bought some fresh bread from my favorite bakery. Do you mind setting the table?"

"Hell no. I'd feel better doing something than having you wait on me."

She smiled. She nodded to a drawer. "Silverware is in there, and I just use paper towels for napkins."

"Since that's my SOP, I think I can handle it."

"SOP? What does that stand for?"

"Standard Operating Procedure."

"Huh, that sounds almost military."

Mateo inwardly winced.

Focus!

"My friend Jase was in the Navy. Now he works construction and plays on our soccer team. I must have picked that up from him." He eyed the paper towel holder under the cabinets next to the crock pot. The crock pot was plugged into an extension cord with multiple outlets. So was her coffee maker, blender, food processor and toaster oven. They weren't plugged into the outlet that was right there on the wall.

It was a long extension cord. It wound all along the bottom of the wall, going past the sink, until it was plugged into a socket ten feet away, past two other sockets. At least he was ninety-nine percent sure the cord was, since it was covered by silver duct tape.

What the everloving hell?

"Lainey?"

"Yeah?" She didn't look up from where she was plating the empanadas.

"What's with the extension cord?"

"Oh, a lot of the electric plugs are broken, so I figured out a workaround."

Hmmmm.

She finished putting the last empanada on the serving plate, and he was almost drooling. Still, the extension cord. That was just too weird to let go.

"Why not call maintenance?"

"I called maintenance three times. Every time they fixed it, it would last for two or three days, but then it would break again. When I called the fourth time for them to replace them, they said they were working fine. He sounded really exasperated, so I didn't ask him to come the fourth time. Then I figured out my solution."

Lainey's grin was like a beam of sunshine. Mateo couldn't look away.

"I got an extension cord with multiple outlets, like we use at work, and plugged it into one of the outlets way over here. That one never broke."

She pointed to the outlet on the other side of the kitchen, with very little counter space.

"I was kind of scared of getting water on the cord, so I used waterproof duct tape and taped it with two layers. It's really safe," she assured him.

Mateo glanced at the 'broken' outlets and saw the two white test and reset buttons between the outlets.

This couldn't be real. He went over and tugged at the duct tape. Yep. It was stuck like glue.

He bit his lip.

Well, at least now he knew what she couldn't do.

"Honey, can you come here a moment?"

"I'm prepping the pumpkin gourds for the stew. Can you hold on?"

"I'll try."

He bit his lip harder.

Don't laugh. Do. Not. Laugh.

He watched as she washed her hands and brought one plate with the pumpkin bowl over to the counter where he was leaning. "Okay, I'm here. Did you want to show me something.?"

"Maintenance never showed you how they fixed the outlets, did they?"

She shook her head as she nudged him out of the way so she could start ladling the stew out of the crock pot and into the pumpkin bowl.

"Honey, can you hold on for a minute? I think I can show you how they fixed it."

She stopped ladling and turned to him, her eyes bright and excited. "Really? I YouTube'd and everything, but they just showed me pictures of the electrical backing of the surface of the outlet, you know? I figured that's how they fixed it, but it was too much for me. If you could show me how to fix it, that'd be wonderful."

God, he hated to do this. She was going to feel so dumb.

"Okay. See this bottom button that's popped out?" Lainey nodded. "It's the reset button. Just press it until you hear a click. Now the outlet is operational again."

"It's that easy?" Lainey's eyes were enormous. "Oh my God, that's wonderful! I mean, the extension cord was working, but getting to use all the outlets instead is great. Do you think this will work for the one in my bathroom too?"

Mateo chuckled. He couldn't help himself. How in the hell could such a competent woman be so damned inept? "Is there duct tape involved in the bathroom, too?"

"Yep." She grinned. "You do not know how excited I am. You're getting two more homemade meals for this."

He gazed into her excited blue eyes and felt ten feet tall, all for pressing a button. "Calm down, Lainey, this is not homemade meal worthy. Anybody could have done this."

She giggled. "Obviously not anybody. Now grab the paper towels and set the table so I can bring out the food before it gets cold. I don't think we want to microwave the empanadas."

"That would be sacrilege."

"So, hustle up."

Mateo opened his mouth to say, 'aye aye,' then closed it at the last second.

Dammit, there was just something about Lainey that threw him off his game. Maybe it was because deep down he knew she couldn't have anything to do with the Kraken. It was just impossible.

15

Hopefully, the *FLAN MIXITO*, which was really a total pain in the patootie to make, would result in more kisses. She'd practiced making it after watching four different YouTube videos. The dulce de leche was the simple part, but the flan? That had taken three different tries. The first two were only good enough for the garbage disposal. The third she took over to Lars, who was having a party that night.

He came over the next day to tell her it was a hit with his guests. Of course, he hadn't eaten any. Lars also wanted to know when she was going to show up to one of his parties as he leered at her breasts. Once again, she told him she wasn't interested in going for a run or spending time at the gym, and he quickly smiled at her and remembered that he was late for a personal training appointment. Not unlike Matt, when he had shot out of her apartment the week before. Hopefully, all the flowers Matt had sent meant that he wouldn't pull that nonsense again. If he did, it wouldn't matter if he bought out an entire florist shop and sent twenty pounds of chocolate. He would have been dead to her.

"Lainey, this is the best food I've had since my *abuelita* cooked for me back in Argentina."

"Abuelita?"

"My mom's mother. She passed not long after we moved to the States."

She reached across the table and placed her hand over his. "I'm sorry."

He turned his hand over and threaded his fingers with hers. "There's nothing to be sorry for. It's the way of life. Old people die. It's the young people dying that rips a hole out of your chest."

She tightened her grip on his hand, and he gave her a sad smile.

"Do you want to talk about it?" she asked softly.

He shook his head.

"In that case, how about dessert?"

"I don't know if I can eat dessert at this point. Maybe a little conversation?"

"Okay. Would you like coffee? I have fernet to go with it."

"My God, you've really gone all out. I only get fernet at just a few South American restaurants in DC and Baltimore."

Oh, that smile. Hopefully, she'd win the same kind of smile when she served the flan. Or better yet, after he kissed her.

"What are you smiling about?" His voice was quiet. Hushed.

"I like your smile."

"I like yours too, Lainey. Was that all that was making you smile?" He was still whispering.

She shook her head, her hair brushing her cheeks that she knew were turning red. Matt reached out and pushed a lock behind her ear.

"You don't want to tell me?"

"I was just wondering what else I could do to make you smile."

"Oh *corazón*, you make me smile all the time. Couldn't you tell by all the flowers I sent?"

"Then why did you leave like there was a firecracker up your butt?"

Lainey ripped her hand away from Matt's, then covered her mouth with both hands. Did she really just say that? What kind of codswollop, twaddle-minded idiot was she?

Matt burst out laughing. "That is wonderful. Did you really think that? I was pretty sure you thought I shouldn't let the door hit me on the ass on my way out."

Lainey slowly dropped her hands to the table. "Actually, I was thinking bottle rocket," she whispered.

Matt chuckled again. "I like you, Lainey Simpson. I really like you. And so did my boss, Jada."

"She did?"

"She absolutely did."

"In that case, let's break out the fernet. I haven't tasted it. I hope it's good."

He winced. "It's kind of an acquired taste, but whatever you don't drink, I'll finish."

"Okay. It's not like Jägermeister, Everclear, Moonshine or Absinthe, is it?"

"You've tried those?" He sounded surprised.

"I did go to school in the South. Clemson might not have been known as a party school, but I was in a sorority. It was kind of expected. I couldn't get away with not attending some fraternity parties."

"Shit, Lainey. You should have been more careful, drinking shit like that? You could have gotten into some dangerous situations."

"I always had a sorority sister with me. That was a rule I took very seriously. And I always kept it to a two-beer maximum. And if I tried something wild, like those shots, I would only drink a sip or two. Heck, that was all I could really handle. That stuff was awful."

"That's good to hear."

"But I do like lemon drop martinis. Those are really good."

"Well, why don't you make some coffee and I'll open the fernet? But let me help you with the dishes first."

It took her a moment to take in what he'd just said. There he was, all big and muscled, sitting at her table. She'd eaten with her father and brothers many times when it was just family and she'd cooked. Never once. Not ever, had they even offered to take their plates to the kitchen, let alone offer to help with the dishes.

"You don't have to do that," she assured Matt.

"You cook, I help clean. Them's the rules."

"O-o-okay."

"I'll clear the table while you start the coffee. Then I can load the dishwasher."

WHEN HE TOOK the plates into the kitchen, he shook his head again at the extension cord. He was going to have to help her get that taken down. What in the hell was maintenance going to think when they saw all the touch-up painting they were going to need to do? Actually, probably nothing. After all, they'd been called three times to reset her outlets. He grinned to himself.

"What are you grinning at?"

"Just how many flowers are in your living room. I didn't realize how big the bouquets were going to be until I told the florist I wanted to spend the same amount on the daisies. When they handed me this big handful, I got an idea of how I might have overdone it. But then again, I did leave like my ass was on fire."

"There was that," Lainey agreed, with a twinkle in her eye. "Why don't you just leave the dishes in the sink? The coffee's ready, and I want to taste the fernet."

"I like your sense of adventure. I would never have expected this from a banker."

"Something tells me that even though you're a scientist, you like to be challenged, and not just mentally. I bet you're the type who likes adventure sports."

"Busted," he said as he took the two mugs of coffee from her. "I remember my *abuelo* telling stories about the old days. He was quite the adventurer himself. He made his living as a *gaucho*. But that didn't stop him from going mountain climbing in the Andes."

"Really?" Lainey's eyes were wide. "Your grandfather was a cowboy and a mountain climber?"

"You know Spanish?"

"Just the little that one of my nannies taught me. Tell me more about your grandfather."

"He roamed all over Argentina before he met my *abuelita*. He said the day he met her, his wandering days were over. All he ever wanted to do from that day on was stay next to her and start a family."

"That's so romantic. Was it the same way for your mother and father?"

He picked up the bottle of fernet and poured a little bit into her glass and a healthy amount into his. He took a large gulp, then set it down. "No, not really. Mom met my dad in college when she was getting her master's degree. As she explained it, she had lived a sheltered life, and I believed it. My *abuelita* and *abuelo* were strict Catholics and sent her to an all-girls Catholic school until she was ready to go to college. She was at the top of her class. When she wanted to go to university, they were so proud that they scrimped and saved and made it happen."

"Mom was an only child, and they spoiled her, but she never acted like she was spoiled. She was one of the kindest people you could ever meet. But sheltered. Maybe even naïve. Actually, there was no maybe about it."

He paused again, and this time poured some of the fernet into his coffee. "Are you going to try yours?" he asked, indicating her untouched glass of alcohol.

"I forgot. I was too hung up by your story." He

watched as she took a dainty sip. Her eyes lit up. "Oh, this isn't bad at all. I like this, Matt. I've been meaning to ask you. Is your name really Matthew? That's odd that you would be named that when you were born in Argentina."

"Are you the woman who didn't know about the reset buttons on the electrical outlets?" he teased.

"Why? Am I right? I bet your name is Mateo or something like that, right?"

Shit!

"Yep, that's the name I was given when I was born. When I came to America, Mom just went with Matt so that when I went to school, it made me fit in better. It kind of worked. But my brown skin still made me stand out like a sore thumb in Wilmington, Delaware."

She winced. "I can imagine." Then she winced again. "That is to say, I'm sorry that happened, and I can't really imagine being in your shoes, because I was never in your shoes, you know?"

Mateo chuckled. "I get what you're saying. Don't worry about it. As soon as little league soccer and football started, nobody gave a shit. They all wanted me on their team."

"Yeah, I could see that," Lainey smiled.

"If you like the fernet, you should pour just a little into your coffee, then you'll be living large."

He watched as she carefully poured some of her drink into her mug, making sure she didn't spill a drop. It was funny to watch how perfectly she tried to do things. Thank God she used paper towels instead of cloth napkins and extension cords for perfectly good outlets. Otherwise, he'd be intimidated by her.

She took a sip of her coffee. "This is good, Matt. Really, really good. I'm glad I'll now have a bottle of it around." They quietly sipped their coffee for long moments. It was nice that she didn't feel like she had to fill every second with inane chatter.

"Is being a banker hard?" he finally asked.

"Not really. A lot of what I do has been repetitive. But three weeks ago, I got transferred to this new department, and the boss who was supposed to train me immediately went on vacation. That hasn't been a walk in the park."

"Why were you transferred?"

"I got a job as a management trainee. This is a fast track to becoming a personal banker, and that's where I can do those loans I was telling you about."

"Tell me more about the management trainee program. Did many people apply?"

"Unfortunately, yes. The only other person in my current department applied, and she's kind of bitter that I got the position. I can't tell if she is really kind of incompetent, or if she is doing things on purpose to make my job tougher."

"Like what?"

"She's handing me things that I can't read, and I'm supposed to decipher them before I can properly enter them into the system. Or she'll tell me that somebody called and won't give me the right number. Stuff like that. Since I only worked with the head of the department for four days, I don't know if he puts up with this kind of malarky or not. I would hope not, but when I called her on it, she said she just shows her cleavage and she gets along with Mr. Pine just fine." Lainey shuddered. "Can you imagine?"

Talk about sheltered. If she only knew how many straw-blonde, painted up, mini-skirt wearing, thong-showing *Frog Hogs* had actually flashed their tits at him and his fellow SEALs, just to get their attention. She'd probably die of shock.

"Hmmm," he shook his head noncommittally. "So, what do you do when you have trouble with the numbers?"

"Eventually, I can figure it out. There was this one time I had to call down to the Cayman Islands and validate an account number. I had to talk to someone else who was new. He was busy telling me his life story, and how his uncle was the vice president of the bank. Took me forever to validate the account. You wouldn't believe how many cryptocurrency transactions flow through the Cayman Islands."

"Aren't they known for being a big tax haven?" Mateo asked, trying to sound ignorant.

"Yeah, and they are also known for money laundering. Thank God we have strong policies in place that look for those types of things. However, I'm going to recommend that we bring on a strong cyber-security programmer like some of the bigger banks use. That's just an added layer of protection."

Bingo! Just wait until I tell Gideon and Kostya about this!

"I think I'm ready for that dessert now," Mateo said with a wide grin.

I knew it.

His gut reaction had been right all along. There had been no way that Lainey Simpson could ever have been mixed up with the Kraken, or some kind of money laundering scheme, or even cheating at cards. His woman was way too fucking honest. Bonnie, Jada, Leila, Amy, Lark or even Nolan's Maggie didn't even come close to Lainey when it came to honor or kindness. She had it in spades.

She got up from the table, and he started to get up as well.

"No, stay where you are. The dessert is a surprise."

"Okay." He flashed a smile at her. He was curious to see how she intended to top tonight's dinner. He liked pies. Maybe pie?

He heard the refrigerator door open. Then he heard the whoosh of one of the burners being lit. Okay, it wasn't pie. He waited, and then the wonderful smell of dulce de leche wafted out of the kitchen. His absolutely full stomach, a stomach that had had three helpings of *cabonada* and three empanadas, suddenly felt empty. But seriously, who couldn't want dulce de leche?

He watched her come out to the table. For a second he looked at the dessert, but then he focused on Lainey. He watched as her hips swayed as she carefully took each step. Then, before he thought it couldn't get any better, her breast brushed against him as she placed the dessert in front of him.

He didn't need to look up to know it was an

accident. When she sat down with her plate in front of him, her cheeks were bright red. Yep, a total accident. He looked down at the dessert. The flan looked perfect, and the scent of the *dulce de leche* took him back to Argentina. He closed his eyes for just a moment, flashing back to a dinner with his mom, Luis, and his *abuelo,* as they all waited impatiently around the table for his *abuelita* to bring out the *flan mixto*. He opened his eyes and sighed.

"The whipped cream is the kind from the can, but everything else is homemade. I hope you like it."

How in the hell could she sound hesitant? The woman was a miracle worker. No wonder Brax had told him to be careful. Mateo was definitely in over his head.

He continued to stare at Lainey in the soft light of the dining room. He watched as she bit her lip. She looked worried.

"Aren't you going to try it?"

"Oh yeah. Fuck yeah, I'm going to try it. I'm probably going to ask for fourths. Then I'm going to want the rest of it for breakfast."

"Uhmmm." She was blushing again. Finally, after he'd picked up his fork, she responded to what he'd implied.

"That could be arranged. But it's really important that you heat the *dolce de leche* up properly. You have to use two pans. One on the bottom filled with hot water, and the pan on top you fill with the chilled caramel. Otherwise, it burns. I could teach you before you leave..."

Mateo put his fork down. He reached over to where her hand was balling up her paper towel. "How about I sleep over tonight and you heat it up for me in the morning?"

"We can't—I mean, you can't sleep in my bedroom. Xena's in my closet. That's her safe place."

Oh yeah, the three-legged dog. But it definitely sounds like Lainey is getting on board with the idea of us sleeping together.

Thank Fuck.

"Corazón, I wasn't thinking about us going to bed together. It's too early. We'll work it out a little later. How about that? Right now, I want to savor this gift." He picked up his fork and scooped up a small bite of flan, whipped cream, and dulce de leche and tasted heaven.

16

Lainey bit back a giggle. Apparently that old saying that the way to a man's heart is through his stomach was true. She took three bites of her dessert and two sips of her coffee and heard Matt groan. She looked up to see him wiping his face, and she couldn't stifle the laughter this time.

"You ate your second piece that fast?"

"Woman, you're lucky I showed some self-control."

She laughed harder. "I'll take that as a compliment," she said when she could finally control herself.

"That was how it was meant."

"Do you want a third helping?"

Matt leaned forward, his forearms on the table. When had he rolled up his shirtsleeves? God, his arms looked spectacular, all muscled and strong, with just a sprinkling of hair. She frowned. His watch looked really industrial. When she looked at it closer, she saw that the time was set to military time.

"Hurry up and finish your dessert, Lainey." Matt's voice was deep and rough. She'd never heard him sound like that before, and it sent an electric current from the top of her spine down to her pelvis. She let out a long breath.

"I'm not sure I'm hungry anymore," she whispered.

"That's good." He got up and rounded the table so that he was hovering over her. He pulled out her chair, then held out his hand. She trembled, but not from nerves. She was excited.

Danged excited.

She put her hand in his and he drew her up so that not even a sheet of paper could come between them. Matt lifted both of her hands and put them around his neck. She could see the pulse in his neck beating fast. Good, she wasn't the only one who was worked up.

"I'm going to kiss you. Just like I should have done the other night, before the bottle rocket went off."

Even though this was the sexiest and most romantic moment of her life, Lainey laughed. She continued to giggle until she felt the hard press of Matt's erection against her tummy and her laughter died an abrupt death. She couldn't help the little shimmy she did against his body, then it was his turn to make a noise, and what a noise it was. She savored it as he groaned out her name.

"Lainey."

She opened her mouth to say something, but he dipped his head and plunged his tongue into her mouth. There was no warning, no chance for her to overthink or worry. Instead, he just took over and she gave way and let him control everything.

Maybe not everything because soon her fingers were threading through his gorgeous, short, curly hair. She scraped her nails over his scalp and felt him shudder.

I did that. I made this warrior of a man tremble in my arms.

She didn't know how, but she was scooped up in his arms, and he was heading to the living room. Lainey knew he was heading to the couch, and there was no way that she wanted the first time they made love to be on her couch. Because, to heck with the three-date rule, she wanted to make love.

Now!

"Wrong way," she murmured. "Down the hall." She snuggled closer to him, her head resting against his chest.

Matt changed direction. He strode past the guest bathroom and ignored the guest bedroom and her office. "Stop, Honey. Not my bedroom. Go back."

He gave her a curious look.

"My dog, Xena. She gets easily scared. She won't know what to do if a man ever went into my bedroom. We need to use the guestroom."

"Guest room it is." Matt pushed open the door with his shoulder and chuckled. Lainey understood why. It was made up for a woman spending the night, not that she'd had anybody spend the night here. But if they did, it would be perfect for them.

"You're definitely a Southern lady."

She hit his shoulder. "Don't make fun."

"*Corazón*, I'm not making fun. I promise."

She let out a sigh of relief. "Well, good."

Matt laid her down gently on top of the bed. He did it like she didn't weigh a thing. He was sure strong for a scientist. Then he put his knee on the chintz duvet cover and covered her mouth with his. All thought was whisked away as his kiss ripped away all her inhibitions. Even when he started unbuttoning the front of her dress, she didn't flinch.

"*Dios mío*, you're beautiful." His voice was guttural, like he had swallowed gravel. She loved it. Almost as much as when he flipped open the front clasp of her bra and took one of her generous breasts in his hand and dipped his head to suckle her nipple.

"Matt," she called out. "More."

He covered her other breast with his big hand and brushed his thumb over the tip. Back and forth. Again and again and again. She tried to keep quiet. She really did. She prayed that when she wailed out his name that her neighbors or Xena didn't hear her.

MATEO TOOK HIS TIME, not just because he thought it had been a long time for Lainey, but because to not savor this night would be a sin.

Lainey twisted and let out a disgruntled sound. He looked up from where he was feasting and realized her arms were tangled in her dress and she wanted to touch him.

He grinned. "Something wrong?" he asked.

"Don't you dare tease me," she grumbled. "You got me into this mess. Now get me out of it." It was fun to hear her honeyed Southern accent commanding him.

"And don't you dare laugh. I want to touch you. It's only fair."

"In that case..." Mateo wrapped one arm around her waist and pulled her dress and bra down to her waist. He stopped and looked into her eyes. "More?"

Lainey bit her lip, then nodded. He waited.

"Yes. I want both of us to be naked."

Thank you, God!

He lowered her back onto the soft duvet and unbuttoned the rest of her dress. Each button revealed more of her pearlescent skin. He couldn't stop himself; he had to kiss her stomach, then her belly button, and when her lacy white panties were revealed, he pulled them down and down along with the rest of her dress until he could throw her clothes over his shoulder and admire the beauty that was Lainey.

She said nothing but the way that her legs shifted and her hips swayed, he could see that she was just as eager as he was.

"You agreed you'd be naked, too." Her words were a whisper.

Mateo unrolled his shirtsleeves, then unbuttoned all the buttons on his shirt until he could pull the shirttails out of his pants.

"Yesssss." Lainey hissed out the word and sat up. She reached out for him. But he wasn't ready to be touched yet. He had a lot of things he wanted to do before she was allowed to touch. He took her hands in both of his and kissed her fingertips.

"Lie back. Can you do that for me?"

She frowned. "But? Why?"

"Because I asked you to. Will you do this for me, *querida*?"

Her expression softened, and she gave him a warm smile. "If that's what you want, then yes."

She was perfect. Absolutely perfect.

He took off his shoes, socks, and slacks, and pulled a condom out of his wallet. He only had one. Next time, he'd come prepared. He put the condom on the nightstand and saw Lainey give a grateful smile. That was his job. He would always protect her.

Naked, he stretched out beside her and pulled her close. This time he had no problem with her touching his chest, not when he was planning on touching her all over. She hugged her arms around his back, then started to stroke him up and down. It was as if she were petting him, and he liked every moment.

He thrust his fingers into the dark mass of her hair and positioned her just right for a kiss, one perfect kiss. As if she knew what he was going to do, she parted her rose-colored lips. He slid his tongue inside the warmth that was Lainey and felt his world tilt. For long moments, their tongues brushed against one another, ramping up their passion, taking them to a precipice.

Mateo needed more. So much more. He needed to know how her body tasted. He needed to know how high he could take her. As he slid down her body,

Lainey softly scratched her fingers down his back. Yet one more sensation to revel in.

Finally, he was where he wanted to be. Once again Lainey was moving her legs, eager for more caresses, and Mateo intended to provide them. Positioning himself between her legs, he spread them even wider apart. He heard her gasp. He looked up to make sure she was okay. She had a pillow beneath her head and a satisfied look on her face. He grinned, because he intended to make her feel much more than satisfied.

Mateo noted the shimmer of wet as he traced the seam of Lainey's sex. Up and down, he continued, and when he looked up, she was panting as she watched him.

Good.

He gently pulled back the lips of her sex and stared. She was beautiful everywhere. Mateo thrust his tongue into her, in and out, devouring her. Lainey arched up, eager to experience even more pleasure. He licked her clit, then delicately added teeth to his caress. Lainey's whimpers changed to moans.

"Yes."

She ground her pussy into his face, and he would have smiled, but he was too engrossed in giving this woman the pleasure that she deserved. He could feel her rising higher.

"Matt," she groaned.

Mateo. My name is Mateo.

He kissed his way up her body, then reached over for the condom, tore it open, and put it on. Lainey was trembling underneath him, her head slowly rolling back and forth on her pillow. He couldn't help himself. He tilted her chin up and kissed her. A long, luxurious kiss. The spice of Lainey made him want more, but she pushed at his shoulders.

"Inside me," she begged.

He brought up one of her knees to the side of his thigh, the other he cocked out so that her softness was at the perfect angle for his entrance. Lainey braced her feet and curved upwards, demanding his cock. He slowly slid into her soft, tight heat.

Lainey's neck arched, and she called out the wrong name again. "Matt. Give me everything."

He gently drove into her body until they were merged, his body with hers, until they were fused together. One being, one heart and one soul.

And they spiraled into bliss.

17

LAINEY WASN'T KIDDING; HER DOG REALLY WAS A scaredy-cat. But, as usual, bacon saved the day. She was a pretty border collie. If he had to bet, Lainey took her to a groomer every other week who specialized in abused animals. He'd noticed the high-priced dog food that was in the fridge.

"You're living large, aren't you, Xena?" Mateo remembered the show called Xena, Warrior Princess, and as a teenage boy, he sure wasn't watching it for the plot. Xena was hot.

He crouched down and let Xena nibble half a strip of bacon out of his hand. It reminded him of the pregnant pit bulls at Pepper's place. Gideon had followed up for him, so he knew that three of the girls had lived to give birth to their pups. One didn't make it through the birth. As for the males, they were still being evaluated to determine the best ways to rehabilitate the dogs, or if that was even possible.

The whole thing made him sick.

Mateo stopped thinking about it and turned his attention to the beautiful girl in front of him. He gave her a good scratch under her chin and the dog leaned against him. Yep, she liked to be petted, just like her mama.

He got back to cooking. He would have liked to spend more time in bed, but after years in the Navy, sleeping past oh-five-hundred was impossible. He'd cuddled Lainey for an hour before he had to get up and find something to eat. Despite his promise to eat the *flan mixito* for breakfast, he was looking for some protein, and he'd found it. Lainey was a woman after his own heart. Her refrigerator was packed with good stuff. Mateo even found her waffle iron, which he could now plug in on the other side of the sink.

He wasn't sure what Lainey would want for breakfast, but he wanted to be prepared for anything. Mateo prepped the fixings for a Spanish omelet, and got the batter ready for the waffles, then cut up the strawberries to go on them. He couldn't help himself, though; he had to fry up some bacon ahead of time. A man needed protein, and there was the added boon of having met Xena.

Xena walked into the kitchen and leaned against him.

"You want another piece?"

She walked away from him, toward a half-filled water bowl and an empty food bowl that was on a stool. It was probably raised higher for Xena so she didn't lose her balance.

"I'll get you your breakfast, girl."

He fished out the package of food that was labeled *Xena* and *breakfast*. There was one that was titled *dinner*. Of course. His woman was a bit OCD. Mateo stopped right where he was.

His woman?

Xena came over and rested her muzzle against his thigh. "Just a moment."

His woman?

When had Lainey become his woman?

How about the moment I started defending her to the Lieutenant?

"Dammit," he muttered to himself.

He turned around to get the kitchen scissors so he could cut into the pre-packaged dog food and found Lainey frowning at him.

"Matt, why are you swearing?"

Shit.

"No reason."

"Really? You seemed kind of vehement. Are you regretting sleeping with me?"

He couldn't stand the vulnerable look on her face.

"Absolutely not. I was thinking about what one of my friends said when I first met you. He was totally on point. He said I was going to fall hard and fast."

"And that's something to swear about?"

She was standing there in an oversized sleep shirt, with her hair tousled, looking like her dog had just died. He thought fast.

"I just hate it when Brax knows me better than I know myself. I did fall hard and fast."

Her beautiful blue eyes got wide. "You did?"

"I did. I talked to another friend, Kostya, about you. I told him how honest and kind you were. I explained about you making cookies for the old couple down the hall. I told him how smart you were, and how you wanted to make a difference for lower-income people who wanted to get loans for start-up businesses. I told him how you went out of your way to find an Argentinian recipe to make me cookies from my home, which were delicious, by the way. Then I told him how being around you makes me feel better about myself."

"You said all that?" She smiled big.

Mateo nodded.

"What did Kostya say?"

"He said I'd better spend more time with you." And that wasn't a lie, but goddammit, he better get to tell her the truth pretty damn soon.

"Then that works out great, because I'd like to spend more time with you," she grinned.

MATT HAD LEFT after helping her tidy up the kitchen and taking off the duct tape. Lainey had to admit, being able to use all the sockets in the kitchen really made a big difference. Xena came over and jumped up onto the couch beside her.

"He's a good guy, isn't he?" she asked her dog. "You came out from your doggy bed and everything." She couldn't believe how much Xena trusted Matt. That never happened.

Xena pushed her muzzle under Lainey's hand, demanding to be scratched.

"Do you want scratches, or are you giving me strength to call my mother? You know how she loves her Sunday talks. Whereas I would prefer a tooth pulled without Novocaine."

Xena whined and pushed even closer.

"You understand. You're a good girl. Let's get this over with, shall we?"

Lainey pressed on the key that would call her mother.

"Well, it's about time, MacLaine. I have left four messages for you, without a return phone call. I raised you better than that."

"Mother, I told you that Sundays are my day to call family. I've been telling you that since the day I moved to Virginia."

"Well, this is urgent."

Lainey sighed. "It's always urgent."

"I'm not feeling well, and the doctor says that I need to take things easy, just like your sister."

Lainey frowned. "What exactly did the doctor say? Is there something in particular that is wrong?"

"I have a brain tumor."

"What? Oh my God, Mom. When did you find out? Have they done a biopsy?"

"They've done exhaustive testing. This new doctor, who is an absolute quack, took blood and put me in one of those tube scans—"

"You mean an MRI?"

"Whatever they're called. They roll you into a coffin

and give you terrible music to listen to and tell you not to move. She's a new doctor. For thirty years, I've had the same doctor, and now we have this new woman. Can you believe it? A woman!"

"Have you seen a neurologist? An oncologist? A surgeon?"

"She's a total quack. She hasn't referred me to any specialist like she should. She had the nerve to tell me that my headaches were probably caused by stress, and I probably had anxiety. She said that a lot of women benefit from taking a pill and seeing a therapist. As if I was a common case. She even wrote that down in my official file! MacLaine, it was mortifying. Can you imagine someone calling me common?"

"She didn't call you common," Lainey corrected. She felt a headache starting. Maybe *she* needed an MRI. "What else did your doctor say?"

"MacLaine, weren't you listening? She typed it in my file that I was neurotic, where nurses and everybody could see. I told her to remove it immediately. She said she couldn't because it was her diagnosis. I told her she had to, because her diagnosis was wrong, and if she didn't erase what she had typed, your daddy would get her fired!"

Yep, definitely a headache.

Think about Matt. Think about Matt. Think about sex. Think about really stupendous sex.

"—your father called the hospital administrator to get her fired. We belong to the same country club. Your father assured me that the administrator was going to look into it. But I've called her office every day, and she's still there. So, I'm going to die of a brain tumor and nobody cares."

"Mother, I care. All of your children care."

"When I told Bennett, all she did was complain about the food at Charleston Place and Spa. She didn't even offer to have Trey call his fraternity friend who's a dermatologist."

Lainey tried to bite back a laugh. It didn't work. Of course, she snorted.

Of course she did.

"How many times do I have to tell you to stop that disgusting habit?"

"I'm sorry, Mother."

"Now that you know I have a brain tumor, you have to come home and assist me. There is no way that I will be able to continue to chair the Historical Society by myself."

"I thought Noreen Lancaster has always wanted to co-chair with you." Lainey suggested.

"I can't believe you even brought her name up. She is shrill and uncouth. I can't believe that she actually belongs to the Daughters of the American Revolution. I am still looking into that. I think her great-grandmother forged her documents."

Lainey shoved her face into a pillow to cover her laughter.

"MacLaine! Are you listening to me? This is my hour of need. You cannot deny me."

When she was sure she had her laughter under control, Lainey started talking.

"Mother, I can take off two days from work before

your Anniversary Gala. I don't have any more time accrued," Lainey crossed her fingers at her lie. "That way I can help you with the preparations."

"Lainey, I don't need help with the preparations," her mother said sharply. "That's what the help is for. I need your emotional support. We will have eight of the state's most influential people staying at Magnolia Run for the weekend. Others are flying in from across the country, including from our nation's capital. I will expect you to act as another Simpson hostess. I have recently talked to Luke Abercromby's mother. He and his fiancée broke up six months ago. She and I agree that you two would look very good as a couple for the weekend, if you could lose fifteen pounds. I will arrange to have him at the gala."

Lifeless Luke?!

"Mother, I'm seeing someone."

"That doesn't matter. We need someone of a certain caliber. Normally you wouldn't attract a man like Luke, but as a favor from his mother, he will act as your beau for the evening."

"That won't work for me. Either Matt Agular is coming with me, or I'm not coming. End of story."

"Good God, you're dating a Mexican?"

"No, I'm dating a scientist."

"He can't come. A scientist is even worse. They have no social skills."

"Do you want me there?"

"You *have* to be here. If you're not, people will talk."

"Then I guess Matt will be coming."

"At least tell me he will look good in a tuxedo."

A quick mental view of Matt Aguilar in a tuxedo made Lainey's blood run hot.

"Mother, he'll look good, I promise."

"All right. Be here first thing Thursday morning before the Anniversary Gala."

Please God, let Matt be available.

18

MATEO COULD TELL HIS BOSS WAS PAST BEING TENSE, antsy was no longer in his vocabulary, he'd left agitated in the dust, and now he was downright pissed as fuck. But who could blame him? He and Lark hadn't seen blue-eyed little Romy who was just a little over two years old for over three weeks now. She'd gone to some secluded island with Lark's impossibly rich mother. A mother who had made it clear she would take any other family of the Omega team with her. Beatrice Allen was a kick and a half, but that still didn't mean a damn thing to Kostya because he and Lark wanted their daughter with *them*. In their home. In their arms.

It was going to be terrible after what he and Gideon had to report.

"Okay, I didn't get any usable data on Ely Roberts yet," Mateo started. "He did talk to his old high school buddy Pepper Higgins, but all he wanted from Pepper was his sister's contact information."

"Are you sure you got everything from him?" Jase wanted to know.

Ryker laughed. "You're kidding, right? Mateo is quiet and creative. I'd never want to be on the other side of an interrogation from him."

"Let's just say there were ants and cockroaches involved, and I'm sure I got all the information that was available. Unfortunately, it was not good. I took it to Gideon, and he checked it out. Pepper's sister spent the last ten years working at a daycare in Pennsylvania. She was liked and well thought of. Ely paid her seven grand to quit and apply for a job in Virginia Beach."

Lark, who was sitting in her normal seat in the corner of the couch, gasped. "Not Tiny Tot's Playtime."

Mateo nodded.

Lark reached out blindly with her hand, and Kostya grabbed it. She was white as a sheet. Her head was shaking, and her silvery blonde hair was flying across her face.

"Was it?" Lark's voice was shrill. "Was it Romy's daycare?"

Mateo looked at Gideon, then turned back to Lark. "It was."

"When?" Kostya demanded to know as he picked up his wife and sat down on the sofa with her nestled in his lap. All that could be heard in the room was Lark whimpering.

"When?!" Kostya roared the question.

"Two days after Romy left with Lark's mom," Mateo answered.

"Where is she?" Jase and Linc were hovering near the hallway, ready to go to the daycare.

"Calm down. Don't you think that Mateo would have been all over that if she were still there?" Gideon said sharply. "She worked there for two days. Long enough to find out that Romy was going to be out for an extended length of time. Our assumption is that she reported to Sykes who told her to get the hell out of Dodge. Right now, I'm continuing to check morgues. Mateo and I figure Sykes is not going to want any loose ends."

Mateo's gut clenched. He couldn't get the picture of the little girl holding her cat out of his mind. Christina Higgins was definitely dead to his way of thinking.

"I've been working on something with Jada when it comes to Ivan," Linc spoke up.

Mateo's gut clenched again. He didn't want to hear about Ivan's account with Lionel Security and Trust Bank. Lainey was officially off the table.

"Linc, before you talk about what you've found, I want to bring all of you up to speed about MacLaine, Lainey Simpson," Mateo interrupted.

Linc nodded, and Kostya said 'Go ahead' from where he was sitting. Lark still had her face shoved into his neck.

"You know that I've been undercover with her for almost three weeks now. A few days ago, she mentioned that she was going to recommend that they bring on a strong cyber-security programmer to make sure all of their cryptocurrency and other types of complicated transactions were given an additional level of scrutiny."

"That's very promising," Gideon said slowly.

"What do you mean by promising?" Mateo demanded to know. "That's more than promising. Why would she want someone to come in who would find out her illegal activities? She has to be on the up-and-up."

"Mateo, I still haven't been able to track down where the gold came from. She didn't inherit it. She didn't earn it. I've searched her father's records going back thirty years. He has not purchased gold. Where did that come from? I'm sorry, man, she's still on our watch list."

"Well, I'm the one who has been with her for the last three weeks, and I'm telling you she is not part of the Kraken."

Jase took a step away from the hallway toward Mateo and glowered. "Just how have you been *with* her? Have you taken your eye off the ball?"

"No, I have not. I know what my job is, and I've done it. Everything about her screams innocent."

"Find out about the gold. Find out why she made that transfer. Then we all will be with you," Kostya said. "Okay, who's up next?"

Mateo listened to what Linc said he'd found about Frank Sykes' son Ivan. He tuned out what Brax said about Amanda Melton, and he was just fucking happy when the meeting was over.

He was almost at his truck when Brax grabbed his arm.

"Wait up."

"I'm busy."

"Let's grab a beer," Brax tried to insist.

"I told you, I'm busy."

"I believed you. Now let's go to your place and have a beer. I'll follow you. It should be easy since you're driving this heap."

"Brax," Mateo started again.

"I really don't want to hear your shit," Braxton growled. "Get in your fucking truck, drive to your place, let me in, and offer me a goddamn beer."

Mateo saw something in his friend's eyes that caused him to nod. "Fine."

"Geez, you sure are a stubborn asshole."

"As the saying goes, takes one to know one."

Brax shook his head and headed for his vehicle. Mateo headed back to his place.

It was the middle of the day, so they were out on Mateo's patio. The sun was shining, the trees were in bloom. It should have been perfect, and it would have been if his lieutenant and his second-in-command would have just believed him about Lainey.

"Want another one?" Brax asked as he pointed to Mateo's beer.

"Nah, I might be driving up to Annapolis tonight."

"I thought you weren't going to see her again until this weekend."

"Yeah, that was the plan. But thought maybe I'd ask her to lunch, too. It depends on how much of Janice's work she has to do."

"So, you know about her co-workers, huh?"

"That's the job, isn't it? I need to know what's going on at the bank, so I should know about her co-workers. Janice is a bitch and is constantly foisting things onto Lainey. But she doesn't sound smart enough to be working for the Kraken."

Braxton started picking the label off of his beer.

"What?" Mateo said.

"What, what?" Braxton asked.

"You've got something to say, so say it."

"You've slept with her, haven't you?"

Mateo said nothing. He watched as a hummingbird buzzed by on its way to a sprig of cherry blossoms.

"Well?"

"It's worse than that."

"How can it be worse than that?"

Mateo could hear the judgment in his friend's voice, and he didn't want to. He'd been hearing it in his own head for the last ten days.

"Ah fuck."

Mateo's head dropped, and he looked at his shoes.

"It was just like I said. She was perfect for you, and you've fallen for her."

"Don't say it like that," Mateo whispered. "Don't say it like a bad thing. Falling in love with Lainey is the best thing that's ever happened to me. She's... She's... She's joy. I can't explain her any other way. To be around her, you're flooded with joy and happiness. You can't help but smile. Even Jonah, the contrary bastard, would smile after five minutes with Lainey. That's how good of a person she is."

"Mateo, you realize she could—"

"Stop it! Just fucking stop it! There is no way that she is involved with anything wrong. I'm going to find out about the gold and the bank transfer and get the proof that Kostya and Gideon need, but I don't need it. She's golden to the core."

Mateo felt Braxton's hand on his back. He could feel his support.

"If you say so, then I believe you. How can I help?"

19

_____

"You're early."

"That was the plan," Mateo said softly. He'd been hoping to catch her in her robe, and he had.

"I don't have my clothes or make-up on," she breathed out as she looked up at him.

"Let me in, Lainey."

"Okay." She stepped back, and he walked into her home and closed the door behind him. Lainey stepped backward. It was as if she could sense he was on the hunt, and he was.

"I th-th-thought you said the reservation was at seven."

"I did. I got off work early and realized I was hungry."

Her eyes got wide.

"You mean you want to?"

His smile was slow, his eyes at half-mast. "Yes, I want to. Take off the robe, Lainey."

She looked around the room. He'd already scoped it

out. Her curtains and blinds were all closed, but she still bit her lip. "Lainey, take off your robe."

She plucked at the belt with nervous fingers.

"Now, *Corazón*. I need you. I need you right now."

It seemed like hours before her robe dropped to the floor and revealed tangerine panties and bra. So pretty. He watched as her nipples tightened, and her breath bellowed in and out, like she couldn't take in enough air.

His gaze traveled further down, and he thought about all the time he would spend there, bringing her to orgasm. Before dinner. After dinner. Before breakfast. After breakfast.

"You're staring at me," she whispered.

"I'm looking at what's mine." He couldn't help that feeling of possession. It might not be politically correct, but the other night she'd given herself to him, and now she was his.

"Yours?" Her body was trembling.

He stepped forward until they were inches away from one another, close enough for him to tilt up her chin for a ferocious miracle of a kiss. He devoured her, his tongue claiming the molten heat of her mouth. Lainey met him, stroke for stroke, whimpering as her nails bit into his biceps, as her entire body pressed closer to his. Never had a woman matched him so well.

He reached behind her and unclasped her bra. She released him, then did a sexy little shimmy that had her bra falling to the floor. He watched in delight as her breasts were even more appealing as they swayed and danced just for him. He took one in his hand and smiled as he both felt and saw how well she fit, her softness driving him out of his mind.

"Bedroom," she gasped.

She grabbed his hand and led him to the hall. They walked past Xena who was eating her dinner, showing no interest in them. Lainey led him to her bedroom that had a four-poster bed, and was awash in yellow, which was only fitting since she had brought sunshine into his life.

When she bent down to throw back her covers, he had time to admire the perfect globes of her generous ass. She was all-woman. Soft and curvy as she should be. Mateo tore off his t-shirt, then closed the distance between them and pulled her back to his front, keeping her bent over, until her forearms were resting on the bed.

She turned her head around to look up at him. He saw the question in her gaze.

"Matt?"

"I enjoy feeling you against me. I love everything about you. Did you know that?"

She shook her head.

He moved her hair to one side, then kissed the nape of her neck. She trembled. He licked where he had kissed, and she shivered. She continued to shiver as he made his way down her spine until he got to her tailbone. Lainey dropped down, her head, chest and arms dropping to the duvet cover as if she couldn't hold herself up. That was when he finally knelt behind her and pulled her pretty panties down.

"Lift your leg, *Corazón*."

He caressed her calf as she did what he said. When she totally stepped out of her panties, he kissed and licked one cheek of her ass, then the other. Lainey wailed his name, but he wasn't done. He went back to the first and scraped his teeth downward, giving her a gentle love bite as he pushed her legs apart.

He did it to the other side and pushed her legs apart even further. From this angle, he could see the soft shimmer of her arousal. Everything about her at this moment was shredding his control.

It was easy; he had to. Mateo flipped her over and was rewarded with wide eyes filled with surprise, wonder, and passion. She was precious. Mateo wanted to find all the world's treasures and lay them at her feet. Lainey pushed herself up onto her elbows as Mateo put her legs over his shoulders, and he bent to her secret flesh.

He was hungry for this. Hungry for the taste of Lainey. Not just the tangy honey and sweet spice of her, but hungry to make her soar. He delved, licked, and suckled, while listening to every exquisite sound she made. Her musical moans meant she was enjoying what he was doing, but better yet, were those high notes meaning he was doing something she especially liked. He glided his fingers inside her hot depths and crooked them so that they could brush against her g-spot while he nibbled at her clit. That was her favorite.

Mateo intended to watch her as she orgasmed. He moved his other hand upward and caught hers, tangling their fingers, and he tugged her into a sitting position.

"What?" She sounded drunk.

"Look." He moved his gaze up and saw her eyes were glimmering, and her kiss-swollen lips had a hint of a smile. "You're so beautiful, and I want to watch you when you come."

"You were," she protested.

"I want to see your expression. Stay seated. I promise a treat if you do this for me." Her half smile turned into a big smile.

"Can you tell me what it is? Please? I hate surprises. Tell me now."

Mateo laughed. He bent down and nipped the inside of her right thigh.

"Ow. Why did you do that?"

"I want your full attention on the matters at hand. Or don't you like what we're doing?"

Lainey sat up straighter and used her other hand to grab his shoulder. "I like watching. I promise. Now, give me something to watch."

With that said, Mateo licked through the lips of her sex, stroke after stroke, with his two fingers inside her. He could feel her shudders, and she started making those sexy, high-note sounds. Mateo took her clit between his teeth, then lashed it with his tongue. Back and forth, back and—

Lainey shrieked out his name.

He had planned to stay the night, so instead of going commando, he had on underwear, which he shoved off along with the rest of his clothes. He would have thrown them over the back of the chair, but Ms. OCD was using that to have tonight's outfit ready to put on later. It's a good thing she'd never see the inside of his condo. She'd run shrieking into the night, never to be heard from again.

He moved Lainey so that she was lying on the bed north to south, her head on her many yellow-and-orange-flowered pillows. He pulled out some condoms and tossed them on the nightstand, but one he took immediately and started to roll it on.

Lainey was no longer lying on her back. Now she was on her side, head propped up on her hand as she watched him perform that task.

"You find this interesting?"

"Next time can I do it?"

"It depends."

"On what?"

"On how desperate I am to have you. And Lainey, I'm desperate. It's been a week, and you're all I've been thinking about. So, if you rolled a condom on my dick right now, I'd come right in your hands, and that's not how I want this evening to start."

She started to get up.

"Uh-uh. Stay right where you are." Mateo put his knee on the bed and one arm over her body. "I've got you right where I want you."

"You do?" That husky voice went straight to his cock.

"Yep, I do." He made room for himself between her legs, and she gave him a smile of pure satisfaction.

"I think you have it all wrong. I've got you exactly where *I* want *you*." She arched up and the warm heat of her core pressed against his sensitive flesh. So, this is how he was going to die. Not in the field. It was going to be on a flowered bedspread in Lainey's arms.

"We're going to take this slow; we've got all night."

His stomach growled.

"I think I remember something about dinner reservations." Lainey giggled.

"Okay, right now it might go a little fast, but when we come home, it will be nice and slow."

She bit her lip, and he did what he'd been dying to do, ever since he'd first noted that habit. He kissed her mouth and sucked her lower lip into his mouth then he gently bit it.

"That's going to be your punishment every time I see you hurting yourself by biting your lip, I'm going to bite it instead."

"That's not a punishment. That's more like an inducement." She giggled again.

"However you take it, I get to kiss you, so I'm good with it," Mateo grinned.

When had he ever laughed with a woman in his bed before?

Never.

It was hot.

She was hot.

This moment was pure beauty.

Lost in the splendor of her sparkling eyes and the feel of her soft body beneath him, he had to have her or he would lose his mind. She reared up as he pressed down, and their lips met in an amalgamation of fire. He would never get enough from this woman. As he tasted her, sweat dripped down his back. He knew he was holding on by a thread, but it didn't matter; the riotous pleasure that was ripping through him from just this kiss was out of this world, but as her nails scratched down his back, he knew he needed more.

He wrenched away from their kiss.

"No!" she cried.

He got up on his knees and pulled her thighs around his waist.

"Yes," she sighed. "Oh, yes."

He watched as he slowly penetrated her warm, soft depths, glorying in the sweet high notes of her pleasure. For a moment, just a moment, he looked up to ensure that she was feeling as much pleasure as he was. Then he was trapped. Trapped by the glow that was Lainey. As his cock plunged deeper into the heat of her body, it was as if he were magnetically pulled down to place gentle kisses along her temple, her jaw, her neck until she gripped his hair and pulled him down for a fiery kiss as his body began the primal rhythm that nobody but the two of them had ever felt before.

As she sucked his tongue deeper into her mouth, her tongue dueling with his, she arched up, clasping his hips tight, as if she never wanted him to leave her.

For a brief second, they broke away from their kiss for air, and they cried one another's names, trying to invoke all the adoration and maybe even love they were feeling for one another.

"*Dios mío, corazón mio, eres perfecto.*"

"God, Matt, you're perfect."

Mateo, my name is Mateo!

But even that discordant thought could not stop his

feeling of pleasure beyond measure as he continued to move in ways that continued to bring Lainey to higher and higher peaks. Her cries became undecipherable, but Mateo didn't care. All he knew was that at any moment they were going to reach the sun together.

Every muscle in her body clamped around him.

"Yes!" she screeched.

Mateo was lost as they shot into the sun.

20

"I can't believe you did this," Lainey marveled as he helped her up the gangplank. "No wonder you knew we wouldn't be late for our reservation."

"I wanted to do something special for you, and after all the amazing meals you've cooked for me."

"I've only cooked you three meals," Lainey protested.

"Three meals from my home country. You don't know how much that has meant to me."

When she stepped onto the boat she was met by a table covered with a white tablecloth. Above it was an arbor that was filled with fairy lights. There was also a beautiful bouquet of pink roses in a low vase, so that they could still see one another across the table.

Matt pulled out a chair for her, and then, instead of sitting across from her, he sat in the seat next to her. She felt cherished. As soon as that word entered her mind, she shook her head. Surely that wasn't Matt's plan. She was blowing things all out of proportion.

"What? Have I done something wrong?"

Leave it to him to think he had done something wrong when he had been nothing but perfect. "No, you have done nothing wrong. I'm just amazed by all of this." She waved her arm at the lights and the table. "I don't want you to think this was something I would ever expect."

"Lainey, you've never given me a reason to think that you expect this kind of treatment, but I wanted to do this for you. For us. I wanted a special night for the two of us.

"Well, you've succeeded."

"We haven't even started. Let's see if the meal lives up to the hype, shall we?" He waggled his eyebrows, and she giggled.

Then, like magic, a server appeared out of nowhere and brought them their water glasses and a breadbasket of warm bread. He also handed them each a small menu. "This is what our chef has prepared for you tonight. You're in for a treat. He has selected different wines with each dish, and you will not be disappointed."

My God, this must be costing Matt a fortune!

As soon as the server left, Matt leaned in and gave her a gentle kiss that made her heart melt.

"What was that for?"

"Because you look beautiful sitting there with your wide eyes sparkling under the lights. But after dinner, when the music starts and we dance, I want them to turn the lights off, so it will be just us, the stars, and the moonlight."

Lainey felt like she had been transported to a different dimension. When the first course came out with the buttery chardonnay to complement the crab, she sighed with pleasure. Next came a glass of Riesling to go with the scallops. Each course was small, each glass of wine was small, so that she was ready to sample the next scrumptious course. When the Malbec and the lobster Thermidor came out, Lainey could only eat half.

She glanced over at Matt, who had already finished his serving. "I don't suppose I could talk you into eating this other half, could I?"

"No, take it home. It'll be good left over," he insisted.

"If I gave you a polygraph right now, and I asked you if you were lusting after my Thermidor, what would it say?" she asked.

"That's not a fair question." Matt's voice was low and deep. "If you asked me any question with your name and lust in the same sentence, I'd break the machine."

She threw back her head and laughed. When she was finally done, she picked up her plate, and deftly switched it with Matt's. "There you go. I have plans for you later on. You need to keep your strength up."

———

THEY WERE STILL LAUGHING by the time they made it back to her house. The first order of business was to take Xena out for a walk. Matt waited for Lainey to change out of her dress, then the three of them walked a couple of blocks around the streets of Annapolis, then headed back to Lainey's building.

While they were waiting for the elevator to take them to her floor, Matt leaned over and whispered into Lainey's ear.

"Do you want me to kiss you right here?"

"Huh?"

"You're biting your lip."

Lainey released her lip and grinned. "I think my mother would disapprove if you did."

"I'm not sure that's a deterrent. From everything you've told me about her, it might be fun to upset her applecart."

They stepped into the elevator. Matt slipped his arm around her waist and she dropped her head onto his chest. She liked how they fit together.

"I think something's been bothering you tonight," Matt said as they left the elevator. Matt took the keys from her and unlocked her door.

"Are you clairvoyant?"

"I just like to observe things."

"That probably makes you good at your job."

"It does," he agreed.

"You've never told me much about what you do at your company besides making presentations."

"Lainey, I'll go over my entire job description some other time. Right now, I'm not going to let you deflect anymore. Tell me what's bothering you." He helped her out of her jacket and hung it up in her coat closet.

She went over to her refrigerator and pulled out a bottle of water. "Would you like one?"

He shook his head. "Come sit on the couch with me. I need you in my arms."

How did he know exactly what she needed?

She went to the couch and cuddled beside him. When he had her wrapped up in his arms, he said, "Tell me."

"It was just a crazy idea I had. It's nothing."

"Lainey, we're past that point. If you have a crazy idea, or any kind of idea for that matter, and you want to discuss it with me, then go ahead. I'm not going to judge you. I promise."

There had to be something about being wrapped up in his arms, and the spicy scent that was all Matt, that cleared away all of her angst about what she was going to ask him. Well, most of her angst.

"Interested in an all-expense paid trip to Charleston?" She mumbled the question into his chest.

He answered her without any kind of pause. "Not if you're footing the bill." He tipped her chin up. "So, tell me why we're going to Charleston together."

When Lainey looked up into Matt's eyes, all she saw was kindness and acceptance. Something that was sorely missing when she was growing up. "It's my parent's fortieth wedding anniversary, and it's going to be a weekend-long extravaganza. I mean we're talking a real-life ball. Can you imagine growing up in a house with a ballroom?"

She watched as Matt's eyes widened.

Lainey pushed out of Matt's arms and reached for

the water bottle on the coffee table. He took it out of her hands and untwisted the top, then handed it to her.

"I see the look on your face. You can't imagine it. A ballroom, for goodness' sake. Granted, it's small, but still a ballroom. She's hosting probably eight different couples there at the house, and probably rented rooms at the highest-end hotels in town for thirty others that she deems worthy. I don't want to think how many more servants she'll have on hand."

"More servants? You grew up with servants?"

Lainey took a sip of water. "Don't hold it against me, okay?"

"But Lainey, I thought those old plantation houses were smaller than that."

Lainey sighed. "They definitely are. My great-great-grandaddy made his money in tobacco. And my great-grandfather wasn't much of a traditionalist, he was more of a rub-it-in-your-face kind of man. Our mansion was kind of on the small side, so he did some add-ons in the back, leaving the front as it is. He added about fifteen thousand square feet to the back. I think it's still the largest house in South Carolina."

Matt whistled. "Shit."

"Wait till you see it. It's got oak trees and Spanish moss leading up to it, interspersed with magnolias." Lainey gave a dejected sigh.

"It sounds like you didn't like it."

"I was supposed to conform and be a certain type of woman. I hated it."

She jumped when she felt Matt cup her cheek. His

thumb brushed her lower lip and pulled it down so she was no longer biting it.

Lainey rubbed her cheek against his hand like a cat would. Heck, she was almost purring.

"Would you like me to go with you?"

"God yes." She blew her bangs off her forehead. "Mom has one potential suitor lined up to escort me, but only if I lose fifteen pounds."

"What?!" Matt sat up straight, and Lainey toppled against the arm of the sofa. "Tell me you're not serious."

Lainey gave a half-hearted laugh. "Wish I was. But it's par for the course. I don't dress right, don't laugh right, and I bite my lip."

"Did she really call this idiot a suitor?"

"Nope, she called him a beau."

"Shit, Lainey, this is something out of Gone with the Wind. The next thing you're going to tell me is that your house has a name."

She shook off his arm and took another sip of water.

"Holy fuck, it does have a name. You gotta tell me what it is. Come on, baby, tell me. This is too good. Tell me."

"I told you about the magnolia trees, so it kind of makes sense?"

"Lainey." Matt's voice was full of laughter. His brown eyes were twinkling.

"Magnolia Run." She chugged down half the bottle of water as Matt laughed his butt off. When he continued to laugh, she started to get ticked.

"Feel free to stop anytime now."

"I'm not sure I can," he continued to chuckle.

"Well, try." Her voice was sharp.

"Let me tell you something. I sure as hell am going to be attending this shindig with you. That's for damn sure."

"It's going to be one of the lowest levels of purgatory, you know that, don't you? I mean, you're going to have to wear a tuxedo on the night of the ball, and everybody is going to be judging you the entire time. They judge me. I hate it."

"Ah, *mí amor*, I don't give a damn about me, unless it reflects badly on you. As for you, nobody better do anything that makes you feel bad in my presence, or I'll rip their head off and shit down their neck."

Lainey jerked backward, her eyes wide. "Did you just say that?"

Matt didn't look like himself. He looked dangerous. "I sure as hell did. Look, Lainey, you're one of the sweetest, most loving and generous people I've ever met. If somebody thinks that they can do something to put you down, I'm not going to allow it. End of story."

"Uhm. Okay."

This was definitely not the reaction she was expecting from a scientist. Weren't they supposed to be a little more mild-mannered? A little more cerebral?

"You don't have to worry about me. I'm used to it," she smiled.

"Well, get un-used to it. And you're damned right I'm going, and no you're not paying for me. I've got my own damned money. Let's not stay at Cherry Bud Walk. Let's stay at one of the hotels."

Lainey giggled. "It's Magnolia Run, and you know it. We have to stay there; it will be expected. All the family will be there, except maybe my sister. She's pregnant and currently on bed rest."

"Oh. I didn't know that. Is she okay?"

She enjoyed hearing the concern in his voice. But then again, what didn't she like? Strike that. What didn't she adore about this man?

"Don't worry, her doctor said she's just fine. It was Bennett's idea to go on bed rest. And speaking of bed. I'm tired of talking about my family. I think it's time to go to bed. What do you think?"

"I'm all in," Matt grinned.

21

"Lainey, there's a valet in front of your house." Mateo laughed.

"Yeah, well, you're the one who somehow had a Mercedes coupe waiting for us at the airport to rent."

Mateo smirked. He thought that had been a pretty smooth move. "You told me I needed to make a good impression. I figured that was a good way to start."

"You're right," Lainey mumbled as she shrank down in her seat. "I can't believe Mother has people arriving so early. She told me they weren't coming in until tomorrow."

"Guess she lied." Mateo got the feeling that Lainey was going to be in for a lot of surprises this weekend, and none of them good. He really didn't like any damn thing he'd heard about her family so far.

They didn't have to wait for anyone in front of them, they just drove up to the valet. He opened Lainey's door and helped her out of the Mercedes, and it rubbed Mateo wrong. That was his job. He got out and popped the trunk. Before he had a chance to get his hand on any of their luggage, somebody appeared.

"I've got that, sir."

Mateo took out his wallet and grabbed two ten-dollar bills. As he got to where Lainey and the valet were standing, he slid his keys into the man's hand as well as one of the bills. The man took the keys and the bill and smiled. "What name should I put with this?" he asked.

"Agular."

"I'll take good care of your baby," he promised.

"Miss Simpson, your mother has put the two of you in your old room," the man with their bags said.

"Thank you, Fortnum." Lainey smiled. It wasn't one of her genuine smiles, it was a resigned smile. The man preceded them into the house, where a young woman stood beside the open door. Fortnum set their luggage down on a massive marble floor that covered the foyer. Obviously, someone at a lower level was going to take their luggage upstairs. Mateo shoved his other ten-dollar bill back in his pocket. He figured Fortnum would turn his nose up at a tip.

"Let's go upstairs, Matt," Lainey said as she turned to him.

Fortnum cleared his throat. "Your mother expects you in the blue room as soon as you arrive."

"I want to freshen up first," Lainey said, with hardly any trace of an accent.

"She was sitting near the window facing the drive," the old guy told her.

"Fortnum," Lainey said through gritted teeth, "I want to go to my room first."

"You know your mother likes things done a certain way."

Mateo watched the exchange, and he was done. He picked up their bags before the crypt keeper could say another word. "Come on *Corazón*, show me the way to your room."

She gave him a grateful smile. "Follow me." She started up the grand staircase and at the top, she went to the right, down a long hall past five doors, before taking a left. Her bedroom was at the end of the hall. At least they were going to have some privacy.

When she opened the door to a room that looked like it had been designed by Pepto Bismol, he laughed.

"You sure have laughed a lot since I first told you about this trip," Lainey noted.

"That's because there's been a lot to laugh about." He placed her two bags on the light-pink upholstered bench at the end of her bed, and she snagged her cosmetics bag from him.

"I have to freshen up before seeing Mom. I don't need to hear any of her guff."

"Lainey, you look great." Mateo looked her up and down. He'd been surprised when he'd picked her up this morning and she'd been wearing white slacks, an orange linen top, and orange sandals. He figured that when you flew somewhere, you wore something comfortable, like jeans and a t-shirt. It'd been hot, and he knew it was going to be even hotter in Charleston, so he'd been wearing his cargo shorts and a white t-shirt, but taking a cue from her, he realized he'd better change. He'd grabbed his suitcase from his car and brought it into Lainey's place, then put on slacks and a button-down shirt with a pair of loafers.

Now, from the open door of the bedroom's connected bathroom, he watched as Lainey looked over her make-up and hair, and then turned around to check the back of her hair. In all the time he'd known her, he'd never seen her this worked up about her appearance.

"How are the back of my slacks? Are they very wrinkled from the plane? Should I change?"

"You look fine," he assured her. "As a matter of fact, you look great."

She bit her bottom lip.

He took three steps into the bathroom and pulled her into his arms and nibbled her bottom lip into his mouth.

"What?—"

"I told you, the next time you bite your lip like that, I'm going to do it for you. Those are my lips to torture."

She melted into his arms, and he kissed her properly. He stroked his hand up and down her back until he felt all the tension flow out of her body. He pulled away, and she looked up at him.

"Hiya, sugar." She smiled, her eyes hazy.

"Hi." He smiled back. "Are you doing better?"

"Much." She reached up and wiped her thumb over his lip. Must have been lipstick she was wiping off. He didn't really give a shit. She could have asked him to put on scarlet lipstick to meet her mom, and he would have gladly done it.

"We've been summoned to the blue room, and I have my head on straight again. Thank you."

"It was definitely my pleasure."

MATEO WAS PLEASED that Lainey was still relaxed when they entered a room that was most definitely blue. Were those actual peacock feathers in that vase?

He turned his attention to the only person in the room, and she looked just like Lainey would in forty years, if Lainey decided to eat a constant diet of lemons.

"MacLaine, you were told to greet me as soon as you arrived."

Lainey's Southern accent was like warm honey that dripped over Mateo, all sweet and warm. Mrs. Simpson's accent had an almost fake feel. It was as if she was stretching out every syllable, forcing people to listen to her longer. Bottom line, it was grating.

"I wanted to freshen up before seeing you, Mother." Lainey went over to the blue armchair where her mother was sitting and gave her an air kiss on both cheeks. Mateo had seen air kisses before, but certainly not between a mother and daughter.

Lainey moved back toward Mateo and waved toward a couch that was diagonal to her mother's chair and they sat down.

"MacLaine, persimmon is not a pleasant shade for

you. It makes you look sallow. Please tell me you are not wearing other clothes this color while you are here. And really, what were you thinking wearing white slacks? A dark color would be so much more slimming."

Is this woman for real? She has all the motherly instincts of a black widow, and they eat their young!

"Mother, I'd like to introduce you to my boyfriend, Matt Agular."

"Hello, Matthew. My daughter has not told me much about you, other than that you are a scientist. That sounds promising. Tell me more about yourself."

Mateo stuck to his cover story, which was an amalgamation of his brother and mother. "I was born in Argentina. My mother got her PhD in chemistry and authored a white paper that got her recruited by the DuPont Corporation when I was four years old and my brother was eight years old. We moved here. I followed in her footsteps."

"So, you work for DuPont?"

"No, I work for a pharmaceutical company in Baltimore."

"Hmmm." She looked up at the entry to the room and, as if by magic, the crypt keeper appeared. "We're ready for our refreshments."

"It will be just a moment, ma'am."

Mrs. Simpson turned her attention back to Lainey. "MacLaine, the first of our guests will arrive at four o'clock this afternoon. I expect you to be wearing your great aunt's pearls, your hair up, and the navy blue dress I have hanging in your closet."

Her mother leaned forward. "Wait a moment. Are you wearing your grandmother Simpson's earrings?"

Mateo watched Lainey touch the pretty garnet flower-shaped earrings with the good-sized cubic zirconia in the middle.

"Yes, they are," Lainey said with a big smile.

Mrs. Simpson gasped. "Where did you get them? They were never found after her death."

"Gran left me the contents of her safe deposit box." Lainey grinned wider.

Mrs. Simpson gripped the arms of her chair.

"That wasn't in the will."

"No, she made me the co-signer when I was eighteen. It didn't have to be declared in the will. After she died, I opened it up. She left me a beautiful letter."

"I don't care about the letter, what else did it have?" Her mother's voice was harsh.

"Just some gold coins and bracelets and stuff," Lainey said casually.

Gold coins! Not a payment from the Kraken! She's innocent.

"The Simpson jewels! You know your father has been trying to track those down since his mother passed. Why haven't you told him that you had them? They belong to him."

"Actually, they don't. They belong to me."

Her mother's face was almost purple. It went with the color of the room. "I'll have to talk to your father about this. As an attorney, he'll know the correct course of action."

Lainey smiled. "I look forward to it."

Mateo was positive his girl had her ducks in a row.

"Back to the matter at hand. As I said, there is a navy-blue dress hanging in your closet. since you declined to tell me about your weight, I was forced to assume the worst, so I had it fitted for a size fourteen. You must really get your eating habits under control."

Mateo grabbed Lainey's hand and let her try to crush his bones.

"Fortnum, put the tea service here," Lainey's mother indicated the table in front of her. "MacLaine will serve. Take away the scones. They're not needed."

"Actually, I'd like the scones, Mrs. Simpson," Mateo said.

"Very well," she grimaced. "Mr. Agular, I would assume that my daughter told you how important this weekend is? Her father, Mr. Simpson, will run for the state senate next year, and he is gathering his supporters now. After he wins and serves a couple of years, he will then run for a national seat. It is important that the Simpson family be seen in the best light. Do you understand?"

"Your daughter explained a lot of things in great detail. So far, I see she was quite accurate."

"Is that supposed to mean something to me?"

"Take it however you want to," Mateo invited.

Lainey's mother sniffed and turned her attention back to Lainey.

"Today is informal. However, besides family and close friends, there will be a couple of key potential donors who are staying here with us. We'll be having cocktails and hors d'oeuvres out on the back lawn. Your father wanted a barbeque. Can you imagine?"

Lainey shrugged, which seemed to be enough of a response for her mother to continue. "I'll need you to ensure that you've talked to every single person at this gathering. Don't tell them what you're currently doing up in Virginia. That's just gauche. Say you're taking a gap year or some such thing and considering opening your own interior design firm. Dottie's daughter has been considering opening her art studio for fifteen years now. She's in every magazine and seen with everybody who's anybody. Maybe you should say you're considering opening up an art studio."

"Don't you mean gallery, Mom? A studio would show I'm an artist." Lainey reached down to pour tea.

"God forbid, not an artist. Yes, you must say gallery. I guess all that schooling was good for something. Please say you're not putting all that sugar in your cup of tea."

Mateo watched as Lainey's hand tightened on the silver sugar spoon until her knuckles turned white.

"Now, you." Lainey's mother turned to look at Mateo. "Did you rent a tuxedo? If you did, we need to get Lainey's father's tailor in here immediately to fit you for a proper tuxedo. You must look your best. I suppose you do have that tall, dark, and handsome thing going for you, so that's good."

"No, I didn't rent my tuxedo. It's already been fitted, so I won't need your husband's tailor."

The old witch raised an eyebrow. "And you're a scientist?"

Mateo shrugged. There was no way he could tell her about the whirlwind shopping trip that Jada Harlow had taken him on. He was amazed how fast clothes and shoes could add up to thousands of dollars just for a few days' worth of outfits.

"What brand? Who's the designer?"

"Mom, we're done." Lainey stood up and pulled Mateo with her.

"Sit back down, MacLaine. You're embarrassing yourself in front of your young man."

"No, you are being rude to me and to Matt. We're leaving."

"Fine. Be down here at three-thirty so we can go over who will arrive first. I want you to know their names." She turned to Mateo. "If you do not feel comfortable talking to someone, then don't. The last thing we need is for you making others uncomfortable. Do you understand?"

"Mother, you didn't understand me. We're leaving, leaving. You've just attempted to ravage my self-esteem in front of a man I care deeply about, and now you are going to start picking him apart. I won't have it. We're getting a hotel, and then we're flying back to Maryland tomorrow."

'Atta girl!

Mrs. Simpson came halfway out of her chair. "You can't do that. I need you. I can't do this without you. What would people think if I didn't have one of my daughters in attendance? If I had Bennett I could, but I don't, so I need you."

"Get Bart's wife, get Lee's wife. They might not be

blood relatives but they married into this menagerie. They're Simpsons. They can take their turn at bat."

"They've refused. No matter what I've said to Bart and Lee, they will not command their wives to assist me with any more of my functions."

"Well, good for them. Maybe now Lee won't get a divorce."

"Bite your tongue. Simpsons don't get divorces."

"It's amazing they got married after—"

Mateo gave Lainey's hand a gentle squeeze and she shot him a grateful smile. He was pretty sure she didn't want to burn the bridge too far.

"You can't leave me in my hour of need, MacLaine. This is my fortieth wedding anniversary. Does that mean nothing to you? If you won't do it for me, think of your father."

"You mean his campaign."

"Yes. His campaign. This is something he wants. Are you going to deny him this? He's already extremely successful, now he wants to be even more. What's wrong with that?"

"I thought going into politics was to serve the people you represent," Lainey countered.

"I'm sure he's going to do that, too. But how will he be able to do that without you assisting us?"

He watched as Lainey blew her bangs off her forehead.

"Mother, if I do this, promise me you will not pick on Matt. Not one word. I'm used to the putdowns. This is our little love language, but Matt is off limits."

"Actually, Mrs. Simpson, if you pick on Lainey, I will

take Lainey home. I care about her too much to see her belittled."

"Belittled?" Lainey's mother was now standing on her tall pointy shoes in her dusty blue sweater set, looking like a puffed-up robin. "I do not belittle my daughter, and how *dare* you try to interfere in our relationship."

"Let me make this clearer. I adore your daughter. I cannot believe how lucky I am to have found a woman like her. I will protect her from any kind of threat, be it physical, mental, or emotional. You, ma'am, are an emotional threat, and that stops now, or we're leaving."

Mrs. Simpson opened and shut her mouth three times, reminding Mateo of a guppie fish. It took everything he had not to laugh.

She whipped her head around to glare at her daughter. "Are you going to let him talk to me like this?"

"Heck, Mom, I'm thinking about making out with him, right here in front of you."

Mateo started laughing. The older woman whirled around at him and burst out shrilly. "This is not funny!"

"Yes, it is, Mom. Now, are you going to play nice with me so I can help you and Dad with his campaign and celebrate your fortieth anniversary, or are you going to be mean and force Matt to whisk me away?"

"For the last time, I'm not mean to you. I only say things to help you improve yourself. But if these things hurt your feelings, I will desist."

Lainey rolled her eyes and looked over at Mateo. "Will that do?"

"Again, as long as you're not hurting, I'm good. Let's take some of these scones, butter, and jam up with us to our room." Mateo bent down and grabbed a plate. He winked at Lainey's mom as he led Lainey out of the room.

22

Tonight was the night of the formal, informal dinner. Tomorrow was the main event. Tomorrow was the eight-hundred-dollar gown. Tonight was the Macy's dress that Lainey and Penny agreed looked divine. It was off-the-shoulder, lavender with an ombre effect from the waist down. It really showed off her figure, and Matt had tried to talk her into staying in her room and bailing on the dinner once he saw it. Guilt had forced Lainey to refuse his offer. That had been a mistake.

There were people still showing up, and a few people milling around when her mother spotted the two of them.

"Hello." She gave them both a sunny smile.

Lainey knew she was in trouble. Her world was going to be blown to smithereens somehow. Rose Simpson did not do 'sunny.'

"Matt, would you be a dear and get me a glass of champagne?"

"Mom, the waiter is just over there." Lainey pointed to the server twenty feet away from them with a tray of champagne.

"He doesn't have the pink champagne I like," she said, as she gave Matt a wide smile. "Be a dear and go to the bartender we have set up under the pergola and ask him to pour a glass of champagne for Mrs. Simpson. He'll know what to give me."

Matt looked down at Lainey. "You good?"

She nodded. "Hurry back." The idea of having someone at her back was intoxicating. He gave her waist a squeeze and kissed her cheek.

"I'll be right back with your drink." He smiled at her mother.

As soon as Matt left, her mother started in. She did her best to mentally ignore everything she was saying and was relieved when she saw Matt on his way back to her. Her mother's back was to Matt as he returned, so she didn't see his thunderous expression as she said, "If you would just wear a girdle, you wouldn't look so ridiculous—"

He set her mother's glass of champagne on the tray of a passing waiter. "I guess you hadn't heard me. That's a shame. We'll be leaving, but not before I've had my say."

"Mr. Agular, you have no place in this conversation. MacLaine has a certain image she needs to project for this family. I'm well within my rights to correct her errant behavior."

Lainey was beginning to feel light-headed. Had her mother always been this vicious? Or was it because she'd been gone so long that she could notice it more? Or was it because Matt was here that she felt so humiliated?

Matt slid Lainey to the side so that he could close in on her mother, who was forced to tip back her head to look at him. "Look, lady, I've listened to enough of your bullshit," he said quietly.

Lainey checked around. The only people who were looking their way were Lee and his wife. Then she turned her attention back to what Matt was saying.

"I think I have you figured out. You're jealous of Lainey. She's living more of the life that you wanted to be living. She's not stuck in your little mold of stuffy parties, perfectly fake smiles, and endless diets that result in hair inserts."

Her mother clutched her chest and gasped.

Score five-hundred-and-seventy for Matt. Who knew my mother is using hair inserts? Lainey leaned in closer and darn it all, *he was right!*

"Your daughter is gorgeous, funny, loving, and well-liked by everybody she encounters. Her body is gorgeous and healthy. I don't even need to know how much she weighs to recognize that. Do you know why? Because I know the woman I love is perfect. And if you were blessed with any kind of nurturing gene, you would know she's beautiful just the way she is. Lainey has put up with your bullshit remarkably well. She's even called it your 'love language.' I'm putting a stop to it right now. We're going."

He loves me?

Her mother reached out and grabbed Matt's wrist. He looked down at her hand with contempt.

"If you leave now, everyone will notice."

"And I give one shit why?"

He loves me? Me?

"It will hurt her father," her mother pleaded.

"As far as I'm concerned, he's complicit in the way you've treated Lainey. He's allowed this all along. We're packing up our shit and getting out of here."

He loves me!

"Lainey, please, I'm begging you, don't make a scene."

Lainey looked at her and realized her mother was close to tears. She wished it was because Matt had finally opened her eyes and she felt bad about the way she'd treated her all these years, but Lainey knew it wasn't. It was because she didn't want Charleston society to know their family was having a ruckus.

"Hey, folks," Lee said as he came up beside her mother. "How is everything going?" He gave Matt a pointed look.

"Not so good. We're just leaving."

Lee nodded. "I should have done that a few times earlier in my marriage. Instead, I left Elizabeth open to a lot of hurt. I'll be sorry to see you leave. I've enjoyed meeting you." Lee held out his hand to Matt.

"Lainey, can't you do something?" her mother begged.

She shook her head, trying to clear it, when all she really wanted to do was hug Matt and tell him she loved him too. But not here. Not in this toxic city.

"Lainey, don't let him take you away. It'll be noticed."

"The ball is in your court, Mother. I just don't think you have it in you to play nice." Lainey shook her head. It was all she could think to say. She was in a daze.

"Matt," her mom started. "Will you allow me to explain?"

"Lady, there is nothing to explain about your wretched behavior. You either own it and apologize for it, or you own it and admit that's who you are and you're always going to be a bitch."

Lee laughed. "Well said."

Her mother looked from Matt to Lee to Lainey and then back to Matt again. "But I didn't mean—"

"My advice, Mom? Own it and apologize. Elizabeth only got a little taste of your acid tongue. Lainey's been getting it in spades, since the first guys started asking her out at fifteen."

She turned to Lainey. She looked confused, then she straightened up. "If I apologize about what I had to say about your gown and your weight, will you talk your beau into staying?"

"Jesus, you're a piece of work," Matt growled.

"What?" she hissed at him. "I'm apologizing just like you told me to."

"This is as good as it's going to get, man," Lee said with a chuckle.

"Lainey?" Matt said as he pulled her in close.

Lainey didn't care about one darn thing. Her mother could go to the head of the table, clink glasses and ask everyone to quiet down while she told everyone how much Lainey weighed, and how bad her acne had been, and how long she'd had to wear braces. She wouldn't give a hoot. Matt had said he'd loved her.

Matt said he loved me.

Matt said he loved me.

"Lainey?"

"What?"

"Do you want to go?"

She snuggled closer to Matt.

"Tell your young man that I've apologized to you and that you accept it, and we're done with the matter and you'll mingle like I've told you to."

"Matt, I'll even show you where they hide the beer in this place," Lee said.

She looked up and Matt was staring down at her, his eyes warm and anxious.

"We can stay."

He bent down and touched his lips to hers.

"And no more of that. That's inappropriate." Her mother just couldn't help herself.

"Seriously, Lainey, you've gotta stop doing this to me. Your mother has put together such a hellish itinerary we've only been able to fuck twice today, and then you put that dress on. That's not fair."

Lainey turned around in front of the tall standing mirror in the corner of her room and smiled. The champagne foil knit-draped dress was ruched at the right side of her waist and hid the little bit of tummy she'd been forming since she'd been taste-testing so many fun recipes. But you wouldn't know she was hiding anything, because it flowed over her body like it was made for her. Actually, it was, since she had a seamstress alter it so it would fit perfectly after she bought it.

She loved it!

She was halfway to biting her lip, then stopped.

"Ah, come on, do it. Bite your lip. I just want a little taste," Matt begged.

"The dinner and dancing will eventually be over," she promised.

He went over to her old bedroom closet and opened the shoebox she had brought with her.

"Come sit down, Cinderella, so I can help you into your shoes."

If he thought the dress was something, the shoes were going to blow his mind. Lainey stifled a giggle. She sat down on the pink bench, lifted her gown, and Matt knelt at her feet. Then he pushed back the tissue paper and groaned. "Are you fucking kidding me?"

She threw back her head and laughed. He carefully pulled out the glittery champagne-colored shoes with the five-inch heel, peep toe, and two ankle straps. She'd had Matt in mind when she'd bought the shoes. She and Penny had agreed that every man would think these shoes were sexy.

"We can be twenty minutes late," he cajoled as he guided the first shoe onto her foot.

"We were late to this morning's brunch, and we got the stink-eye."

"No, we didn't. Your mama loves me." Matt kissed the bottom of her second foot before guiding on her shoe and taking his time to clasp on the ankle strap.

"My Mama is both scared and respects you. I don't know the word for it, but that's what she is, so she's currently letting you get away with things," Lainey corrected.

"You're right about the scared and respect thing. It's an animal thing. She recognizes me as her alpha. It's as easy as that."

"Whatever. I just know I have big plans for you after we leave my childhood bedroom. I adore making love with you, but I'll like it even more when I'm not looking over your shoulder up into a pink canopy."

This time, it was Matt's turn to laugh.

"Tonight, I'll work harder. Obviously, if you have an opportunity to concentrate on the canopy, then I'm not doing my job right."

Lainey felt her core tingle. "I can't even imagine how good it would be if you try harder."

"Well, tonight, you'll find out."

THEY ARRIVED thirty minutes before people were going to be seated for dinner. In the ballroom, they had seating for one-hundred-and-forty guests, and that still left room for a dais for the family to sit at, a DJ booth, and a substantial amount of floor space for people to dance.

"You made it. I was worried it would be like

brunch," her mother said as she came up and grasped Lainey's hands and gave her air kisses. Then she did the same thing to Mateo. "You both look marvelous. Don't forget to mingle. Have you seen your father?" she asked Lainey.

Lainey shook her head and then her mother walked off. Lainey turned to Mateo and motioned for him to bend down, not that he had all that far to go with her in five-inch heels.

"This alpha crap is horse manure. You're a scientist. You brewed up something to give her a personality transplant."

Mateo chuckled softly. "Swear to God, I didn't. Let's go somewhere close to a beer to mingle."

"If we find Lee, we'll find a beer."

Mateo looked around the big room and thought he spotted his dark head. He pulled Lainey's hand through the crook of his arm and led her through the throng of people. Lainey did a great job of mingling. He was surprised by how many people she knew, but he shouldn't have been. After all, she had grown up here.

"Lainey, Mother's looking for you," Bennett said with delight.

"What are you doing here?" Lainey asked the pregnant woman who looked like her. But once again she looked like she was training for the Olympic event of lemon sucking.

Bennett leaned into Lainey and they did that creepy air kiss.

"I just couldn't miss Mother and Father's big night.

I'll go back to the hotel after the festivities are over. Really, Lainey, is that gown the best you could do?"

Lainey sighed. "Let me introduce you to my date, Matt Agular."

She put out her hand. "A pleasure, I'm sure."

Jesus, she's as bad as her mother.

Mateo shook her hand.

Mateo gave Bennett's husband a chin tilt. He'd already met the man and didn't much like him. His face was looking red, which told Mateo that he'd already hit the sauce pretty hard. That was just great, because rumor had it they'd all be seated together tonight, hopefully not too close together.

"But what did Mom have to say about your dress?" Bennett asked.

Enough already.

"Rose said your sister looked marvelous," Mateo said.

"Rose? Trey didn't call Mother Rose until we were engaged," Bennett squawked.

"Don't know what to tell you. She told me to call her Rose at brunch today."

"The brunch you were late for?" Bennett asked.

What a snide bitch.

"Yes," Lainey answered.

"I see Lee waving to us. Gotta go," Mateo said as he grabbed Lainey's hand and led her away from the bad seed.

"Did you really see Lee?"

"Yeah, but he's heading outside. But he was near

that bartender, so I've got high hopes I can get a Heineken."

"Lainey, you're looking lovely."

Mateo turned to see another older couple coming up to greet Lainey.

"Hello, Mr. Morrison. Mrs. Morrison. I'm so glad you could make it tonight. I'd like to introduce you to my date, Matt Agular."

The couple turned to him and they exchanged pleasantries for a couple of minutes, then Lainey extricated them so they could continue on toward the bar. There were only two people in front of them, when her mother came up to them.

"There you are, Lainey. I want to introduce you and Matt to Captain Hale and his wife. He's high up in the Navy. Not an Admiral, mind you, but still very high up."

Captain Hale? Mateo felt the blood rush from his head and his muscles clench.

Rose tapped the silver-haired man standing in front of Mateo on the shoulder and he turned around.

"Mateo Aranda?" Captain Hale said slowly.

Mateo grimaced. Shit, he'd only exchanged words with the captain twice. What were the odds he'd remember one Chief Petty Officer when he had over a thousand men in his command?

Rose went on, oblivious. "Captain Hale, this is my daughter Lainey and her beau Matthew Agular. He's a scientist."

"Hello, sir, it is nice to meet you. If you're in the Navy, where are you stationed?" he asked, attempting to cover.

He didn't dare look at Lainey to see if she'd caught his real name. Mateo watched the captain's eyes flicker. If the captain knew who he was, then he'd realize that Mateo would know damn good and well that he was currently living in Virginia Beach, and that would tell him he was working undercover. Shit, Kostya was going to get an earful tonight. He just hoped he'd have time to give him a heads-up before the captain called him.

Make that two earfuls, judging by the look on Lainey's face.

He was positive now that she'd caught his real name.

The captain's wife turned around just then and smiled at Mateo and Lainey.

"This is my wife, Scarlett. We live in Virginia." He said to both Mateo and Lainey.

Scarlett smiled. "We have it on good authority that the man behind the bar has bottles of Heineken hidden away. My husband is really hoping that the rumors are true."

"Yes, it sure is upsetting when things turn out not to be true, isn't it?" Lainey responded to Elizabeth as she pulled her arm away from Mateo and took a step away from him.

Fuck!

23

CAPTAIN HALE KNOWS MATT? OR SHOULD I SAY, MATEO Aranda.

And now he's suddenly acting like he doesn't.

Little things about Matt started adding up in her head. His watch set to military time. His alpha attitude. The way he looked so dangerous—no, deadly—when he was angry.

He's not a scientist. Is he in the Navy? Why is he lying?

Why is he lying to me?

Lainey heard the chimes, which meant that everyone needed to take their seats.

"It looks like we made it just in the nick of time." Scarlett smiled as Captain Hale took his beer from the bartender. "I told him that you wanted one too, Mr. Agular," she said to Matt.

"I don't think there's time. But thank you, Mrs. Hale." Lainey smiled. She watched and waited as the couple drifted away.

Matt—or should she be thinking Mateo?—was

making a point of looking at the bartender and not at her. "Come on, we need to get to our seats. As for the beer, you're just shit out of luck."

He reared back. "Did you just say shit?"

"Yep. And I'm going to be having a few more choice words to say to you tonight, *Mateo Aranda*, so start thinking on whatever bedtime story you want to try to shovel down my throat. Now let's get up there and make nice, and then I'm on the first flight home to Maryland."

The problem with trying to stalk away in five-inch heels from someone who was well over six feet tall, is that they were going to surpass you. Which Matt did. She tried to walk around him, but he moved with her.

"We look stupid," she told him. Stop this."

"Lainey. You need to let me explain."

"Sure, I will. Tonight. As I'm packing my suitcase, you can explain all over yourself. And I'm not going to believe one fucking word that comes out of your mouth. You love me. Let's start with that bullshit, shall we?"

Lainey bit her lip and looked up at the huge chandelier in the middle of the ceiling, praying to God that she wouldn't cry. Matt's hands landed on her shoulders.

"Oh, God, Lainey, don't cry."

The chimes sounded again.

"We've got to go sit down."

He pulled her in for a hug and kissed the top of her head. "Whatever you're thinking, it's not that bad. I promise you."

She let him lead her to the front of the room. They walked up the three steps to the top of the dais and she saw that her life, the shitshow, was going to get even worse. Her mom and dad were in the center. She was seated between Matt and Trey. On the other side of Trey sat Bennett. So, her handsy, drunk, brother-in-law was going to be sitting right next to her, where his hands would be hidden by a long white tablecloth. Goodie for her.

"You look gorgeous tonight," Trey said as Matt pulled out Lainey's chair so she could sit down next to Trey.

She muttered a thank you to Trey.

"What about me, you haven't said I look gorgeous." Bennett pouted.

"You're pregnant. You look as good as you can with your stomach out to there," Trey said, laughing as he made a hand gesture to show her large stomach.

Maybe I should be drinking.

Their salads were already at their place settings along with the bread and butter. Matt stared at his, not looking happy.

Good. He shouldn't be.

"It's true, you know," Trey said to Lainey. "You were too skinny before. I like how you fill out your dress now. Very nice." Trey leered.

Lainey ignored him, and chose to breathe through her nose. She picked up her roll, broke it in half, and buttered it.

"Yep, you keep buttering that thing," Trey whispered. "I like a woman with a big booty."

Matt leaned back and grabbed the back of Trey's tuxedo, forcing him back so they could talk behind Lainey. "Look, asshole. One more word, and I'm going to take you out. Got it?"

"Hey, I'm just giving my sister-in-law a compliment. I've known her since she was fourteen. I think of her as a little sister. This means nothing. No need for you to get your panties in a twist. It's all good. Just eat your dinner."

"Remember what I said," Matt growled.

Bennett leaned forward and hissed across Trey at Lainey. "You keep that oaf under control. He better not cause a scene."

"He's not the one out of line. Maybe if you were actually home where you belonged, Trey would be too interested in you to be vulgar to me."

"What are you talking about?" Bennett looked truly clueless. It was sad.

Lainey leaned back in her seat, just as Matt and Trey sat up and stared at their food. Lainey didn't know if she was going to eat anything. Not with Trey on one side, and a liar on the other.

HE NEEDED to get out of here and talk to Lainey. She knew he was lying to her about his identity, but other than that, she knew nothing. But shit, that was bad enough. He took another bite of his raspberry tart and felt Lainey squirm and move closer to him.

What the fuck?

He pulled back the tablecloth and looked underneath in time to see Trey's hand high on her thigh.

Motherfucker!

He stood up and Lainey grabbed his wrist. "Don't."

Mateo had no idea what the 'don't' was for. Was it for him not to make a scene? Not act as her protector? Don't let the door hit you in the ass as you leave?

He took three deep breaths, then pulled out Lainey's chair. "Your mother would like you to sit next to her while the toasts are being made, so we'll change seats. Okay?"

She gave him a grateful smile and slid into the seat he had just vacated. He sat down in hers. Lainey was already switching their dessert plates, like that mattered. He knew what he was hungry for, and that was vengeance. This motherfucker had taken advantage of Lainey when she was in a spot where she could do nothing about it, and was doing it while he was seated right next to his pregnant wife. It didn't matter that his wife was a snide, jealous bitch. She was his wife. The woman he married and had children with. This man wasn't even worth the title.

Trey gave him a cautious look when Mateo settled down into Lainey's seat. Mateo took a few bites of his food, not even knowing what it was he was eating, just biding his time. He wanted the asshole to get a little complacent. After Trey took his second sip of scotch, Mateo leaned over. "Put your hand on my thigh," he commanded.

"What?" Trey looked at him in shock.

"It's what you were doing to Lainey," he whispered quietly, not wanting either of the two women to hear. "Now I want you to put your hand on *my* thigh."

"What, you want me to jerk you off?" Trey gave a harsh laugh. He picked up his glass of scotch to take another sip.

"Put your hand on my thigh, and maybe I won't arrange to have your hands cut off tonight."

Trey dropped his glass.

"What the hell, Trey." Bennett hissed. "My God. You're a mess. Don't have another drink tonight." She waved for a server to come over with a towel, and they cleaned up the mess.

"Now, drink water for the rest of the night," Bennett said.

"Put your hand on my thigh," Mateo whispered.

Trey put his trembling hand on Mateo's thigh and Mateo held his hand down with his right hand.

"Now, Trey, I'm going to need you to be really quiet. Can you be quiet?"

"I was just complimenting her." Trey mumbled.

"You were touching her, weren't you?"

"Well, yeah."

"Is this the first time you touched her?" Mateo whispered the question as he looked across the crowded room.

"No. I mean yes."

The servers began taking their dessert dishes, and Mateo knew the toasts would soon start. It would be Lee, Bennett, Bart, and Lainey. There would be applause. He would time things just right.

"How many women have you touched when they haven't wanted you to touch them?" Mateo asked.

"None!"

Mateo listened to the clinking of the glass and heard Lee's voice as he said something that he couldn't care less about. Soon, there was clapping all around the room.

"We need to clap," Trey hissed.

"Actually, we don't," Mateo smiled. "Just nod your head."

Lee had been on the left far end, now it was Bennett's turn on the right far end. She got up and Mateo again tuned out what she was saying.

"We need to clap."

Mateo smiled. "No, we don't."

"You should have clapped," Bennett hissed when she sat down.

"Sorry, honey."

Bart was up next, and again Mateo ignored the toast. He could feel Trey squirming in his seat, wondering what the hell Mateo's game was.

Thumb or middle?

The applause died down, and now it was Lainey's turn. Mateo reached out with his left hand and touched her shoulder. "You've got this, beautiful."

She gave him a grateful smile as she stood up.

There's still hope.

Her toast was sweet, funny, and kind, just like her. The applause was loud.

It didn't totally mask Trey's shriek of pain as Mateo broke his middle finger.

He'd have preferred his thumb, but in order to break Trey's thumb, he'd have to use two hands. Mateo broke Trey's finger with one hand by isolating it and twisting it backward, which he did easily.

People at the two tables closest to the dais turned their attention from Lainey to Trey. However, after seeing him slumped across the table, everybody just assumed he was drunk.

Lainey looked over at Trey, who was sobbing with Bennett shaking him. Mateo gripped her elbow and said, "it's time to go."

Her eyes narrowed. "You're right. It is."

24

"Who are you?" Lainey asked as soon as her bedroom door was shut behind them.

Matt didn't immediately respond.

Lainey stalked to the middle of the room and turned around, her eyes blazing as she stared at the man she loved, a man she *thought* she knew. "Let's make this easier. I'll tell you what I know, and you tell me when I'm wrong."

"My name is—"

"Uh-nuh. Not your turn. Your name is Mateo Aranda, and you're in the Navy. That's courtesy of Captain Hale. Should have known you weren't a scientist when I saw your watch was set to military time and the minute you said you were going to rip off someone's head and shit down their neck."

"Lainey, you know you don't want to be swearing," Matt protested.

She started to tremble, so she crossed her arms over her chest. "Stop right there. You have no right. No right whatsoever to pretend to know what I want or don't want. You've been playing me since the beginning. You're a liar."

"Stop right there. Just stop." Matt rushed forward and settled his hands on her shoulders.

She threw them off.

"Don't you dare. Don't you *dare* touch me. Matt Agular the scientist can touch me. He's the man I fell in love with. Not some liar."

"I'm the same man," Matt insisted.

"I'm right, aren't I? Mateo Aranda is your real name, isn't it?" She hissed the question into his face.

"Yes."

"You're in the Navy?"

"Yes."

"What do you do for the Navy?"

"I'm a Navy SEAL."

"Why would someone special forces need to pretend to be someone else and get to know me? Why would—?" Her eyes got wide as saucers. "You did something to make my tire go flat, didn't you? You actually did that. You were lying to me from the first word you ever spoke."

"I had to. We needed to find out if you were working with the Kraken."

Her eyes were still huge as she stared at him. "The who? What are you talking about?"

Matt looked devastated. "We had evidence that pointed to you being involved with a terrorist organization and we needed to find out if that was true, so someone needed to find out. I volunteered. To begin with, I thought MacLaine was a man. When you were a woman, I had to change tactics."

"Those tactics included sleeping with me?"

She could feel the burn of tears at the back of her eyes. She couldn't handle this conversation much longer without falling to the floor and sobbing. And what was worse? She wanted Matt to be the one to pick her up, hold her and tell her everything was going to be all right.

"I need you to leave the room while I pack," she whispered.

"I can't do that, Lainey. I can't let you go thinking that everything I've said, everything I've done, is a lie. Because it wasn't. I love you. I've meant every word I've said to you. Yeah, finding out things about you started out as a mission, but falling in love with you brought me back to life. It wasn't a lie; I swear to you."

She shook her head sadly. "But it was the fruit from the poisonous tree, wasn't it? It doesn't matter how it ended up. It started from lies, so it has a foundation that's rotten to the core. It would never work. I should have known this was too good to be true. Things like this never happen to me."

"You're looking at this all wrong," Matt said desperately.

"I'm begging you, Matt. Not as the man who professes to love me, but as the man who took an oath to our country. Just leave me alone for an hour so I can pack and call an Uber and leave."

"Where are you going to go?"

"Somehow, I'm going to get a flight out of South

Carolina and go home. Then I'm going to get Xena out of doggie jail and she and I will talk about how all men are crud-buckets. So, will you leave? Please?"

Matt nodded. He lifted his hand as if to touch her cheek and then dropped it. "This isn't the end, Lainey."

"Yes, it is," she disagreed.

He walked to the bedroom door and opened it. "In your heart, you know it can't be the end. I'll give you this time, for now. But what we have together is too good to be thrown away. I love you, *mi Corazón.*"

She looked at the closed door for long minutes after Matt walked out. It was only fitting that he called her his heart, since he was taking her heart with him.

MATT GOT his car from the valet after tipping him fifty bucks to set it aside in the shadows so he could easily follow Lainey's Uber when it showed up. He followed her all the way to the Holiday Inn next to the airport, and from his vantage point could see her check in and head toward the elevators. After that, he parked his rental in the hotel lot and called Kostya.

"Mateo, a heads-up would have been nice," his lieutenant growled.

"I was trying to fix things with Lainey."

Mateo was met with silence. Damn it, he hated it when Kostya did that. He always won.

"She said she can never forgive me."

"You ended up falling for her, didn't you?"

"Yes," he whispered.

"Goddammit, Brax sure called that one."

"He told you?"

Kostya sighed. "Yeah, he did. He told Gideon and me, it was a bad idea for you to be the one to be assigned to MacLaine as soon as we found out she was a Lainey who adopted a three-legged rescue dog."

"Well, you all were wrong. Meeting her was the best thing that ever happened in my life."

"And Captain Hale blew your cover by calling you Aranda, right?"

"That about sums it up."

"Mateo, we still can't be a hundred percent positive that she isn't working for the Kraken. There is still the problem with the—"

"I know how she got the gold. Her grandmother left her the contents of her safe deposit box. It contained jewels and gold. Because it was a safe deposit box, which her grandmother had her co-sign on when she was eighteen, there was nothing mentioned in a will. I found out about that yesterday when she was wearing her grandmother's earrings and her mother went apeshit."

He heard Kostya sigh. "And the transfer?"

"I don't know. But I'm thinking whoever was handed that paperwork would've had to have made the transfer. It was just Lainey's unlucky day to do it. Kostya, she's not part of the Kraken."

Mateo could hear the desolation in his own voice, and apparently Kostya could, too.

"I believe you, Mateo. Linc is working the Ivan lead, and Brax says he'll have something to report tomorrow about Amanda. I'll need you here tomorrow night."

"Yeah, I'll be there."

XENA WHINED as she nosed her way under Lainey's arm.

"Not now, baby."

The dog licked her hand.

"Xena, I just took you for a walk and you have food and water in your bowls. Mommy needs to be left alone, okay?" Her voice was rough and raspy from all the crying she had done over the past week. It had been easy for Mr. Pine to believe her when she said she was sick. But she hadn't been lying. She really was sick. She never wanted to leave the comfort of her couch ever again.

Woof.

Woof.

Woof.

"No, Xena. No barking. I'm begging you."

She'd been doing that every time Lainey's phone would ring. She couldn't turn it off in case it was work calling, but instead it was always Mateo Aranda calling.

She should just block him. She should.

"I should."

She picked up her phone and watched as the last two rings stopped. The call clicked over to voicemail. She waited another minute, and then she saw Mateo text her. She didn't read the text. It was bad enough that she still had a picture of him on her phone that came up every time he called or texted.

She'd called in sick all week. Penny offered to come over tonight, but she still needed the whole weekend to get herself together. Maybe she could shower tomorrow morning. Then on Sunday she could go to the grocery store, instead of just having ice cream delivered.

There was a knock at her door. It couldn't be Mateo, since he'd just called and texted. Lainey looked down at her ratty Bettie Boop t-shirt and red heart leggings. She frowned. Why was she wearing leggings with hearts on them?

The doorbell rang.

Woof.

Woof.

Woof.

"Xena, be good. Go to your doggy bed," Lainey said as she slowly hoisted herself off the couch. Xena stood in the middle of the living room looking at her and then turning and looking down the hall. "Go. Go to your doggy bed. I'll see who's at the door."

The doorbell rang a second time, and Xena headed down the hall.

Lainey looked through her peephole and saw a blonde girl with a ponytail holding a big bouquet of flowers.

Lainey unlocked her door and opened it, leaving the security chain on. She saw the delivery girl was a little older than she originally thought. "I don't want any flowers."

"Okay, but I'll need a signature saying you refused them," the woman said.

Lainey looked at the oversized bouquet. It had daisies and sunflowers. She bit her lip and tried not to cry. She closed her door and thanked God she at least had a sleep bra on, then unhooked the chain and opened the door.

"Thanks, Miss Simpson. Can you hold them while I get my clipboard?"

Lainey nodded and took the bouquet. She took a deep breath, taking in the glorious scent.

"Darn it, I can't find my pen," the woman said.

"Come on in and I'll use one of mine."

Lainey turned around. She felt something press against the side of her neck, and then she was catapulted into a world of agony.

She tried to scream but couldn't, not even when she heard the vase shatter when it hit her hardwood floor. She couldn't even scream when the glass dug into her arms, shoulders, neck, and chest as she fell into a trembling heap.

"Quick!"

Woof!

Woof!

"Fuck. A dog. Get it!" It was a man's voice.

Woooooofffff!

Another jolt of excruciating pain coursed through her as she heard her baby cry, then everything went black.

25

"WE'VE GOT A PROBLEM," GIDEON SAID ON THE SECOND meeting six days after Mateo got home from Charleston. Every man in the room was on edge. It had now been four weeks since the bombing of Gideon's house. The Lainey lead had turned into nothing. The one lead they had regarding Ely Roberts had turned into nothing, especially after Christina Higgins' body was found washed up on the shore of the Elizabeth River.

That left Ephram Brady, Hick's little brother Lloyd who they still didn't have a handle on, Amanda Melton that Brax was pretty sure he had pinpointed, and Ivan Sykes who Linc still had to update everyone on.

"What's the problem?" Jase's voice boomed loudly in Kostya's living room. God, Gideon really needed to get his house rebuilt soon. Kostya's place was nice, but just too small to contain so many big men.

"Linc is going to tell you. I'll put him on speaker."

"What's the problem?" Jase practically yelled again.

Out of all of them, everybody knew Jase was having the hardest time being separated from his family.

"I tracked down one of the nurses who took care of Ivan after Decker International put him on disability. This is before Ivan fired them all. She actually stuck around off the books. She admitted to having a relationship with him until he became too dependent on the opioids he was taking for the pain. She tried to get him help, but he refused. That was when she bailed." Brax continued. "She's kept in touch with him through an email address, and I gave it to Gideon."

Everybody turned to look at Gideon. "I was able to hack that email account, but he's only ever used it to communicate with her."

"So, it's a dead end," Mateo said bitterly.

"Not really," Linc continued. "I asked the nurse to send him an email asking to meet for old time's sake, basically promising sex. I figured that would get him to respond, and it did. Gideon was able to figure out his IP address and find where he was emailing from."

"Well, don't keep us in suspense," Jase roared.

"It was a Starbucks in Annapolis."

"Motherfucker." Mateo jumped up from the ottoman he'd been sitting on.

"Calm down. We don't know that anything is wrong," Kostya said. "As a matter of fact, this might just mean he's scheduling a meeting with his contact at Lionel Security and Trust Bank. If you're right, Mateo, and Lainey isn't their contact, we'll know soon enough."

"God dammit, how often do I have to tell all of you,

Lainey is innocent? If Frank Sykes' psycho son is in Annapolis, then Lainey's life is in danger!"

"Hold up, you need to hear about Amanda. Brax is going to report on her, too," Kostya ordered. "Now sit back down."

Mateo stayed standing. "What?"

Kostya turned to Mateo's friend. "Braxton?"

"Amanda entered the US five weeks ago. She flew into LAX, from France. She then took a plane to DFW."

"Was Dallas her final destination?" Jase asked.

Brax shook his head. "She flew into Virginia two days before Gideon's house blew up."

"So, she's in charge of the Kraken," Kostya said.

Mateo could give one good shit about Amanda.

"How do you know this, Braxton?" Kostya asked.

"I have a contact who works at Interpol," Braxton explained. "They used their facial recognition software and provided her current passport information. She's traveling under the name of Alice Law."

"Do you know where she is now?"

Braxton shook his head. "She hasn't used any planes since she flew into Norfolk. No credit cards under the name of Alice Law have been used, nor has a driver's license been reported."

"Gideon, is there any way that you can isolate the time that Ivan was using the Starbucks' IP address and see other emails that were being used during that time period?" Mateo asked.

Gideon looked over at Jada. She shrugged. "It's definitely worth a shot. It'll take a while. We won't have anything for at least twenty-four hours, but it's a good thought."

"I've got to go." Mateo headed for the door.

"Mateo, we don't have a plan. I don't want you going off half-cocked." Kostya said.

"You all will come up with a plan. I'm going to visit my girlfriend."

He moved to the hallway, and Jase stood in his way.

"The lieutenant told you to stay."

Mateo looked Jase in the eye. "If this were Bonnie, would you stay?"

Jase stared at him for six seconds, then stepped aside. Mateo was not surprised when Braxton followed him out the door.

"You better not be trying to talk me out of this," Mateo said as he jogged to his truck.

"Fuck no. I'm here as your wingman."

"Good."

WHEN SHE FINALLY OPENED HER eyes after being tased, she was in her dining room. The pretty light fixture that she was so happy to have found was smashed on the floor. Her dining room table had been shoved up against the wall, and her chairs were tossed in a pile in her living room. She was hanging from where her light fixture used to be, her hands duct taped together. Her mouth was duct taped shut.

The crazy florist was grinning up at her. There was a man at her kitchen island taking apples and oranges out of her fruit bowl and putting them into one of her pretty pillowcases.

Lainey looked around the room and saw no sign of Xena. Maybe she ran away and was hiding in her doggie bed.

Please God, let her be hiding.

"You stole our money," the blonde woman said.

Lainey shook her head.

"Yes, you did. And we want it back. It's really simple. Tell us where you've hidden it, tell us how to get it, and we might let you live. Do you understand?"

Lainey shook her head wildly, her hair flying around and stinging her face.

The woman looked over her shoulder at the man. "It's a pity. We're going to have to do this the hard way."

"I like the hard way." The man grinned. He tied a knot in the pillowcase where the fruit was bundled, then, with the rest of the free material, he swung it around. "I'm going to enjoy this."

"You don't get to play today, Ivan."

He frowned. "What the fuck are you talking about? I'm the one who gets information. Not you."

"Ah, but she's more delicate, and if you do the swinging, you'll bust her up inside and we'll never get our answers. If I do the swinging, she'll just be in a lot of pain, and probably won't bleed out before we have a chance to find out what we need to know."

Lainey couldn't believe what she was hearing.

"Wait a minute. Did you put apples in this thing?" the woman asked.

"Yeah," Ivan shrugged.

"You dumbass. Those are too hard. We need oranges, or grapefruit. They have some give." Lainey watched as he untied his knot and took out the three apples. He re-tied the pillowcase and shoved it at the woman. "Here."

Lainey trembled.

"Are you going to tell me where the money is?"

Lainey nodded vigorously. She had no idea what the wench was talking about, but she needed to stay healthy. Now she understood what Matt had been talking about. These were the terrorists. The *clackling* or something. But it was all going to be okay, because she knew down to her bones that Matt would rescue her. Now she needed to stall for time.

"You know what, sweetheart? I don't believe you. I think you're scared, and you'd lie to me right now. What I need to do is tenderize you a bit, and then I'll get your cooperation. I'll try to stay away from major organs as best I can. I want you to last for a bit."

The woman took one end of the pillowcase and swung it backwards, then brought it forward, and it landed on Lainey's hip. Lainey screamed behind her gag.

"Oh, that's nice," the woman said. "That looked like it hurt. Let's do that again." She pulled back the pillowcase and hit Lainey's upper thigh, and Lainey screamed a second time. Once again, it sounded like a muffled gurgle.

"Oh yes, this *is* fun," the woman smiled. She looked over her shoulder at Ivan. "No wonder you wanted to do this."

She turned back to Lainey. "You're going to end up telling me everything you know, right down to what you got on your first birthday." She took another swing. This one hit Lainey in her stomach.

Lainey didn't know how long it took, but finally, her fondest wish came true, and she passed out.

"What's your plan of attack?" Brax asked as they sped along the streets until they got to the Chesapeake Bay Bridge Tunnel that would spit them out toward the peninsula.

"I don't have one," Mateo admitted. "I'm just headed for Lainey's condo."

"Is it like yours, or does it have someone manning the front desk?"

"Someone is manning the front desk, but he's barely awake most of the time. Anyone could get past him. But Lainey told both shifts I was on her approved list."

"Sounds good. Are you loaded up?" Brax asked as he motioned toward the toolchest in the back of Mateo's truck.

"Damn right I am, but I don't think we're going to be able to walk in with rifles without causing a stir."

"Pistols?"

"And knives."

"Try calling her," Brax suggested. "Or has she blocked you?"

"Amazingly she hasn't." For the first time in the last three hours, Mateo felt a grin forming.

"So, there's still hope," Braxton said.

"That's been my take." Mateo took his phone out of the side pocket of his cargo pants and handed it to Brax. "She's number one on my speed dial."

"I thought after our time together at Gideon's place, I was number one. I'm hurt," Braxton teased.

"Shut the fuck up and dial her number."

Braxton put it on speaker and even over the rumble of his old Dodge truck, Mateo could hear Lainey's honeyed accent as she told the caller to leave a message. He yanked the phone out of Brax's hand.

"Lainey, this is important. Yeah, I need to grovel again. Yeah, I need you to believe I love you. But this is a matter of life and death. Call me, *mí amor*. Call me."

He handed the phone back to Brax. "Text her, will you? I don't want you saying the I love you part. That has to come from me. But the life and death part. Text her that part."

"Gotcha."

They were silent for the next two hours, until Mateo had to stop for gas. The truck was not really known for having good gas mileage.

"I'm going to go grab some water and whatever. Is there anything specific you want?" Brax asked as he jumped out of the passenger seat.

Mateo shook his head and willed the gasoline to flow faster.

When they got back on the highway again, Braxton's phone rang.

"It's Gideon," he said as he picked up. "I've got you on speaker," Brax told Gideon. "We're about ninety minutes outside of Annapolis, right?" Braxton glanced at Mateo.

"Seventy," he muttered as he pressed harder on the gas pedal.

"We're seventy minutes outside of Annapolis unless we get pulled over or crash. What do you have?"

"Mateo's idea paid off, faster than we thought," Gideon said. "We were able to nail down another e-mail address that Ivan was using. Amanda's been banging on Ivan to track down a missing payment. Apparently, they finally tracked down that the client deposited their payment into Lionel who then converted it to cryptocurrency," Gideon explained.

"After that, Ivan found that half of the currency was correctly dispersed into smaller amounts and deposited into the accounts of other Kraken members throughout the world, as planned. The final problem was that the remaining half never made it into the Grand Cayman Island account. Amanda's account. Ivan's been in charge of figuring out why not."

"Gideon, if you now fucking think that my woman is stealing from the Kraken, I'm going to make it so you and Jada will never be able to have sex again. Am I making myself clear?" Mateo practically yelled.

He heard both Gideon and Jada laughing.

"He doesn't think that, Mateo. I promise." Jada said. "We're really thinking that there was some kind of glitch with the transaction, or somebody in the Grand Cayman bank is trying to pull a fast one. Lainey's in the clear as far as we're concerned."

"And?" Mateo prompted.

"And we've got to find out where she is as soon as possible," Gideon said. "I've checked with the bank. She hasn't been in all week. She apparently has the flu."

"I know that," Mateo said. "Since I was stuck on base, I called Mr. and Mrs. Morrison across the hall and asked them to report on her status. She's been out walking Xena every day. But hell, I left a message for them yesterday, and they haven't gotten back to me. I know Saturday is their bridge night."

"Bridge?" Jada asked.

"It's a card game," Gideon explained.

"I'll call right now, but they might be at church," Mateo said.

"By the way, Kostya and Jase left fifteen minutes after you did. So, hold your horses before rushing into anything."

Mateo sat up straighter in his driver's seat. "They did?"

"Mateo, yeah, we always like the black and white truth, but we always have our brothers' backs. You should know that."

Braxton chuckled. "What are they driving?"

"Jase's Mustang. I'd say they're going to be passing you pretty soon."

"They don't even know which way we took to get to Annapolis," Mateo scoffed.

Jada laughed. "If you don't think Gideon has a tracking device on everyone's vehicle, you're deranged."

Mateo felt a headache coming on.

"Gotta go," he muttered. "Hang up," he told Braxton.

Braxton stopped the call. "You okay?" he asked.

"Too much laughter. Lainey's in trouble. I can just feel it."

"We don't know for sure," Braxton said.

He had Braxton call the Morrisons but it went to their answering machine. Of course they didn't have cell phones.

Mateo pressed down harder on the accelerator.

———

How long had it been since she'd opened the door? Lainey watched as the two of them were now sitting down across from her at her dining room table, eating chicken parmesan and gnocchi with bruschetta and sparkling water from her wine glasses.

"You keep looking at our water glasses," the unhinged harpy said as she poured more water into her glass. "Are you thirsty?"

It had been Friday when she'd opened the door, right? Or was it Saturday?

Was today Sunday?

She watched as the beautiful fall of liquid poured into the glass with a smooth swishing sound. Then she heard a snap and crackle of the sparkling bubbles. The blonde, who she now knew as Amanda, set down the green bottle and slowly picked up her glass and swirled the precious liquid around.

Lainey watched as she brought the glass to her lips and took a sip. A second sip. A third sip. She watched her throat work as she swallowed down the water.

How many hours? How many days had it been since Lainey had had something to drink? Did she open the door on Friday or Saturday? Why wasn't her brain working? Her head drifted forward but was then yanked back by the duct tape sticking it to the back of her dining room chair.

"Please" she moaned, praying they would understand her.

"Please."

Amanda laughed as she picked up a piece of bruschetta. "Are you ready to tell us what you did with our money?"

Lainey carefully nodded her head, trying not to hurt herself, but still she felt some of her hair being torn out of her scalp.

"Ivan," Amanda said as she turned to the man. "You know something?"

He shook his head as he continued to eat his meal.

"I think I believe her. I think she is ready to tell us the truth."

"Great," he said as he continued to eat.

If she could just get some water she could think. She just needed to stall for some time. Matt would come. She knew he would. Matt would come and save her, she just needed to stay alive.

"Ivan, you need to go take off her gag."

"She's going to make noise. They always make noise when you yank off the duct tape. It rips off their skin."

"Dammit, do I have to do everything?!"

Amanda picked up one of Lainey's good white linen napkins and touched it to her lips, then got up from the table and walked around to where Lainey was duct taped to her chair. She tilted Lainey's chin up.

"Damn, it looks like it's on there pretty good."

All Lainey could think about was how the paint came off the wall when Matt tore off the duct tape on top of the extension cord.

"I know you don't want me to kill your crippled dog, so you won't scream when I eventually take off your gag. But I'm thinking you're not going to be able to help it if I just yank this off." She dug her phone out of the back pocket of her jeans and her fingers flew across the screen.

"Google knows all. Got it."

"You got olive oil?" she asked Lainey.

Lainey carefully nodded.

"Then we're in business."

The blonde eventually came back with a cloth, a bowl of warm water, and the olive oil. "This is going to hurt somewhat, but if I use the oil to loosen the adhesive, then it shouldn't be too bad, and you might still have lips by the time we're done."

Lainey zoned out while Amanda used the oil to remove the duct tape. Having Amanda touch her made her skin crawl.

Crack!

Lainey's cheek stung where Amanda smacked her, and her eyes went wide. "What?!"

"You weren't paying attention. You weren't listening to me. I said, are you ready to talk now?"

"Yes." Lainey knew she said *yes*, but it was so raspy even she couldn't understand it.

"Make sense!" Amanda said as she held up her hand as if to slap her again.

"Water." Again, the word was indecipherable.

"Jesus, I can't make heads or tails of what you're saying."

"She said water," Ivan said with his mouth full, then continued to chew.

"Oh yeah, your throat's probably dry."

Lainey tasted copper and her lips were on fire. *Guess olive oil didn't work after all.*

"Open your mouth, you stupid bitch."

Huh?

She felt water trickling into her mouth, mixing with the blood. She opened her mouth and tried to gulp.

"Now you're being stupid. You're going to throw up if you drink too fast."

The water stopped coming, and Lainey opened her eyes. Oh yeah, the blonde woman. Amanda.

"Are you ready to talk now?"

Lainey nodded, and fire went through her scalp. Oh yeah, her hair was duct taped to the back of the chair.

Crack!

Her head whipped sideways from the blow.

"Are you ready to talk now?

Lainey bit her lip and whimpered. What was she supposed to talk about?

Money. Oh yeah, money.

"You want to know about the deposit that came in from India, right?"

"There you go. Now you remember." Amanda turned to the man who was now eating some kind of dessert. "Did you hear that, Ivan? The bitch remembers what we've been talking about."

"It came from a textile plant," Lainey said.

"Good girl. Keep going."

"It was in our bank for six weeks, before we exchanged it into cryptocurrency."

"Yes, and you divided half of the money into eighths and deposited them into eight different accounts."

Lainey started coughing. She couldn't stop. It went on and on and on.

Crack!

Lainey still coughed.

"Give her some more water," Ivan said.

Amanda grabbed her chin, forced her jaw open, and poured water down Lainey's throat. "Drink, you stupid bitch."

Lainey tried to drink, but the coughing wouldn't stop. She needed to lean forward to spit out the phlegm.

"Ivan, give me your knife."

Oh God, this is it. Matt isn't going to get here in time.

Ivan reached down under the table then came up with a huge knife. He leaned across the table and stabbed it into the wood. "There."

Lainey continued to cough.

"You couldn't have just brought it around to me?" Amanda asked as she pulled it out of the table.

"No." Ivan pulled another dessert out of the take-out bag and started eating.

Amanda went behind Lainey.

"Stay still." But Lainey couldn't as the coughing continued.

I'm not going to cry. I refuse to give the bitch the satisfaction.

She felt her hair being pulled. More hair ripped from her scalp.

"Ow," she mumbled.

Then her head was free. She bent over and spit out the phlegm that had been tickling her throat.

"That's just gross." Amanda said.

Lainey was only sad that she hadn't thought about spitting on the bitch.

At least her cough had stopped.

"Water." Lainey begged.

Amanda put the glass up to Lainey's lips and she sipped slowly.

"Now talk."

"I transferred the money into the Grand Cayman account that was listed on the file."

"You did not," the man said. "It never arrived. You stole it."

"I swear to you, I didn't steal it. I transferred it."

"What was the account number?"

"I don't remember account numbers, they're too

long. All I remember is that it was given to me by a co-worker and because I had trouble reading a number, I had to call the bank down at the island."

Amanda jabbed the knife into the table right in front of Amanda. "Do you mean to tell me this is nothing but an accident? We've lost thirty-five million dollars because of a fucking typo?"

"Get it back," Ivan said as he took another bite of tiramisu.

"I don't know if I can."

"Well, you're going to try. Tomorrow you're going to go into the bank and talk to whatever idiot you talked to in the Cayman Islands and explain the mistake and get them to put it into the right account."

That wouldn't work in a million years.

"Okay," Lainey said. "I just have to talk to the same man I talked to last time."

"You're going to have to clean her up." Ivan said to Amanda.

"Bullshit. I'm leaving her like this until tomorrow morning,"

"All right, but if she pisses because you gave her water, I'm going to make you clean that up." Ivan pointed his fork at Amanda. "There is no way I want to be smelling that. It's bad enough that we have the dogshit smell coming from the back bedroom. I told you we should have killed that thing."

"And I told you, we needed that pup for leverage, to keep this bitch from screaming."

"Whatever."

"Do you have to go to the bathroom?" Amanda asked.

Lainey nodded.

27

"FUCK!" MATEO EXPLODED, AS HE TOSSED THE PARABOLIC listening device back to Brax sitting in the passenger seat, who immediately pointed it back at Lainey's window.

They all looked at one another. Yeah, Lainey had bought herself some time, but she'd lied through her teeth. There was no way that she'd be able to reverse that transaction.

Thank God his truck was a crew cab. Eventually someone was going to notice they'd parked in the back alley that Lainey had parked in the first night they'd met.

"Did you hear that bitch slapping her?" Mateo asked nobody in particular. "And how long have they been denying her water?"

"Yeah, but there was good news too," Kostya said in a calm voice. "They have to take care of her if they want her to go to the bank tomorrow and call the Cayman Islands."

Mateo turned around to look in the backseat. "Gideon, when was that email conversation between Ivan and Amanda?"

"Thursday."

"And they mentioned Lainey by name?"

Gideon shook his head. "They were like us. They were calling her MacLaine. My guess is they were looking for a man."

"So, like us, they were calling the bank, asking for a Mr. Simpson," Mateo muttered.

Gideon nodded.

"So, let's say they figured things out as fast as Thursday, and the worst-case scenario, they found out where Lainey lived, and got to her on Thursday. They've had her since then. It's possible she's been without water since then."

The very thought tore him apart.

"Wait, that's not possible!" Mateo practically shouted. "I talked to Mrs. Morrison. She saw Lainey taking Xena out for a walk Friday morning."

"Okay. Okay. So, it's fifteen-hundred hours on Sunday. Worst case is what? Eight-hundred hours Friday?" Kostya asked.

Mateo nodded. "So, fifty-six hours. My woman's strong. She can do this. She's already coming up with bullshit for them about how she can get them their money. She's figured out a way to get out of her condo. She's smart."

"That's right," Kostya said calmly. "We just have to wait until tomorrow morning. Everything's going to be fine. We'll take shifts watching her window."

"I'll take the first shift," Mateo said.

"I'm going back to my Mustang and put the seat back. I saw a Teeter's grocery store parking lot not so far from here."

Brax got out of the passenger side door so Jase could get out of the backseat.

"Brax, go with Jase," Kostya ordered as he followed Jase out of the backseat. "I'm going to take this shift with Mateo." He took Brax's place in the front seat.

"It's like you said, boss, nothing's going to happen," Mateo protested. "You don't need to stay."

"If I get too bored, I'll crash in the backseat," Kostya said. Mateo knew he wouldn't.

Fuck, am I going to get some speech about getting involved with a suspect?

As soon as Jase and Brax walked away, Kostya jerry-rigged the listening device so that it was still pointed toward Lainey's big living room window, but all had gone quiet. Then he turned to Mateo.

"You got something to say?" Mateo asked Kostya. He really didn't want to drag this out.

"I've always listened to your instincts when we've been out in the field. If you've had something to say, I knew I had to give it weight. You never talked a lot, but when you did, it was important. Your gut was normally right, and I should have known it was in this case, too. I'm sorry I doubted you."

"You just thought I was thinking with my little head, not my big head."

Kostya nodded. "It was a shitty thing to do, when all of us who have fallen for our women have been right on the money. All I can say is that this thing with the Kraken has me all twisted up. Being on a mission, risking my life, that's fine. Yeah, leading a team, it's killed me when men under my command have died, but we have all signed up for the same thing. But our children? Our families? Mateo, this has ripped out my soul."

Kostya looked away for a minute, then turned back to Mateo. "Apparently, it's ripped out part of my brain too." He chuckled. "I should have listened to you sooner."

"Hell, Kostya, if you did, you might have taken me off this assignment. That would have been the worst thing in the world."

"I'll try to find solace in that," Kostya whispered.

They sat there in silence, waiting for some kind of noise to come over the amplifier, but nothing did.

"You got any pictures of Romy?" Mateo asked.

Kostya grinned. "Sure do."

At Romy's christening, she had been christened Romana Beatrice Barona. Lark explained that Romy was named after Kostya's brother Roman who had died as a child. Beatrice was the name of Lark's mother. He had heard Lark call Romy, Romy Bea.

"Here she is." Kostya handed Mateo his phone. "Beatrice has her playing in the shallow water. The kid started out a water baby."

She looked adorable with her red polka dot sun hat and matching swimsuit. He laughed out loud when he saw Beatrice Allen wore the same hat. "Your mother-in-law is a kick."

"Tell me about it." Kostya laughed. "Damn lucky to have her at times like these."

They stopped talking when they heard the doorbell ring in Lainey's apartment.

"Are you expecting anyone?" the woman asked.

"No." Lainey's voice was raspy.

"Ivan, go see who it is."

There was a pause.

"It's some skank with red hair."

The doorbell rang again.

Mateo heard Xena bark.

"Make your dog shut up before I slit its throat," the man said.

"Get rid of the bitch at the door," the woman said. Mateo assumed that was Amanda.

"If you hurt my dog, I won't go to the office tomorrow and get your money."

"Lainey! I can hear you talking in there," A woman yelled through Lainey's door.

"It's Janice," Lainey said. "She won't go away until I talk to her."

"Don't do anything funny, or I will let Ivan kill your dog," Amanda said. "And don't open it up all the way, keep the security chain on."

What in the hell is Janice doing at Lainey's door? They hate one another.

"Janice, you know I'm sick. You shouldn't be here."

"Yeah, sure. That's why you have company, too."

"It's a doctor. She's making a house call."

Out of the corner of his eye, Mateo saw Kostya shaking his head at Lainey's pathetic lie.

"Oh really? And who's the man that I heard? Is he helping her give you the collagen lip injection? I have to tell you; they're doing a shit job of it."

What the fuck is she talking about?

"Janice, why are you here?"

"I've been talking to Arnie since you've been sick. I showed him all the mistakes you've made."

"What? What mistakes?"

"Oh, you poor thing. Someone had to go into your user account while you were out sick to make sure everything was handled. So I took care of that."

"How did you get into my account?"

"I told you, Arnie likes cleavage."

"What did you do?"

"I changed a lot of the past transactions you processed. It turns out you broke seven different laws because of the way you processed those accounts. Arnie was furious."

"You can check your email. Arnie's probably also left a message. You're fired. And do you want to hear the best news? I'm the new bank management trainee."

"Kostya, we've got to move. They're going to kill her now!"

"Why don't *you* come inside now that Miss Simpson is worthless to us?" Mateo heard the man ask as he and Kostya bolted out of his truck.

Then they were across the street, through the lobby, and pushing through the door for the stairs.

Before Mateo could start up the stairs, Kostya grabbed his arm.

"Wait." Kostya had his phone to his ear. "Get to her condo, now! They're going to kill her."

Kostya paused as he listened.

"Yes, we're going in."

Kostya let go of Mateo's arm and pulled out his pistol. Mateo pulled out his.

"Kostya, we've got Lainey and Janice in there. They might kill Lainey if they think Janice can do what they need, but my bet is that Lainey will convince them that only she can do what needs to be done."

"That's a hell of a bet." Kostya looked at Mateo.

"You gotta listen to my gut, boss."

Kostya nodded.

———

"WHAT IS GOING ON?" Janice screeched.

"Shut up, bitch," Amanda said as she pulled out her gun and put it to Janice's temple.

"I won't shut up," she yelled back at Amanda. "I demand to know what is going on."

"Let me have her," Ivan said.

"My pleasure," Amanda said.

Lainey watched in horror as Ivan grabbed Janice's arm and cut her from her sternum down to her stomach. It was a very shallow cut, but it started to bleed, and Janice started to cry.

"Why did you do that? Why did you do that?"

Amanda changed places with Ivan. "He did that to get your attention. Do we have your attention now?"

"It hurts." Janice was now sobbing.

Her cut was bleeding, but very little. She needed to pull herself together before they got that bag of oranges. Lainey still couldn't stand upright.

"God, is she always this whiny?" she asked Lainey.

"Yes. Stupid too. If you're planning on her calling the bank at the Cayman Islands, it won't work. She won't even know which deposit you're talking about. You're stuck with me."

"Bitch, she was smart enough to get you fired," Ivan said.

Lainey flinched. That was true.

"You're right, but she still won't know which file it was, or who it was I talked to down at the Cayman Bank. So, you're going to need me alive."

Ivan and Amanda looked at one another.

She had them.

"She's lying," Janice said. "I got her fired. I can do anything she can do, only better. You need me. Kill her."

God, Janice had the self-preservation instincts of a cat. Scratch that, she had the self-preservation instincts of a rat and a cockroach put together.

Lainey turned to Amanda. "I'm telling you; she won't know my contact down at the Cayman Bank."

"Sure, I do. It's Bertrum."

"That's a lie." Lainey sighed.

Janice turned to Lainey. "Then who is it?"

"I'm not telling you, so you can use it after they kill me. But good try, you skank." God, it felt good to call her that. Lainey turned back to Amanda. "You see how she wanted me to tell her? That's because she doesn't know. You need me alive."

———————

MATEO HAD BEEN ready to break down the door, but one thing he'd learned on his job, always try the easiest route first.

It worked.

After bringing Janice in, they'd forgotten to lock the door. Thank God for confusion and stupid terrorists.

Mateo and Kostya had listened as Janice tried to convince Amanda and Ivan to kill Lainey. His woman had been right all along. Her co-worker was a bitch of epic proportions.

Mateo crouched low. Kostya was high. Amanda no longer had her gun pointed at anyone. Lainey's arms and legs were free, but the duct tape that had been used to secure her was all over her pajamas. There was some in her now-short hair. Ivan was still holding his knife outward, pointed between Lainey and Janice. In one quick move, he could stab either of them.

Mateo pressed the door open a little more to see if the security chain was on. It wasn't.

"I want them alive," Kostya ground out. Mateo knew he meant Amanda and Ivan. He didn't blame him.

"Agreed," Mateo said in an almost silent whisper. "I've got Amanda."

"Right, I've got Ivan," Kostya said.

Mateo nodded.

"Count of three?" Kostya asked.

Mateo nodded again.

"One."

"Two."

"Three."

Kostya pushed forward through the door. Mateo lunged up from his crouch. They burst through the doorway. Amanda yanked her gun up and aimed toward Lainey. Mateo took his shot. It was a head shot. He didn't care about taking her alive. All he cared about was that Lainey lived.

28

"You came." Lainey croaked out the words as Mateo gently lowered her to her couch.

"You saved me."

"*Mí amor*. Don't talk. An ambulance will be here soon."

Lainey heard the commotion, but it seemed far, far away. All she could see were Matt's—No, Mateo's—beautiful brown eyes looking down at her.

"You came," she whispered again.

"Let me get you some water."

When he tried to get up, she grabbed at his arms. "No! Don't leave me."

He pressed a kiss on her forehead and she closed her eyes. Then quickly opened them again, wanting to make sure this wasn't a dream. That he was really here.

"I'm here. I'm not leaving you."

His voice sounded shaky. Then he shouted over his shoulder. "Jase, bring over a couple of bottles of water. Now."

Out of the corner of her eye, she saw an enormous guy drop a whimpering Ivan to the floor, then he went to the kitchen.

"Lainey, what happened to you? Why do you have blood all over your arms and chest?"

Jase handed Mateo two bottles of water that he held in one of his big hands. He set one down beside the couch.

"Let me have my hand, Lainey."

She released Mateo's hand and he opened the bottle of water. She tried to sit up, but she couldn't.

"Fuck," he muttered.

Before she knew what was happening, she was lifted and then cradled in Mateo's lap, her head resting between his shoulder and jaw. "Let me help you drink this."

She took long, grateful sips.

"Okay, *mi amor*, that's enough for now."

He was right. Already her stomach was cramping, and that just hurt all those bruises she had inside and out.

"Besides the cuts and being thirsty, what else? I can tell you're hurting."

"Goddammit!" The roar cut through all the talking in the room.

Lainey gripped Mateo's shirt in a panic as she heard the yell coming from her kitchen. She glanced over to see who made that noise. Was it Ivan? Had he gotten up off the floor? Was he going to kill Mateo and his friends? Was he going to get her?

It was the same man who had given Mateo the bottles of water; he was holding up her pretty pillowcase filled with oranges.

"What's in it?" another one of Mateo's friends asked.

The big man who roared ripped her pillowcase open and oranges fell onto her counter and then bounced onto her floor.

"Motherfucker!" he roared again.

"Aw, Lainey," Mateo whispered. "How bad are you hurting?"

"Bad," she admitted. "She said she wouldn't hit my kidneys, so at least there was that, right?" Lainey tried to smile.

Mateo dropped his head into her shorn hair and breathed in deep. Then he lifted. "Where the fuck is that ambulance?!"

THIS TIME, it was his turn to sleep in the uncomfortable hospital chair, and Mateo couldn't give one good shit. He was just happy as hell that Lainey was out of surgery and it turned out to be relatively minor. What he found out; a person could live pretty well without a gallbladder. He just wanted her to wake up.

"Mateo, have you had something to eat since yesterday? I'm worried about you."

He looked up into the warm, blue eyes of Rose Simpson. Who would have ever guessed that her eyes could be warm?

"I haven't been hungry."

"I knew you were going to say that. Lee's wife is bringing some soup for you from the cafeteria. Lee's parking their rental car. Conrad is outside having a cigar, waiting for him." Rose held out her hand for him to take.

"I just want her to wake up, you know?" Mateo said.

"I know, honey. She will. The doctors expect her to wake up today. Her body's been through a lot."

Mateo got up out of his seat. "Here, sit down."

"No, that's your seat," Rose protested.

"My mama would tan my hide if I was sitting while a lady was standing," Mateo said with half a grin. Rose sat down in the empty chair.

"I bet your Mama and I would have liked each other."

Now was a good time to deflect, because he knew for sure that those two women would not have gotten along, no matter how much of a turnaround Rose might have done. "Thank you for forgiving me about my deception."

"What's there to forgive?" Rose asked. "You saved my daughter. You're one of our country's heroes. I can't thank you enough."

"Mateo?"

Mateo rushed over to where Lainey was just waking up.

"I'm here. You're safe. I love you so much."

"I love you too," she whispered. "I just had the most outrageous dream."

"It's okay, you're safe now," he assured her.

"Not that. I dreamed my mother called you honey."

Mateo looked at Lainey in shock for a moment, then he threw back his head and laughed.

EPILOGUE

"She's fitting right in," Kostya said as he looked over to where Lainey was sitting with Jada, Lark, Bonnie, and Leila. Once Lainey's reputation had been cleared at Lionel Security and Trust Bank and Janice had been fired, she could easily get a job in Virginia Beach if she wanted to. Now she was conspiring with some of the other Omega Sky women.

"She's fitting in a little too well, if you ask me. She spends every Wednesday night with them," Mateo grumbled.

Gideon snorted. "Aw, poor baby, he doesn't get to see his woman one night of the week. It must be so rough."

Mateo looked around the group of men here in Kostya's living room. The women were in the dining room looking over some printouts. "Hey, she only moved down here three months ago, it *is* rough. What's more, two of those months were spent finding a house with a big enough yard for Xena."

"I like your dog," Gideon said. "She plays well with Lucy. She has no fear."

Mateo could finally chuckle just a little. When they opened up Lainey's bedroom where Xena had been cooped up, she came out all teeth and claws. All the men had backed up from her, not wanting to hurt her. They were more than willing to let her have at Ivan, though. That fucker had deserved all the clawing and bites that he got, before they'd started to pound on him. Unfortunately the cops had come before they'd been able to get the information they needed. But Xena had been a champ. Mateo still grinned about her turnaround.

But when Xena had found her mama, she'd started to whine and cry, but after she was done, she stood guard. Her snarling and growling started all over again when the EMTs arrived. It took everything Lainey and Mateo had to get her to calm down enough to let the EMTs take Lainey away. According to Kostya, even as the cops were taking Ivan away, they still had to hold onto her as she tried to bite and claw Ivan again. Apparently he had become her favorite chew toy.

Amanda left the apartment in a body bag, which made Mateo extremely happy, after he found out exactly what she had done to Lainey.

"So, when is the housewarming party?" Brax asked Gideon.

"Still four more months. It hasn't mattered how much money I've thrown at this project; it has taken forever."

Kostya laughed and so did Linc, Mateo, and Jase.

"I don't know how my wife got roped into all of this," Linc said.

"They want the translations to be right on the webpages, and Lainey said you can't just trust the AI translation apps."

"Your woman sure seems hellbent on starting up this low-income loan program," Kostya said.

"Yep. But it was your wife's fault. Lainey was planning on getting a degree in non-profits, but Lark said why wait."

Kostya laughed. "That's my girl."

Linc rolled his eyes as he swished another chip through queso and popped it into his mouth. "At least there's food."

"At least I got to come this time," Mateo said.

"So, when are you going to pop the question?" Brax asked.

"Keep your voice down." Mateo frowned at Brax. "I have a plan."

"So, fill us in. Maybe we can help."

"If I needed your help, then I would have asked for your help already."

"Do you have the ring?" Jase asked. "According to my daughter, it's important that there are diamonds in it."

"Yeah, I remember what you told us." Mateo laughed. "Yep, diamonds are involved in the ring. But I have a lot to compete with since she has her grandmother's jewels."

"I hope you ponied up," Brax said.

"I rode a horse, okay?" he gave his friend a pointed look.

"Okay. Okay. Okay." He threw his hands up in the air.

Gideon winked at him.

———————

"HAVE I told you how happy I am that you pulled me in to work on this?" Leila said for the third time.

"Why wouldn't we?" Lark asked.

"Sometimes I feel kind of out of things, since I'm always travelling so much with my job."

Lainey laughed. "And I feel just the opposite, all of you are employed. I'm the lump on the log, just sitting around with pie-in-the-sky ideas."

"Uhm, have the doctors given you the all-clear?" Bonnie asked tentatively.

"Sure they have," Lainey said. "I've been good for ten weeks now. Why do you ask?"

"It's just something Jase said."

Lainey narrowed her eyes. "Which means it came from Mateo. Okay, let's have it."

"Bet you and I heard the same thing," Jada piped up. "Gideon told me that it's only been in the last two weeks that you've been okay to go back to work, and before that we should all take it easy with you."

"I've got to have a talk with Mateo. He is way-over-the-top protective."

All the women around the table burst out laughing.

Finally, after she caught her breath, Lark said, "Good luck with that."

Lainey frowned. "What do you mean?"

"They're all over-protective alphas. If they could wrap us in bubble-wrap and keep us under guard at home 24/7 they would do it."

"Mateo's not that bad..."

Lainey looked around the table at her new friends who were all grinning at her.

"Oh my God, he is that bad."

"It gets worse when you have kids," Lark said.

"We're not even engaged," Lainey protested.

"Not yet," Bonnie grinned.

"Did my girl do good by you?" Gideon asked when he followed Mateo into the kitchen.

"Gianna is an amazing artist," Mateo enthused. "But I don't know how she had time to design Lainey's engagement ring with three kids under the age of four running around."

"Did I tell you that the oldest boy's middle name is Gideon?" Gideon asked.

"Only about forty times." Mateo smiled as he reached into the fridge to take out the vegetable plate.

"Vegetables? I thought we were getting beer."

"Lark made me promise I would try to get us to eat some vegetables."

Gideon chuckled. "I haven't talked to Sebastian for

a while since he took the desk job. Did she say how he was doing?"

"I got the feeling he was just biding his time to get back out into the field."

"That sounds about right." Gideon nodded. "So, how did the design turn out?"

"I gave her pictures of some of Lainey's grandmother's jewels, and she came up with something that was in the same vein. I told her to not skimp on the size of the stones, and she didn't. She even found a jeweler for me to go with."

"I wish you luck," Gideon said as he patted him on the back.

———

LAINEY STRETCHED out on the yoga mat in front of the fireplace. Ever since she had her gallbladder removed, she was more conscious of her body and liked to ensure it was limber and in shape. It also made sex even better!

She heard the garage door come up. Xena got up from her spot by the fire and ran toward the garage door by the kitchen. Mateo came in calling out, "*Corazón*, I brought home dinner."

He did that at least once a week. Even though she currently didn't have a day job, he took what she was doing seriously enough to bring home dinner, and he also cooked once a week. He was perfect.

"No, Xena, this isn't for you. This is for your Mama and me."

Lainey got up from the floor and saw Mateo's eyes widen. "Let me get cleaned up for dinner," she said.

"You know you're wearing my favorite outfit."

She giggled. He did love her yoga clothes. When he saw the one set she had, he went out and bought three more sets. Lainey would never feel comfortable wearing them out in public, but here at home? For Mateo? Sure.

"I'm sweaty," Lainey protested.

"You have a glow," Mateo countered. "Come sit down at the table before the food gets cold."

Lainey liked their new dining room set. There wasn't a chance in purgatory she ever wanted to see her old dining room set again.

She heard a pop and frowned. As she circled the couch and made her way into the dining room, she watched Mateo pouring champagne.

"Is there something we're celebrating?"

"Have a seat."

He looked serious, so she sat down.

"I lost Luis when he was twenty and I was sixteen."

Lainey gulped and covered his hand with hers. "I know, I'm so sorry."

He nodded. "I lost my mom when I was twenty-three."

She squeezed his hand. He turned his over so he could tangle his fingers with hers.

"I had my team of brothers, but it wasn't the same. I didn't have that connection of the heart, that comes with having a family. As I saw my friends pair up, I despaired I would ever have that again. Then I met you."

"You thought maybe I could be your connection?" Lainey asked hopefully.

"You were so much more than that. Lainey, my life is more meaningful with you by my side. You're more than just my lover and the woman that I love. You're the connection that bridges my heart, soul, and mind. We are so intricately entwined that I feel like I can do anything. I've been scared to death at the idea of getting married and starting a family. I never wanted to lose someone I loved ever again, but because of you, I now have the courage to try. Will you marry me, Lainey Simpson? Will you be my wife? My other half? And maybe one day, if God blesses us, the mother of my children?"

She nodded.

She had no words.

She nodded again.

This time, she didn't try to stop the tears.

She kept nodding and saw Mateo's smile.

He untangled their fingers, then grasped her left hand. Through her tears, she watched him ease a ring onto her finger.

She picked up a napkin to wipe her eyes so that she could see the ring clearly.

It was a large emerald-cut yellow diamond, with two emeralds offset on either side, and tiny black diamonds set along the top and bottom of the emeralds. It was the most beautiful ring she had ever seen in her life.

"Are you going to say something?"

She nodded.

"Sometime tonight?" He chuckled.

"Yes," she whispered. "Having you as my husband is my dream come true."

Mateo got up from his seat and came around the table. He pulled out Lainey's chair. "Stand up," he whispered.

"The food will get cold," she whispered back as she stood up.

"Like I care." Mateo laughed. "I just got the most wonderful woman in the world to agree to marry me." He picked her up in his arms and whisked her down the hallway.

Xena knew better than to follow.

Keep reading for a taste of Braxton's story, **Her Eternal Warrior (Book 7),** *The next book in the Omega Sky Series*

HER ETERNAL WARRIOR

Brax looked down at the puppy in his arms. Hell, the puppy was as big as most small dogs.

"What do you mean, she's mine?"

"The Lockharts gave her to you for saving their daughter," Gideon explained. "These Russian Terrier pups usually go for five grand."

"Are you kidding me?" Brax looked down at the black, squirmy bundle in his arms.

"Nope." Gideon grinned.

"My apartment won't allow me to have a dog," Brax protested.

Mateo, who had been eerily quiet, finally spoke up. "Look, you cheap bastard. You know you hate that apartment. You've been bitching about it for four years. Bonnie's friend is planning on moving out of the house she's renting. It'll be perfect for you and Frankenstein."

Brax crouched down and let the pup wiggle out of his arms onto the grass. "Her name isn't Frankenstein, you cruel bastard."

Gideon chuckled. Braxton tuned him out as he looked at the girl starting to sniff around Gideon's yard. She was adorable. Then he thought of something.

"If I'm getting a puppy, why not you?" he asked Mateo.

"I did. He's already at home with Lainey. She couldn't wait to introduce him to Xena."

"So, what did you name him?"

Mateo gave a long, disgusted sigh. "Hercules."

Gideon and Braxton laughed, and as soon as they did, the pup scrambled back to Braxton and pushed her nose into his hand. "What should I name you?" he asked.

"You could name her Buffy," Mateo said. "Stick with the nineties television theme."

"I think not." He picked up his girl. "Nah, your name is Faith, isn't it?" She wiggled her little bottom and pushed against him.

Gideon frowned. "Faith?"

Brax looked over at Mateo and his friend was smiling. He got it. For years, Braxton and his dad had only had faith to carry them through that CiCi would be okay. Now, there was finally hope.

"Yep, Faith." He picked up his puppy and turned to Mateo. "Okay, tell me about this rental."

ABOUT THE AUTHOR

Caitlyn O'Leary is a USA Bestselling Author, #1 Amazon Bestselling Author and a Golden Quill Recipient from Book Viral in 2015. Hampered with a mild form of dyslexia she began memorizing books at an early age until her grandmother, the English teacher, took the time to teach her to read -- then she never stopped. She began re-writing alternate endings for her Trixie Belden books into happily-ever-afters with Trixie's platonic friend Jim. When she was home with pneumonia at twelve, she read the entire set of World Book Encyclopedias -- a little more challenging to end those happily.

Caitlyn loves writing about Alpha males with strong heroines who keep the men on their toes. There is plenty of action, suspense and humor in her books. She is never shy about tackling some of today's tough and relevant issues.

In addition to being an award-winning author of romantic suspense novels, she is a devoted aunt, an avid reader, a former corporate executive for a Fortune 100 company, and totally in love with her husband of soon-to-be twenty years.

She recently moved back home to the Pacific Northwest from Southern California. She is so happy to see the seasons again; rain, rain and more rain. She has a large fan group on Facebook and through her e-mail list. Caitlyn is known for telling her "Caitlyn Factors", where she relates her little and big life's screw-ups. The list is long. She loves hearing and connecting with her fans on a daily basis.

Keep up with Caitlyn O'Leary:

Website: www.caitlynoleary.com
FB Reader Group: http://bit.ly/2NUZVjF
Email: caitlyn@caitlynoleary.com
Newsletter: http://bit.ly/1WIhRup

facebook.com/Caitlyn-OLeary-Author-638771522866740

x.com/CaitlynOLearyNA

instagram.com/caitlynoleary_author

amazon.com/author/caitlynoleary

bookbub.com/authors/caitlyn-o-leary

goodreads.com/CaitlynOLeary

pinterest.com/caitlynoleary35

ALSO BY CAITLYN O'LEARY

PROTECTORS OF JASPER CREEK SERIES

His Wounded Heart (Book 1)

Her Hidden Smile (Book 2)

Their Stormy Reunion (Book 3)

OMEGA SKY SERIES

Her Selfless Warrior (Book #1)

Her Unflinching Warrior (Book #2)

Her Wild Warrior (Book #3)

Her Fearless Warrior (Book 4)

Her Defiant Warrior (Book 5)

Her Brave Warrior (Book 6)

Her Eternal Warrior (Book 7)

NIGHT STORM SERIES

Her Ruthless Protector (Book #1)

Her Tempting Protector (Book #2)

Her Chosen Protector (Book #3)

Her Intense Protector (Book #4)

Her Sensual Protector (Book #5)

Her Faithful Protector (Book #6)

Her Noble Protector (Book #7)

Her Righteous Protector (Book #8)

Night Storm Legacy Series

Lawson & Jill (Book 1)

Black Dawn Series

Her Steadfast Hero (Book #1)

Her Devoted Hero (Book #2)

Her Passionate Hero (Book #3)

Her Wicked Hero (Book #4)

Her Guarded Hero (Book #5)

Her Captivated Hero (Book #6)

Her Honorable Hero (Book #7)

Her Loving Hero (Book #8)

The Midnight Delta Series

Her Vigilant Seal (Book #1)

Her Loyal Seal (Book #2)

Her Adoring Seal (Book #3)

Sealed with a Kiss (Book #4)

Her Daring Seal (Book #5)

Her Fierce Seal (Book #6)

A Seals Vigilant Heart (Book #7)

Her Dominant Seal (Book #8)

Her Relentless Seal (Book #9)

Her Treasured Seal (Book #10)

Her Unbroken Seal (Book #11)

The Long Road Home

Defending Home

Home Again

FATE HARBOR

Trusting Chance

Protecting Olivia

Isabella's Submission

Claiming Kara

Cherishing Brianna

SILVER SEALs

Seal At Sunrise

SHADOWS ALLIANCE SERIES

Declan

Made in the USA
Las Vegas, NV
05 July 2024

91909843R00187